Poison In Jest

Poison In Jest

JOHN DICKSON CARR

COLLIER BOOKS

Macmillan Publishing Company

New York

Macmillan Publishing Company
866 Third Avenue, New York, N.Y. 10022
Collier Macmillan Canada, Inc.

This edition is published by arrangement with
Harper & Row Publishers, Inc.

Library of Congress Cataloging in Publication Data
Carr, John Dickson, 1906–1977.
   Poison in jest.
   I. Title.
PS3505.A763P6   1985   813'.52   84–14919
ISBN 0–02–018400–X

10 9 8 7 6 5 4 3 2 1

Printed in the United States of America

Contents

Poison In Jest

Prologue

The Clock Begins to Strike

DUSK was coming down from the Wiener Wald, and pink sunset had already faded from the low plain where Vienna lies. There was an echo of bells in the air. Spring had begun to lace the street lamps with green shadows, from the double lines of trees round the Ringstrasse; the air was as mild as the bells trembling there, and the noise of footfalls still lingered in a deserted Graben.

They were holding the vesper service in St. Stephen's. From where we sat at the café called The Old Fiddle, we could see the tall fretted spire, half shadow and half glow, outlined against the sky. Tires sang in the street, and a light in our café shone out on the gaudy lettering of a kiosk. St. Stephen's spire climbs incredibly high over grey houses which all have the look of public buildings—or would have, but for their fresh white curtains and their tidy gaiety. From anywhere in Vienna you will see it, dwarfing the City Hall, and the Museum dome, and votive church; and this is only right, because it is Vienna. In the coloured tiles of the roof gleamed now the black eagle of the Hapsburg arms; gleamed, and then faded, like a dying of trumpets in the great, lost anthem.

My companion sat in the shadow of the hedge, so that I could see only the red gleam of his cigarette. On the marble-topped table between us stood two glasses of kümmel. Within reach of his hand, a loose pile of manuscript sheets lay under a yellow-bound book which held the secret to a terror of murder by poison. But we did not immediately speak of the book, or of other things concerned with devilry in a snow-bound house—viz., the tin of arsenic, the hatchet, and the white marble hand. I breathed the fragrance of linden trees, and watched that fading spire. From its pinnacle you may descry the Alps, misty along the west; you may see barges crawling on an oily Danube, where the shields of Rome came, and Bonaparte's sharp-clawed eagles, and hair-and-steel Crusaders moving under scarlet crosses to the Black Sea. Vienna is drowsy now; there is time to remember this. The cafés are deserted. Franz-Josef, the gem-glitter, and the flame of uniforms at the Royal Opera, have clouded into twilight like the Hapsburg arms in the cathedral roof. Ghostly carriages go creaking and spanking round the Ring; King Edward dines, and violins break suddenly into the roll of a hurrying waltz. . . .

"I was thinking," I said, "of the Strauss statue. And of another statue."

My companion's chair creaked slightly. He made a gesture of repugnance.

"That was six months ago," I continued, "and you have never told me how you knew. Do you remember? There was blood on the statue. You put your hand behind it and took the murderer like a rat out of a hole. . . ."

The other shifted uncomfortably. He said:

"I touched a dead body. The murderer was dead when I got there. That was the worst part of it. What you mean is, a rabbit out of a hat. A dead rabbit . . . Poor devil."

"It's pretty hard to feel any sympathy."

"Oh, not for *that* one. I mean the other. Look here"— he touched the sheets of manuscript—"is that why you've written all this?"

"Yes. It's difficult for the rest of the children to be suspected of"—I swung my arm in the air, imitating the stroke of a hatchet, and he winced—"of that. And there's still some suspicion. The truth needs to be told. You were the only one who saw the truth. Running into you suddenly in Vienna like this . . ."

"What do you want me to do?"

"The story lacks an ending. You can supply it."

He was silent for a moment, the end of the cigarette pulsing and dimming.

"I've read this," he said at length, and tapped his fingers on the sheets. "I don't see that I need to explain much. You've got it all in here. That remark Clarissa made was a dead give-away, it's so damned obvious. And those things about the variations in poisons. The real origin of the obsession was clear all the time—so clear I'm surprised it didn't occur to you. Even I didn't have all the information you did when you wrote this. You had a glimmering of the truth. But you were simply applying your theory to the wrong person."

Again he fell to smoking thoughtfully. We were both thinking of the vast jigsaw house where the murders were committed; of gas-lights, and a brandy-bottle, and cellar stairs spotted with blood. An old house, an old town, and the mountains of western Pennsylvania, blue as Vesuvius, had become vivid with terror in the mild Austrian dusk. Somewhere in the city, now, a great clock began to strike. The mellow gong-notes floated across dim roofs, and I counted them idly. One, two, three, four—

The boom of five was dying into silence when my companion spoke. Momentarily the lights of a passing car illumined his face, and I was again surprised to think that this was the man who had seen the truth.

Six, the clock boomed, *seven*—

"Let me show you what I meant when I said you were applying your theory to the wrong person," he said. "For instance. . . ."

Chapter 1

Caligula's Hand

JUDGE QUAYLE half rose out of his chair. He said:

"You asked me that question ten or twelve years ago. You ask it again the first time I've seen you since then. Why do you keep harping on it?"

I felt uneasy. Things were going wrong, somehow. It might have been that I had grown up and could no longer accustom myself to the atmosphere of the Quayle household; yet there seemed to be an uncomfortable, at times almost sinister, difference since the old days.

The judge, who was sitting on the other side of the hearth, continued to regard me with a reddish, suspicious, rather hostile gaze. He was a lean man, who must once have been immensely strong; but now he seemed creaky. His grey-black hair was thin and long, and brushed back from his high forehead as in the engravings of old statesmen. I used to imagine, when I saw him in court, that his whole head came out of an engraving—the long face, fixed and leathery; the slightly projecting teeth, which gave a bunched, dour expression to his mouth; the stern eyes, which in court were without curiosity or interest. When I saw him now in the gloom of his own library, I thought of the picture he presented while listening to testimony: the head resting sideways on two fingers, above the desk of polished wood, and outlined against an American flag. The black robe fallen away from his wrist; the eyes turned obliquely, watching. . . .

It was not that he had shrunk, or that his dignity was any less than what had inspired us all with awe a dozen years ago. He looked a little shabby, it is true. His rolling sentences might have sounded somewhat foolish. But the man was frightened.

We talk of people "throwing a glance," which seems ridiculous. But that is precisely what Judge Quayle did. The dark frozen eyes threw something in my direction, as literally as though he expected me to catch it. A suspicion, an accusation, a doubt, what? Settling back into the padded chair again, he worked his hands up and down the arms of the chair.

"I remember when you asked it the first time. It was snowing that night, too," he said reflectively, and stared into the fire. "Ten—or was it twelve?—years ago. You had just begun to write, and you brought a manuscript to me for criticism."

"It was mere curiosity, sir," I said. "It is now."

He did not seem to hear me. He muttered, still staring at the fire:

"We were happy, then."

"You mean—"

"The family. *My* family." Low, but in his resonant voice, he began to recite the famous lines from Macbeth. "To-morrow and tomorrow and tomorrow—" gripping his hands together now. In anybody else it would have been theatrical. But the tall, harsh man thought in terms like those. . . .

I looked round the library, one of those immense rooms which look topheavy, and have windows to the floor after the fashion of the eighteen-seventies. In an ornate chandelier there were brackets for both gas and electricity. Both had been lighted; the gas gave out a pale, jumpy glow which seemed somehow to dim the electrics rather than assist them, so that the room had a sort of dingy gloom. Old style bookcases ran round the walls. There were dark, very bad oils hanging in gold frames above the bookcases: portraits of Quayles or Malverts, most of them (Mrs. Quayle had been a Malvert). I remembered how, long ago, I had admired those paintings, no less than the doors of the bookcases in figured glass and enamel.

But in one corner of the room still stood the thing which had prompted my question. It was a life-size statue of the Roman emperor Caligula in marble: toga, bulbous nose, loose mouth, standing in witless ugliness with one arm extended. But the arm ended in a stump. Ever since I could remember, the statue's right hand had been missing. It had always been a bogey to the Quayle children. . . .

There was no reason why the judge should remember a casual question, asked a dozen years ago. I recalled the night now. It had been the year before our little crowd in the town had gone away to school. We were in the first triumphant flush of being allowed to drive automobiles; when a room which was to be our own, at a preparatory school, made us feel that we were already men of the world; and when we first learned, with nervous astonishment, that girls liked to be kissed. Young people are more grown up, now. Yet, with sudden sharpness, memories returned. Snow falling past the street lamps, the slur of auto tires, and laughter. A dance orchestra—the polite term was then employed—played "Whispering" and "Dardanella." The dancers jerked a little, but the girls had already got over being gawky. A certain young man felt hot and starchy in a first tuxedo.

We congregated at the Quayle house then. The big place had seemed magnificent. Out of a jumble of scroll- and rufflework, it had great frame towers, crowned in filigree, jutting up above a veranda vast enough for a ballroom. It was covered with frame scales, painted dull brown, and shutters on the long windows gave it an air of secrecy. The lawns and gardens were luxuriant, which made all the more mysterious those big and stuffy rooms, where the shutters seemed to be closed even when daylight streamed in. There was a swimming-pool, too, with stonework around the edges, and trees where Japanese lanterns were hung at night. Oh yes— and a coach-house where we had played robbers at an even earlier date, and a cast-iron dog at the turn of the gravel driveway.

Staring at Judge Quayle now, I tried to fit him into the past. We had all been afraid of him, of course; even the word "judge" was as ominous as "executioner." It suggested rows of calf-bound books, and prisons. On the veranda there had been swings, and wicker chairs covered with chintz; we lounged there when mysterious dusk was coming down from the mountains, and the air grew cool, and shaded light fell through the curtains of the dining-room windows. There was a moist smell of grass after sunset. The mountains were fading, ghostly purple, and car lamps winked along the highway far out past the iron gates. . . .

Sometimes, on these occasions, we would see Judge Quayle coming in from town. He drove a very ancient Hudson, which nobody else would touch; it was built very high, and rattled, and was covered with all kinds of struts like an airplane; but he kept the brasswork highly polished. He wore a dark slouch-hat, tipped slightly forward, and always had a newspaper in his pocket. His back was rigid, which made his great height even greater; he saw few people on the street; he walked as though he were stumping along. Finally, his mouth was bunched up in that dour fashion which made his enemies call him unpleasant things, but which was probably only false teeth. He wanted to be genial. He would try to be, when he met us. But we were uncomfortable, and I know now that he was uncomfortable, too. Occasionally, in the evenings, he would come out on the porch, smoking a cigar; and he would tell us a joke— which nobody thought was funny, but at which everyone laughed. He would try (somewhat bewilderedly) to talk with us. We acted unnaturally, there were long silences, and finally his tall figure would go back to the cluttered library.

I knew him better than most of the others, probably better than his own children, for I had what are politely called literary ambitions. I used to bring my attempts to him, fearfully, for criticism. A vision came back now, of night and the falling snow, and this brown library. The same electrics and jumpy gaslights were reflected in the black windowpanes. Behind the same table which was now in the middle of the room, Judge Quayle sat with a manuscript. He leaned his head on his hand, the fingers tapping at his temple as in the courtroom. His long chin folded out over his collar, and his eyes were half closed. Presently, I knew, he would rise to pace up and down the room, one hand under his coat-tail. He always pulled back his chin a trifle before he began to talk, and fiddled with his cuffs. When he spoke officially (even if it were only to deliver a criticism to a nervous young writer of sixteen) he spoke in the sort of Latinesque prose he was accustomed to write, with Roman heaviness and Roman logic.

Nowadays we make ludicrous mistakes. We say that gentlemen of his generation talk like Latins, when we mean that they talked Latin. We say that they were flowery, when they were exact to the extent of using too many words in order to be exact. Judge Quayle was a jurist, and despised floweriness. He was descended from an old line—the hard-drinking, hard-thinking, whisky-and-spittoon lawyers who did not study laws, but made them. I can see him, gaunt and smelling of bay rum, stalk the brown library while he talked. On the mantelpiece there was a clock under a glass case, and a bunch of cattails stuck behind it. He bade me, like Buckle, "spend my days and nights with Addison." He quoted Lord Bacon and J. S. Black. It was cold, classical advice, mixed with a certain patronizing air towards all novels. And yet his judgment was uncanny. . . .

Looking back on it, I think it did him good to talk. He had few friends. His wife was a small, pleasant, unimpressive woman who smiled and hurried, but seemed to do nothing else. There were five children, three girls and two boys, but they—what? Ever since I had come to the house that evening, I had been wondering about them, for I had seen none of them in ten years.

Across the hearth Judge Quayle still sat motionless. The firelight was strong on his reddened eyelids, and the jumping nerve in his cheekbone; his hair, brushed in that politician's fashion, was much greyer and thinner. That be-damned-to-you decisiveness was gone from his voice. I had been here only a few minutes, in response to his own summons. I had spoken of old times, and made an innocent remark about the Caligula statue—asking, as I had asked once before, why the hand was gone. And suddenly terror had come into Judge Quayle's voice and look. He had demanded, "Why do you keep harping on that?" And now he sat fingering the arms of the chair and blinking. I waited for him to break the long silence.

There had been rumours afloat in the town. Judge Quayle had retired from the bench several years before. While I was in Europe I heard, from some source or other, that he had had a break with the younger son, Tom—who was about my own age—over Tom's refusal to study law. Tom had even been driven out of the house. He was his mother's favourite (they said), and she had never forgiven her husband. But I had lost touch with our eager adolescent group which had so solemnly discussed the future on the Quayle porch, when the moon rose beyond the swimming pool, and nights were full of the gods' laughter and the sawing of crickets. Many dance-tunes had been played since then. I had been very fond of Virginia Quayle, the youngest, at that time; she had yellow-brown hair and large eyes, and she did not talk much. . . .

When I returned to town after a long absence, it was to hear that Judge Quayle wanted to see me. I did not know why. There was a whisper, in town, that the judge had gone mad; that the fantastic house beside the mountains had fallen into sleep and decay. He was not real any longer. But when I drove out to the Quayle house that night, memories had stirred. The lamps of the old town were brightening in winter dusk. The 7:30 train whistled, far away, and you could see the yellow face of the court-house clock. A few snowflakes drifted as shadows across bright and clean-swept streets. They had laid out these streets in the year Washington took command of the Continental army. Through them would always blow the wind of stagecoaches, and the note of the key-bugle from the great days of the National Highway; the town below the blue mountains would keep its rattling hum, its muddy yellow creek, and its ghosts.

When I passed the outskirts, and the road swept arrow-straight towards the mountains, it had occurred to me why Judge Quayle might want to summon me there. Many times, in the old days, he had spoken of the book he some day intended to write. It should be the voice of those dull golden-framed portraits which crowded the walls of his library. It should be the history of this soil, where young Washington fought his first battle at Fort Necessity, and the redcoats buried Braddock beside the trail. It should echo back the warwhoop on the red-lit river below Fort Redstone, and the crack of rifles; and the painful plod and creak of the pioneer march. Well, I had written books of a sort. It might be that my first mentor wanted to find a publisher. . . .

The iron gates of the Quayle house sagged open. The house was as huge and grotesque as ever; but now there was an atmosphere of dinginess about it, and it needed paint. The towers were black monstrosities against starlight, the lawns unkempt. There was a marshy smell from the dry swimming pool. Under the roof of the porte-cochère, a bright light shone on the gravel driveway, where I parked the car. The veranda still had crooked streaks in the dust to show where the porch furniture had been dragged away months before. I entered a dusty vestibule and knocked at glass doors of checkered red and white.

The woman who admitted me I recognized with difficulty as Mary Quayle. That was the eldest daughter: a born spinster, though her sleek black hair was bobbed and she wore new clothes smartly. She opened the door only a little, and said with sharp fearfulness, "Who's there? who's *there?*" It was not until I mentioned my name that she recognized me, and drew her elongated neck back to a reasonable size.

"Jeff! Jeff Marle!" she cried. "Gracious, how you've changed! I didn't know you were here at all. Do come in!"

She was backing away from me in the dimly lighted hall, smoothing her skirt. She had heavy-lidded eyes, and a high-bridged nose destroying beauty. Her mouth, I saw, had become thin; her rather muddy skin had settled into that drawn, dry fixity which seems peculiar to middle-aged virgins. She made several quick efforts to smile, and failed in all of them. That trick of seeming to shoot out her neck, which I had observed before, accompanied all the attempts. She had just been crying—not even the dim lights of the hall could disguise the reddened eyes, or the owl-like hollows under them.

"Your father," I suggested. "He asked me to come out. Er—"

"Did he? Do come in, Jeff!" she repeated, although I was already inside. She was flustered, trying to arrange her hair unnecessarily and acutely conscious of her swollen eyelids.

She tried to grow arch. "Imagine seeing you, of all people! —let me take your overcoat, do. There! You know, we were talking about you only the other night, and those murder cases . . ."

She stopped. The moment she said that word "murder," I thought she looked startled, even speculative and fearful as she studied me. Then she hurried on:

"Please come in! I know papa will be delighted to see you. Pardon my being upset, won't you? Mother has been taken ill, and we've all been in a flurry—"

I hesitated. "Some other time—"

"Jeff, I insist! Papa will never forgive me." A new idea brought a sudden eager gleam of relief into her eyes. "I know! It's about the book, isn't it? Of course!"

Apparently my theory had been right. Still arranging her hair and smiling, she led the way through the hall. A cut-glass lamp burned on the newel post of the staircase, and more gold frames glimmered duskily on the walls. The library door, like all the others, was brown, and had a white porcelain knob. . . .

I do not know what motive—some hazy impulse from the past, probably, for the action was involuntary—prompted me to do what I did then. With the inrush of memories, I recalled a signal Tom Quayle and I used to have. When we had wanted to see the judge about anything, and he was busy in his library, we always used a certain sort of knock. Two slow raps, and three quick ones. Smiling at Mary, I knocked thus at the library door then. . . .

I felt foolish for doing it a moment later. But I was not prepared for the queer look which came into Mary's face. The knocking rattled loudly in the quiet hall. From beyond the door, I heard the scrape of a chair pushed back, and creaking springs; it is impossible to describe what followed, and yet I felt the hiss of indrawn breath through somebody's nostrils, the shock of stiffening of somebody there in the library.

"Who's there?" demanded a voice.

I pushed the door open. Judge Quayle was standing with the firelight red on his face, and white rings showing round his eyeballs. One arm hung over the edge of the mantelpiece. The white fingers were limp, but they twitched. Beyond him, in the corner, I saw the dusty and witless marble statue— which, by some trick of perspective, seemed to goggle with empty eyes just over his shoulder.

The judge's first words were:

"Never knock that way, do you hear? Never knock—that —way."

Chapter 2

Sealed Brandy

IT HAD BEEN my first error. Even after the judge had calmed down, and greeted me with his old rigid courtesy, I knew that he was somehow suspicious of me. The knowledge had made it more difficult to establish any contact with him; we had both mumbled platitudes, and then, by some devilish piling up of unfortunate circumstances, I had made some observation about the statue. . . .

There was a dry sound as he rubbed his hands together. He raised his head from contemplating the fire, and looked at me. His eyes were weak; he did not seem to be able to hold them on anything for long. I noticed that his shoes were very shabby, and protruded with bunions.

With a shade of the old lordly manner, he said:

"Pray forgive me. I should not be so easily upset. But I am much alone, nowadays." A faint smile showed the protruding teeth. "I'm afraid I don't give you a very good welcome, sir. Accept my apologies."

"There's nothing to apologize for," I said. "I shouldn't have come at all. Mary told me that Mrs. Quayle was ill . . ."

He frowned. "Oh, it's nothing serious. The doctor is with her now." That dry sound rustled as he continued to rub his hands together, and frown, and seemed to meditate whether he should go on. "As a matter of fact, she hasn't been well for some time. Dr. Twills is a good man to have around the house."

"Twills?"

"My son-in-law," replied the judge, looking at me suddenly. "He married Clarissa."

So Clarissa, the beauty of the family, was married. . . . I had never known her well; she had been absorbed and

22

princess-like, except when flashes of curt temper disturbed the smooth face; and I remembered her in poses, with a glow as of footlights on her high cheek-bones and her madonna's eyes. In response to my murmur of congratulation, the judge waved a deprecating hand. He seemed to dismiss the matter.

"Oh, they've been married three years now. I have the highest respect for Dr. Twills' abilities. I believe," said the judge deliberately, "he has money of his own. He doesn't practise . . . Yes, he has had Mrs. Quayle under observation for some time. She has been depressed. Moody, you see, and out of sorts."

He hesitated.

"I believe she has been suffering from a mild form of peripheral neuritis. Tonight she had another attack just after dinner, and we put her to bed. Oh, she'll be all right!"

"And the rest of the family?"

Judge Quayle tried to assume a fatherly heartiness. He spoke in a deep voice, he tried to be at once brusque and kindly; but it was a failure. His eyes betrayed him.

"Well, let me see. . . . Matthew is a lawyer now, you know. The boy is doing very well . . ." (You are not thinking about Matthew Quayle Junior, judge. You have no pride in him. Your hands keep straying together again, to resume their brushing.) "Virginia is out of college, still looking for something to do. And Mary—you saw her—Mary is always here. She helps about the house."

I did not dare ask about Tom. But I could see plainly that he was thinking of Tom. His hands slid forward from his knees, and remained clasped; it was as though he were all loose bones inside the shiny black suit; and some hurt brought out the wrinkles on his forehead. Under its glass case, the little gold clock ticked audibly. . . .

I said: "When I heard you wanted to see me, sir, I hoped it was about the book. The book you have always been promising to write."

"Eh?—Oh, yes! The book, of course—"

"You've finished it?"

He sat up straight. "Why, yes. The fact is, hearing that

knock of yours on the door—and other things—well, the fact is I almost forgot it. I have prepared a manuscript," he continued, clearing his throat, "which may or may not be suitable for publication. I observe a very deplorable tendency in the writers of the present day. I am not, thank heaven, familiar with contemporary 'literature,' but certain books of Virginia's which I have chanced to pick up . . ."

I shifted in my chair. He had not lost his shrewdness; he must have seen what I was thinking, for he smiled sourly.

"Don't misunderstand me. I am not speaking of moral values, although I suppose," with bitterness, "they have disappeared also. But there are certain facts of nature, sir, so familiar that we do not need to be reminded of them on every page. There are certain—"

Quite suddenly, his cold calm left him. Blood suffused his face.

"By God, sir, it is not that they anger so much as—as they bewilder me! I can't understand. I wish I could understand."

"Understand?"

"Everything. Whatever I read, whatever I see, seems to turn every standard upside down. I feel that the world is slipping away from me. Nothing is believed to be true any longer. I don't mean sexual morality. I have been on the bench long enough to have known every sordid side of that long before your clever adolescent novelists were born. I mean . . ."

He was spasmodically opening and closing his hands, and now he rose to his feet.

"There used to be values. My family—I don't understand my family."

Whatever we discussed, he could not keep away from that. It was a lonely cry. It came from the loneliness of this room, where an old man puzzled out his days. He remained motionless, leaning on the mantelshelf, for a time. There was nothing I could say. He was only talking *at* me, and seeking some firm grip. Finally he turned, with a crooked smile.

"I still neglect my duties as host," he observed. "There is always a cure for these things."

On the other side of the fireplace there was an old-fashioned bookcase-desk, elaborately carved. Unlocking it, Judge Quayle took out a squat bottle and two glasses.

"This," he told me, "is real brandy; the kind you don't get nowadays. Do you see the seal over the cork? My grandfather put it there. They can't tamper with *this*, anyhow."

He made the last remark grimly, and turned over the dusty bottle to examine it with great care—even taking it over to the centre table and holding it up against the lights. He poured some brandy into the glasses and took up a syphon. When I declined soda, he squirted his own glass full and came over with both of them. He said:

"There was another thing I want to ask you."

"About the book?"

"No. Forget the book. It's been only a kind of—solace. I am given to understand," he lowered his head, studying me, "that you have been concerned in some unusual things since I saw you last. That you have gone in for police work . . ."

I laughed. "Just a spectator, sir."

"For police work," he repeated, "with this man—what was his name?—"

"Bencolin?"

"The head of the Paris police," Judge Quayle said slowly. He stared at his glass for a moment. Then his red-rimmed eyes began to wander about the room; they encountered the statue, and a fishy glaze crept into them.

"Well, sir?"

"I should like to meet him. I—" He seemed suddenly aware of his glass, and took a deep drink. His hand was trembling. "I—They are trying to scare me. They are trying to scare me to death. But they won't. I won't let them. Listen!"

He drank, shakily. Even his lower lip trembled. The lean figure, buttoned up in black, appeared to waver against the jumpy lights. I knew that he was losing control of himself, and I had a ghastly feeling that I myself was concerned in it; as though I were in a car skidding wildly, and unable to control it. He was disintegrating before me. On his wrinkled forehead were small beads of sweat, and his jaw had grown horribly long, like a dead man's jaw falling.

"Judge Quayle!" I said. "Judge, for God's sake!—"

It jabbed him. He got back to the padded chair and huddled into it.

"I am afraid—I am afraid you do not understand. They are all against me. All of them. They—they are not like any children I ever thought of." His voice was now high, the voice of a querulous old man. "They fight me. There is no peace. I had pictured how I would grow old with my children . . ."

A whisper. The room felt very cold.

". . . big table, spread for guests. Everyone laughing. As my father used to have it. Grandchildren. A tree at Christmas. The boys coming to me for advice. They—they don't think much of their old dad, I guess."

The whisper faded, as fingers which slide and find no hold. A light wind rattled at the windows; this room of the gold-framed pictures had turned bleak with the man's words. He had just lifted his glass again, to drink noisily, when there was a knock at the door. . . .

The newcomer had hurried in and addressed himself to the judge before becoming aware of my presence. He was a small, rather harassed-looking man who wore a baggy grey suit and no collar; the brass stud gleamed absurdly at the foot of his scrawny neck. His mild blue eyes were magnified behind big double-lensed spectacles, out of all proportion to the rest of his face. But his forehead was intelligent, the fair hair clipped close above it.

"She'll be all right, father, I think," he said. "I don't understand—"

With an effort the judge recovered his calm. Rising, he set his glass on the mantelshelf, and interposed:

"Walter, shake hands with Mr. Marle. Mr. Marle, Dr. Twills."

Twills started a little as he turned to face me. Then his abstracted eyes awoke, and he grew even more nervous. He had a trick of moving the scalp backwards and forwards on his bulging forehead, as boys do when they try ineffectually to wiggle their ears.

"Oh," he said. "Er—how d'ye do? I didn't know there was anybody here."

"Well, Walter?"

"Excuse me. I wonder," said the doctor apologetically, "whether I could see you a minute in private, sir? It's about Mrs. Quayle's condition. If you will pardon us, Mr. Marle?"

The judge looked at him heavily, gripping the edge of the mantel.

"She's not worse?"

"It isn't that! It's . . . well!—"

Bowing, Judge Quayle followed him out into the hall. The lovely Clarissa's husband? The lovely Clarissa's husband, this rabbit-like, middle-aged man with the nervous hands? I wondered whether these outbursts and jumpy antics on everybody's part represented an ordinary evening at the Quayle home; it was growing just a little mad. I was just lifting my glass when I heard the judge's snarling voice raised beyond the door.

"You're lying," it said. "You're lying. I don't believe it. She never said anything of the kind—"

Twills murmured something, which was cut short.

"You're lying," the judge repeated. "It's a damned plot, and you're in it. I won't listen to any of it."

His voice had risen dangerously even before he came banging back into the library. The globes of the chandelier tinkled as he threw the door open, and the lights flickered. Twills followed him, trying to talk to his back.

"You've got to listen, sir!" cried Twills. "I tell you—"

On the hearth-rug again, the judge whirled. His hand was raised.

"Get out of here!—"

He had taken a step forward, but he stopped, and in a toneless voice he said: "Oh, my God." The pupils of his eyes were strangely dilated, and he stood rigid for a moment. . . . His right hand darted to his collar; he was trying desperately to talk out of a dry throat which would not let any words through. Then he seized the edge of the mantel, and worked his neck from side to side. His eyes were glassy now. Through his teeth blew a sort of hideous gurgling, so that bubbles formed on his lips.

Twills cried, *"Judge!"* and took a step forward. . . .

The fingers of Judge Quayle's right hand tore loose from the edge of the mantel. He slid down to his knees, gasping; he rolled over, struck his head against the brass fender, and lay motionless with one arm almost in the fire.

We did not move. We heard the stertorous bubbling of his breath and saw his long hair disarranged over the side of the fender; but the thing was so horribly unreal that momentarily we were incapable of doing anything. I felt my arm shaking so that the brandy spilled over on my hand. Twills was plucking at his collar-stud, working his lips without sound.

Then Twills sprang past me. He bent over his father-in-law; when he turned again, he was pale, efficient, and very cool.

"He drank from that glass?" the doctor demanded, pointing.

"Yes."

"You drank from the same bottle?"

"No. That is, I hadn't begun to drink. I—"

"Good," said Twills, nodding decisively. "He's not unconscious yet. Help me get him into my surgery at once. I should have known it when he flew off the handle like that. He's been poisoned. Easy, now; get his shoulders, and I'll take his legs."

Chapter 3

"It Ran Like a Spider—"

WE CARRIED the judge to a small room at the back of the house, which was fitted out as a surgery. A shaded gas-lamp burned on a centre table, where many books lay open and a pencil marked a place in one of them. Bottles glinted dully on the wall; there was a smell of disinfectant. When we had hurried Judge Quayle on one of those padded examination tables, Twills turned swiftly to me.

"You know more about this sort of thing than I do, I dare say," he told me, with a pale smile. "But I can handle *him* alone. I think I know just what it is. Oh, God forgive me!" Suddenly he jammed his fists into his eyes. "I think I'm responsible. Never mind. . . . Take care of those two glasses, will you, and see that nobody gets them?"

He was stripping off his coat and rolling up his sleeves. I said:

"Right. Sure you don't want any help here?"

"Don't need it. Oh, you might telephone the hospital and tell them to send out a trained nurse."

"Bad as that?"

"For *her*. For his wife. She's in bad shape. I still wonder—"

"If that's poison too?"

" 'Fraid so. But this is more of a necessity now. Look here, you might see if you can find the supper tray she used tonight; maybe the dishes haven't been done yet."

"Where are the rest of the family?"

"Mary's in the kitchen, I think. Matt's upstairs with his mother. Jinny and my wife are out.—But don't pay any attention to anybody else, get me?" The mild eyes behind those thick glasses were squeezed up, and stared at me rather fiercely, as though we shared a secret.

I said: "Look here, doctor: what the devil's going on in this house?"

"Crazy work. You'll see. You walked in on the climax of it. Hurry!"

I left him switching on a brilliant drop-lamp behind the screen he had drawn about Judge Quayle. The telephone was where I remembered it; in a closet under the stairs. When I had phoned the hospital, I went back slowly to the library.

My first impulse, to put the brandy-bottle and the glasses in a safe place, was purely automatic. It was brought about by no suspicion, beyond a confused sense of bewilderment. It was (Twills had said it) Crazy Work. But even now I should have been startled at the word Murder. Such things are not brewed at home, where death comes respectably, with sobs and black clothes. In other lands we can take murder unquestioningly, as a deplorable part of the civilization, like the coffee of France or the cigarettes of Germany— inseparable from the weird minds of foreigners. But it does not occur in big dingy houses we have known since boyhood. It does not occur among our lifelong friends, whom we cannot conceive as having any emotions at all.

Crazy Work. A kind of ghastly private theatrical, such as Tom Quayle, I could not help thinking, would have enjoyed putting on. Tom had always been stringing up a curtain made of a bedsheet on a wire, and staging shows; he had been one of the best tellers of ghost stories I ever heard. (I could see him now, the firelight on his dark pointed face, fashioning his words with grisly rollings, and Jinny Quayle whimpering in a corner.) All the puzzling events of this night paraded past me in the dim hallway. The judge's agitation at my knock; his silences and outbursts; the statue with the missing—well, how *had* its hand come to be broken off, anyhow? Crazy Work, purely.

I went into the library, and stared about. It was filled with a hard brightness; one of the gas-mantles hissed slightly. Wind had begun to thrum the window-panes, so that reflections quivered in their black surfaces, and the gimcrack lace-and-velvet draperies twitched about. The plaster frescoes of the ceiling were very dirty, and the dull flowered carpet was worn in several places. Through the seats of these padded chairs, you could see the outline of their springs. They looked drunken; the tassels were broken and frayed. It was all very stolid; the bookcases as respectable as matrons; the bad portraits, complacent in gilt frames, were as sturdy as beef on a big dinner-table. . . .

A commonplace library. You felt, nevertheless, the presence of something leering and ugly. A vibration, a pale terror like the mist on a photographic plate. Then I saw my glass, full of the dark red brandy, where I had left it on the floor beside my chair, and I felt a little sick. Not long ago I had almost drunk that brandy. A physical nausea of relief made my skin crawl now; I looked up sharply, and saw the gaping statue in the corner. . . .

The fire had almost died. That mantelpiece, of brown and blistered wood, was almost as ugly as the house. It had a dusty, knitted cover with red tassels. Beside the clock stood the judge's glass, almost empty.

What was the poison? I looked back at the centre table, where the dusty bottle squatted beside the syphon. Then I went over and picked it up. It was a Ferlac cherry, 1870. I sniffed at the bottle, remembering that the bitter-almonds odour of cyanide could be concealed by cherry brandy. But cyanide was much quicker in its effect; almost, they said, instantaneous.

If some one had wanted to murder . . . oh, nonsense! The idea buzzed like a gnat, ugly and uncomfortable. I slapped at it. It would not go away.

Incongruous, to see a poison-bottle standing on the placid table among the litter. Beside it, on the worn blotter, was a small iron press for clipping fasteners on legal documents, and a few bright gilt fasteners were strewn over the papers there. Penholders, pipes, a tobacco jar. Books were piled round the blotter; apparently all reference-works used by the judge in preparing his manuscript, for I caught some of the titles: Ellis' *History of Fayette County*, Veech's *The Monongahela of Old*, Searight's *The Old Pike*, Doddridge's *Notes on the Settlements and Indian Wars of the Western Parts of Virginia and Pennsylvania, 1763-1783*. All of them had yellow note-sheets protruding from their pages.

This was wasting time. I took up the bottle, along with

the judge's glass and mine, locked them in the cabinet from which he had taken them, and put the key in my pocket. Now to see about that supper-tray from which Mrs. Quayle had eaten.

How still the house was! Judge Quayle had toppled over—I could still hear the clash of the fender as his head struck it—and nobody stirred or ran out. Twills said that Mary was in the kitchen, and young Matt Quayle upstairs with his mother. I had better go upstairs; the tray was probably still there. And how to approach this mission? Well, better say nothing about poison as yet . . .

The steps were covered with thick red-flowered carpet, but they creaked on every tread. Even the stair-rail was wobbly. I felt, somehow, furtive. It was now a question of meeting Matthew Quayle Junior, a prospect which I did not relish. I wondered whether he was the same as when I used to know him. Matt had been the perennial college undergraduate, even before he got to college. He was in all likelihood the perennial college undergraduate even after he had left it. Matt played the banjo, incessantly and well, and he swayed ecstatically while he played. He himself was reminiscent of a loudly twanging banjo, on which some celestial Pollyanna was always plunking chords in order to demonstrate what a happy world you lived in. You felt that you could sympathize with his misfortunes, if only you did not have to put up with his enthusiasms.

Mrs. Quayle's room was at the front of the house, and the door was open. A dim lamp, with a newspaper tied round the shade, burned at the head of the bed. It lit the blue-flowered wall-paper, and the marriage license hanging discreetly framed above the walnut bureau.

In the bed, a white face with untidy grey hair, lay Mrs. Quayle. A stab caught me. Her face was flabby and drawn, with bluish lips, and there were dark pouches under the closed eyelids. A cotton nightgown heaved with her unsteady breathing. Even in sleep she looked tired, baffled, worn out with trying. That face swam in the dim light, as weary as she, and the night wind banged at the windows. She too had been crying.

Somebody got up hurriedly from a squeaky chair beside the bed. Peering at me uncomprehendingly, a face approached through the gloom. It was young Matthew Quayle, but I did not immediately look at him. The face on the bed smacked toothless gums, muttering something in sleep; down the dark ragged pouches under the eyes trickled a few tears. I felt a lump in my throat. She had been—well, everybody had liked her, and she had let us make as much noise as we liked.

I beckoned Matt out into the hall. He was tall, with brown hair, which had begun to thin considerably, parted in the middle; a rather bulbous blue eye, and a reddish face. I knew exactly what he would say. He would say, "Well, Jeff, you old son of a gun!"—laugh genially, and slap me on the shoulder, though we had not seen each other in ten years. He did.

"What in the world," said Matt Quayle, with low-voiced heartiness, "brings you up here?" Stuffing a copy of a magazine into his pocket, he thumped my shoulder. "Come on down to my room. Mother's a little upset, you know, but she'll be all right. Haven't seen you in years!"

"I came to see your father," I explained. "He isn't feeling well, and Dr. Twills asked me if I'd step up here and see about—"

He looked at me in surprise. "About mother?"

"He said something she ate upset her, and he wanted to know where the things she'd eaten had been taken to, so he could find out what disagreed with her."

"Oh! I see! Sure. Well, she had her supper sent up; hadn't been feeling well, d'ye see. Joanna—that's the maid—took the tray downstairs a long time ago. You can probably find it in the kitchen. But what the devil, Jeff; don't make an errand-boy of yourself! Let Walter go get it himself."

"How is she?"

Matthew Quayle looked at me curiously. He must have seen something, for he dropped his assumed heartiness. He became what he was: serious-minded, cautious, and at bottom intelligent and nervous under his professional manners. A shaft of light from the room caught his worried eyes, and he mopped the scraggly hair back from his forehead.

"Look here, Jeff," he said, trying to be whimsical, "you haven't—my God, the old kid I used to play with!—you haven't let things—go to your head and—turned private detective or something, have you?"

"Good Lord, no! Why should I?"

"Well, you can't tell. These writers," he grinned, heavily jocose but nervous, "queer in the head, you know!"

"That isn't the real reason, is it, Matt?"

His eyes narrowed. "How much do you know?"

"Enough to keep quiet. And I may be able to help."

For a long time we looked at each other. At length he answered softly:

"By God, it's worth a try! We're all at wits' end, Jeff. . . . All right. You go see about that tray, and come back here. I'll wait."

"Where are the rest of them?"

"Clarissa's out at her ladies' bridge club. Jinny has a date with some kid from town. They won't be in for some time."

I nodded; he entered and reclosed the door. Everybody in the house! Everybody in the house peering over his shoulder, making mention of an unknown bogey! I descended the stairs again and went to the kitchen. There was a muffled scream as I pushed open the squeaky door. Jumping up from her chair beside the white stove, Mary Quayle let fall a long-handled spoon. Very white, her lips pulled back from pale gums, she stared at me. Then she sat down in the chair again, drew a hand across her reddened eyelids, and said: "I can't stand this! I can't stand—!"

I put my arm around her shoulder, and felt her trembling. She clung to my hand. A stately face, Mary's also, for all its faint lines and its dull brown tinge; but it was smeared over with fear.

"I've got to watch that oatmeal," she told me hurriedly, and hastened to turn off the gas in the range. "For breakfast tomorrow, the way papa likes it . . ."

"You'd better tell me," I suggested; "you'll feel better." On an inspiration I remembered something which I still carried. Bencolin had given it to me when I worked with him on the Tellier case at Deauville, and it was still in my wallet: the famous tricoloured badge, with the staring eye, and the words *Préfecture de Police*. I showed it to her, smiling. "And there's no reason," I said, "why an old friend shouldn't help."

"I can't tell you, Jeff!" she cried desperately, "I mean, about . . . But something frightened me a minute ago, five minutes; I don't know. I was so scared I didn't dare leave the kitchen, because the hall's dark, and I was afraid of the pantry because it's dark too, and . . ."

"What did you see, Mary?"

"It was—Jeff, as God's my judge, this is true!—it was something white."

"Not seeing ghosts, Mary?"

"No, no! This wasn't like that. It wasn't big, like a person. It was small. About the size of your hand."

In spite of myself, my smile froze. "Well, Mary?" I said casually.

"You see there, through the door of the pantry? You can just see the ledge of the cabinet from here—see? The coffee-can's on it. Well, something white ran along the ledge there and back again. It looked as though it had legs."

I patted her shoulder and stepped towards the pantry door. For there had been games like this before, in that weird November night at the Brimstone Club in London when Bencolin and I watched with Scotland Yard to trap a criminal who called himself Jack Ketch. But this was more horrible. The prosaic surroundings, the oatmeal on the stove, the white-tiled kitchen . . . I snapped on the hanging light in the centre of the small pantry. Wooden shelves above the ledge, all as usual; electric refrigerator, sink and drainboard with a head of lettuce on it. A window above the sink was open. I latched it and returned.

"There's some wrapping paper," I told Mary, "on the ledge, and a breeze from that window. That's what you saw."

"I—I hope so," she said. She was regarding me with great black unwavering eyes, and one finger fumbled at her lower lip. "Yes! Yes, Jeff, that must have been what it was! . . ."

"Suppose you go upstairs with your mother and Matt. She may need attention, and he won't know what to do." That caught her; she rose quickly. "But first: is your mother's supper tray still here? Dr. Twills wants to look at it and see which dish upset her."

"The tray? Yes, of course, Jeff—there it is, in the pantry. Didn't you see?"

"In the pantry!"

"Yes, on the chair. I was going to wash the dishes. This is Joanna's night off."

"But didn't you wash them?"

"Oh, no. It hasn't been touched."

I went into the pantry again, and saw a covered tray in a corner where the light did not fall on it. It looked as though some hand had recently plucked aside the covering.

"Did she have the same food as the rest of you tonight?"

"Oh, no, Jeff; she *couldn't*! She's been ailing. She had some milk-toast and tea; that's all. I can't understand why any of *that* would upset her, do you? How can Walter tell?"

"Who prepared it—Joanna?"

"No. I did. Just the way she likes it, the tea strong."

"Did you take it up yourself?"

"No, Jeff; Matt did. He was hanging around the kitchen, you know, kidding Joanna, and he offered to . . ." All of a sudden her eyes clouded, as though with tears, and she spoke so fast that I could hardly follow: "Oh, my God, Jeff, there isn't anything *wrong*, is there? Don't tell me you—" Her fingers opened and shut spasmodically.

"No, of course not, Mary! I just wanted to get the thing straight, that's all. . . . Come along now, and go upstairs. Your mother may need something."

"Matt's so *careless*!" she fretted, smoothing her dress as she rose. "But, Jeff! What on earth are you doing, wandering around like this! I left you with . . . Where's papa?"

"He doesn't want to be disturbed. He's looking over his manuscript before I take it along with me."

She sighed. "I know. I typed it out for him. Oh, Jeff,

it's wonderful! And they won't let papa have any peace! I get so mad sometimes I could kill Clarissa and Jinny— but they don't mean any harm, of course!" She looked at me quickly, as though she thought I believed her guilty of disloyalty; she smiled, and followed me as I took up the covered tray.

I was mortally afraid that Dr. Twills might call out from his room and betray things before I got her upstairs; but I watched her ascend the staircase, and then took the tray to his surgery.

He had drawn a tall screen of white cloth round the table. The brilliant drop-light behind made sharp shadows across it; I saw the doctor's shape grotesquely distorted, weaving in silhouette over a huddle with the shadow of one hand dangling. The writhing shape bent and expanded; I heard the clink of instruments laid swiftly down on porcelain, and smelt a heavy medicinal odour I could not identify. A moaning and gasping followed. The dangling hand clenched its fingers. . . .

Presently Dr. Twills came out from behind the screen, after having turned out the light. He rolled down his sleeves slowly, still pale, and with the corners of his mouth turned down.

"He'll live," said the doctor. "Ah, I see you've got the tray. Put it down there, will you? Got a cigarette? That was a close call."

He sat down wearily, drawing smoke into his lungs.

"Was it—?" I began.

"Yes. Poison. Fortunately what I thought. It's not a common poison, and it's a damned dangerous one, Mr. Marle. If I hadn't been right——"

He gestured, and the pleasant eyes behind his spectacles crinkled up in a smile. "The poison? Hydrobromide of hyoscin. A quarter to a half grain is a fatal dose. You get a little delirium and excitement at first; then the pupils of the eyes become paralyzed, the mouth and throat dry; next drowsiness, unconsciousness, and complete paralysis, death in a few hours."

"Never heard of it."

You wouldn't have; it's not a drug commonly used. Hyoscin is never given by the mouth when it is used legitimately, d'ye see. You inject it hypodermically—in very small doses —as a powerful sedative for mania, or meningitis, or delirium tremens; something like that. Never more than two hundredths of a grain."

He contemplated the end of his cigarette. I demanded, "Then how——?"

"How did any member of this household have access to it? Well," said the doctor deprecatingly, "you see, I own five or six grains myself."

Chapter 4

Hyoscin in the Syphon

It now seemed to me surprising that this was the same vague, timid, weak-chinned man who had scurried in to speak to Judge Quayle. His appearance had not altered, but his mouse-like eyes behind those huge shell spectacles turned towards me amusedly. He wrinkled his forehead in a way that moved the close-cropped fair hair backwards and forwards, and smiled.

"Not guilty, of course, Mr. Marle," he murmured, "else I shouldn't have been quite so quick to revive him, should I? . . . No; I only meant that the stuff belonged to me. When I was on the staff of the Bellevue Hospital, I frequently needed it in the psychopathic ward. Only a doctor could get it, I imagine. It's rather special. And no pharmacist, so far as I know, would carry it in stock."

"And your supply?"

"Gone. I found it out this evening. I was afraid of this." He drew a long breath.

"Why?"

He made vague irritated gestures. When he spoke, his calm had gone, and it was with a weak, almost childish petulance: "Oh, see here, Mr. Marle! You know what this is as well as I do, don't you?"

"So," I observed, "do we face it, or don't we? It looks like attempted murder."

"Yes. But not, thank the Lord, a case for the police—yet. I see no reason why we shouldn't deal with it ourselves. A person got in here—when, I don't know, because I hadn't looked in that particular cabinet for days——"

"The surgery is never locked?"

"No. We've," he suddenly spoke with bitterness, "no kids around. And I don't practise; it's just a laboratory. As I

39

was saying, somebody got in here and took a bottle containing six grains of a deadly poison. In addition to that, there are two other poisons floating around this place."

"Two other poisons?"

" 'M, yes. I suspected what was wrong with the old lady tonight. I treated her for it, without letting the rest of them know, or they'd have been scared to death. When I look at the contents of that tray, I shall be positive. Somebody's been giving her arsenic for several days. I only suspected it tonight, when I found the hyoscin gone. Arsenic poisoning, you know, isn't something that jumps up and hits you in the face, unless you have reason to suspect it."

"But a *third* poison?"

Dr. Twills crushed out his cigarette, asked for another, and lighted it. "That," he responded, after a nervous scowling at the screen, "isn't something I want to discuss. Somebody has designs on the old lady and . . . but, I tell you, I've got to be sure first! In the name of heaven, there mustn't be any scandal!"

He got up and started to pace about, flinging his arms.

"I don't know. Maybe I'm morbid, or something. But, understand, I can't get along with that gang! They scare hell out of me. I don't know why. When I'm with anybody else, I'm all right. Give me a case to handle, or some kind of problem I can study without anybody watching me—well, I breathe deep, and my nerves relax, and I'm *all right*. They all look at me as though they were saying, 'What good are you?' I can't play golf, and I can't play bridge, and I'm damn glad of it—oh, and I don't dance, either. And I'm no good socially, and my clothes look all cockeyed. D'you know Clarissa?" he demanded, blinking at me from mild eyes.

"She's the beauty," I nodded.

Twills said bitterly: "She's the beauty, yes. I'm telling you this—d'you mind if I get a load off my chest?—because I'll respect your discretion. Because you can do all the things I want to do. I studied in Vienna. I want to go back there and specialize. I want to eat rolls and coffee in the morning and see the Hapsburg arms in the roof of the cathedral over the roofs, and smell geranium in my window-boxes; I want to work all day in a laboratory, and drink a glass of beer at night and listen to waltzes in a beer-garden before I go home and work some more." He checked his restless pacing. "Never mind. I've got to get at that supper-tray."

"But can't you?" I prompted. "Go to Vienna, I mean? Clarissa would like it. And since you're not—impecuni-ous——"

He shook his head, slowly. The queer, likeable whimsicality of his eyes deepened into a grin. "Off my nut for a minute, eh? Sorry. We'll talk later. I'm going to get the judge to bed on the couch here; I often sleep here, and there'll be blankets. I wish you'd break the news to the rest of them. He's out of serious danger now. Oh, and the nurse ought to be in any minute now. Send her in, will you?"

"Just a minute," I put in. "There are a couple of things I'd like to ask. If I'm not intruding . . ."

"You're not. This is going to be settled. Well?"

"We'll face it. Should you say that anybody in this house was anxious to—to get rid of the judge or his wife?"

Twills started to answer, but paused. "No. Not yet. I'll tell you later. Give me a chance! I've got my own ideas."

"Well, then. Did anybody here know that the judge invited me here this evening? Neither Mary nor Matt seemed to; and I should think that if he telephoned they couldn't help knowing."

"I don't think so. H'm. You think—he had a purpose?"

"No, not exactly. . . . Did he always stay in his library in the evenings?"

"Always," said Twills, looking puzzled. "Wrote every night, six-thirty to ten, regular as clockwork."

"Usually have a drink?"

"Always, but not very much. A glass or two. It didn't hurt him."

"The same stuff—brandy?"

"Brandy or whisky, nothing else. By the way, where are those glasses?"

I told him they were locked in the cabinet. I was still wondering how the poison had been introduced into the brandy. If, of course, Judge Quayle had been in the habit of taking a glass every night, then the task of an attempted murderer would be very simple. On the other hand, I recalled that he had commented on the unbroken seal of the bottle he produced, and his grim words, "They can't tamper with *this*!" He suspected poison, then? Or did he merely mean that nobody could sample his stock without his knowledge? Now if he got that bottle for the special occasion of welcoming me—instead of his usual bottle—the murderer could not possibly have anticipated it, even if (as seemed unlikely) the occupants of the house knew that a guest was to be present. The dust on the bottle seemed to indicate that it had been selected from the bins that very day, probably not earlier than this evening. . . .

As I came out into the hallway again, the doorbell rang. A stout, very capable-looking woman, with a coat over her dress of starched linen, announced that she was from the hospital, and gave her name as Miss Herries. I sent her back to the doctor, and then went upstairs after Mary and Matt. They could leave the patient, for the nurse would be up in a moment, so I brought them downstairs to the library.

Explaining that there had been an accident, I told them what had happened, and assured them that their father was entirely out of danger. I went through the recital very slowly, watching their faces. The moment I mentioned that Twills was taking care of him in the surgery, Mary bolted out of the room. I heard her wailing, "Walter! Walter!" in the hall, and then a muffled banging at the surgery door.

Throughout, Matt had not moved. I was trying to trace him out, to get a grip on the undergraduate bumptiousness which was just below the surface of his nature. He stood beside the table, with the strong light on the side of his ruddy, impassive face, slowly running a hand up and down his lapel. He still carefully wore Rosenberg suits and Frank shoes. He was merely a taller, more fleshy version of the earlier Matt I had known, as the sham Tudor buildings of his college were a larger version of the sham Tudor buildings at his preparatory school. Pink jowls swelled over his collar. His boiled blue eyes, without brows, had assumed an expression of conscious cunning. His lips were pressed to-gether. After a long time he remarked:

"Not so very frank, were you, Jeff?"

"There was no need for telling," I said, "until the danger was over."

Still his hand moved up and down his lapel. "Oh, *I'm* not worried. I had nothing to do with it. . . . How foxy are you trying to be?"

"You can go to hell," I said.

"Oh, come on, now, Jeff!" He looked injured. He wrinkled his nose, to indicate apologetic friendliness. "I didn't mean anything! Only I didn't want any of the foxy-detective stuff put over on me." Then he took out a silk handkerchief to mop his moist pink forehead, demonstrating Overwrought Feelings. "Look, old fellow, I'm all upset! This thing has just about finished me. Why, we've been friends since we were kids! Why, I wouldn't have you take offence——"

"Can you get it through your head," I interposed, "how serious this thing is? If you'll try to be natural, and drop that fraternity-brother talk for a minute——"

He sat down. "I get you. But I *am* upset. Look here, this poison business doesn't concern mother, does it? I mean—*she* hasn't been poisoned?"

"You'll have to ask Twills that. I don't know."

"Say, Jeff—listen. You wouldn't—I mean, you won't say anything about this, will you? It would ruin me. You have no idea!"

I controlled my temper. "You realize, then, that some-body in the house has tried to kill your father and very probably your mother?"

"Jeff, that's impossible! Ho, what a crazy idea!" He rolled back in the chair, his mouth twisted with fantastic jollity. "That's out of the question. Unless—why, sure! Why didn't I think of it? Listen: it's that maid. She's a Slav or some-thing, and . . . Listen, Jeff!" He had become terribly earnest, and rather piteous. "You know there's a mistake! You *know* nobody would try what you're talking about!"

"Please quite down. You promised to talk this thing over a while ago. Why can't we do it? Then, possibly——"

"But what is there to talk over?"

I passed him my cigarette-case, and we both took one. We were silent for a time after lighting the cigarettes. A clock ticked.

"Well, the domestic atmosphere, for instance . . ."

"Oh, pshaw!" he snorted. "It's like any other house. Good home—why, I *love* this place, Jeff!" He kept growling "domestic atmosphere," puffing.

"All relations cordial?"

"Look: I'm wise. I stay out of all that. In this world, old boy, we've got to look out for Number One; I'm on good terms with everybody, thanks. . . . Jinny fights dad; so does Clarissa, and especially mother. But me? Well, you see how it is, Jeff. I just stay out of his way. If he says, 'Come on into the library, Matt, and let's have a chat, the way we used to,' I just say, 'Sorry, dad; got to go out,' and, believe me, I *hike*. He looks kind of funny sometimes," said Matt, reflectively. "But, listen, Jeff! He prob'ly wants to read me his silly book, or something. What have I got to talk about to him? Why, he never even went to law school!" Matt made this remark earnestly, as though he were stating some deep and rather shameful secret. "Would you believe it? And dad a judge! But it's true."

(Matthew Quayle Junior, I should like to wring your neck. Under the shadow of the great lawyers whose voices boom from the old days, you will grub forever among deeds and minor litigations and catchpenny knavery, and on your grave shall be written, "He went to law school." But now, Matthew Quayle, I will question you carefully, and trap you if I can.)

I heard Matt strike the arm of his chair.

"By the Lord!" he muttered, and as I glanced at him interrogatively, "Poison . . . I believe I've got something!"

"What?"

"I wish I could remember who said it, that's all. We were talking about poisons not a week ago."

"Who?"

"All of us. At the dinner-table. Wait a minute; let me think; I'd forgotten all about it." He waved his hand and scowled. "Yes. We had roast lamb that day. H'm. Somebody told a story about some Roman guy . . . You know, Julius Caesar or Nero or somebody like that; I never could keep 'em straight. Well, it seems that somebody's relative wanted to poison this guy, but he was pretty cagey. He had a taster who took a mouthful of everything before he'd touch it. And then one day they brought him some soup that was hotter than hell. The taster said it was all right, but to put some water in it from a cooler they had there. So they did, and it seems the relative had put poison in the water-cooler—so it killed this fellow, after all . . . I don't suppose that's much help . . ."

"Who told the story?"

"That's what I can't remember. I think it was one of the girls. Probably Jinny; she's reading that junk all the time. Oh, well, what's the difference?" asked Matt, rising and shaking himself. "Don't mean anything, anyhow. I——"

He paused as we heard a motor in the drive, and saw the lights of a car flash past the front windows.

"That's Jinny or Clarissa coming home," said Matt, snapping his fingers. "They'll have to be told. I'd better do it myself. You might—er—you know!" He was manifestly excited; for what reason, I could not conjecture. "Now you just stay here," he continued soothingly, "and I'll attend to everything. They might get excited; you know how women are. If you'd like to talk to them, I'll send them in here. Just wait a minute. I'll shut the door—eh?"

He was blossoming into artificial smiles, backing towards the door with a writhing motion, and generally behaving like a man who has to obey an urgent call of nature. He bustled out as steps sounded on the veranda.

But I was thinking of other things. It seemed that "one of the girls" had been reading Suetonius, the tale of the soup with which Agrippina slew the elder brother of Nero. As dinner-table conversation, it hardly seemed to fit smoothly into the Quayle household. Caligula's statue, over there in the corner, had drawn back its flabby lips in a chuckle.

Oh, yes. The dwellers in the Golden House knew refinements too subtle for the modern criminal. When Claudius was ill, surrounded by guards, they killed him nevertheless by poisoning the feather he thrust down his throat to aid in vomiting. The present-day murderer has no such delicate ingenuity; he dumps white arsenic (old when Olympiodorus used it) into his victim's coffee, or else—scorning such effete methods—he goes about his business forthrightly with a machine-gun. But that story from Suetonius . . .

Good God! I stared at the Roman statue, and then whirled back to the table, because there had come some presentiment of the truth. I had been asking myself heretofore how the *brandy* could have been poisoned. On the table were still scattered pieces of the seal which had been over the cork. The wax was clearly too old to have been tampered with. Besides, the poisoner could not have known there was to be a guest; he could not have known Judge Quayle would go after a bottle from the cellar that afternoon; and, even if he had been aware of these things, he could not have known which bottle, among many, the judge would select. No. The poisoner wanted to be sure that his victim drank the hyoscin *no matter what bottle or what kind of liquor* was used. And Judge Quayle never drank without soda-water. . . .

Somebody had listened too well to that story of the deadly water-cooler. Somebody had introduced hydrobromide of hyoscin into the syphon.

The door opened. I started guiltily, my hand on the syphon. The introduction of a dead Roman's craft at murder into this prosaic house by the mountains, while Caligula's statue grinned at the stump of his arm, made it all the more horrible. . . . I turned, and saw Virginia Quayle looking at me from the door.

"I—are they all right?" she said breathlessly. "Are they all *right*, Jeff?"

Her face was flushed with the cold. I had forgotten her eyes. They were wide, and greenish, and long-lashed; they were suddenly so familiar, so strong with the vividness of the past, that I could not speak.

Then she hurried forward in her galoshes, which made a clinking sound in the quiet room. You got the impression, somehow, that she had been running. She had flung off a small brown hat; her very heavy bobbed hair—of that tawny richness which seems always to be flowing—was pushed back from a high forehead, and quivered against her cheek. Her mouth was twitching at one side, as though for a crooked smile. There were gleams of melted snow on the collar of her camel's-hair coat. *Clink, clink, clink-clink* slapped the galoshes. I took her cold hands; she was trembling.

"They're all right, Jinny," I said. "Entirely!"

Her eyes doubted; then they grew fixed, and regarded me with sombre nervousness, like a child's. She said in a low voice:

"It's—it's pretty awful, isn't it? What are we going to do?"

"There's nothing to do, Jinny. I suppose Matt's told you?"

She let out a little attempt at a laugh. "Yes. He's told me—what to say, and what not to say. Damn him. It— it *was* a shock. I came home expecting to get the devil from father, and find . . . Can I see him, Jeff? I mean, I care a lot about him, in spite of what they say . . ."

"Better you don't, for a while. He's in good hands."

She nodded, still in that sombre fashion. She was breathing less heavily now.

"Yes. Walter's a good egg, Jeff; Walter's a peach and an angel. The only sane person in the place, if you ask me.— Listen! I mean: You're not joking, are you? He isn't *dying*, is he?"

She spoke with terrible vehemence, searching my face again. I said:

"Good Lord, no! It's no more than glorified indigestion. He'll be up and about tomorrow. There's absolutely no reason for alarm."

I released her hands, and she went over slowly to sit down on the arm of a chair. Staring at the floor, she kept slapping her hat nervously against her side; her face was in the shadow of that rich-glowing hair, but I could imagine its pinched and shuddering determination. . . .

At last she said in a muffled voice:

"Matt—ugh! Acting like a dirty little shyster. . . . All he could say was, 'Now you mustn't answer any questions, you mustn't answer any questions.' About his own father. Jeff, you wouldn't——?"

"You know better than that."

"Then—will you let me ask *you* a question?"

"Naturally. If I can answer it."

"Well, then." She moved the tip of her galosh about on the floor; she seemed to be straining forward to utter each word. "Well, then . . . Did he—that is, did he do it himself—I mean, did he try to—commit—suicide?"

"I don't think so, Jinny."

She said in a whisper: "Oh, my God, I knew it."

"What do you mean?"

"Oh, not that!" she cried, gesturing. "I mean, I didn't know *what*. But I knew something was going to happen. Something awful. Every time I come into the house I'm in a cold sweat, expecting it. And when Matt was talking I suddenly thought—!"

"Listen, Jinny. You've got to brace up. Take off your things; have a cigarette. . . ."

"You'd brood too," she said viciously, "if you had to live in this place very long. Oh, well!"

She drew a long breath. She kicked off her overshoes, slipped out of the coat, and tossed her scarf over the back of the chair. There was a wistful wrinkle between her brows, a wryly humorous expression about her eyes, as she looked up smiling, and knocking one foot slowly against the side of the chair. "After all, I haven't even said howdy, have I? And all these years!—I'm all right now. Yes, give me a cigarette. You look a lot older."

"So do you. And beautiful."

A pause. She was taking a cigarette from my case, and she looked up steadily. She said:

"I don't mind that from *you*. But I won't—I tell you I *won't* sit out in parked cars with halfwits who tell me how well they're doing in the real estate business, and how soon they expect to have—! Thanks." She lit the cigarette and blew out smoke hard. "—expect to have this, and that, and a sum here, and a sum there, and what-the-hell. That's fine; let 'em do it. But why inflict it on me? *I'm* not interested."

"Meaning that you've been listening to it tonight?"

" 'M. Well. Let's not talk about it. I wonder whether men go through life serenely imagining that women are interested in their businesses?"

"What about women in love?"

"Oh, that's no different. They just think about the person. They imagine him heroically buying real estate, or dauntlessly selling it, or cornering the market with dashing gallantry, or whatever it is you do with real estate; I'm not sure." She frowned reflectively. "Anyhow, it's the person. S'posin'—just s'posin'—I were in love with a brick-layer, d'ye see? Well, I could listen for hours, absolutely entranced, to a lecture about the science of bigger and better bricks. But all I'd think about would be him wielding the trowel."

This was better. Watching the reflective green eyes, which grew so absorbed in everything occupying her, and which seemed always to be groping out after some slightly puzzling idea. I felt that somehow I had always been wanting to talk to Jinny Quayle. She was at once a stranger and an old friend. The tingle of stimulation with a new, eager girl; the druglike charm of relaxing with an old friend. Once we used to walk in an avenue of willows, dead grey-green under the moon; there was an arched bridge with water falling under it; and, through a rift in the trees, you could see one impossibly small star. I remembered the mysterious sound rushing water makes at night-time, and the cool of willow branches. We always began by joking; we always finished with some monstrously solemn conversation, far into the night, about Life.

"Penny?" she said.

I dragged my thoughts back to a poisoner's house. "It's this place. The way people have been acting tonight—crazy work——"

"What do you mean?"

"Well, for instance. What do you know about 'something white,' which runs along pantry shelves or window ledges?"

Intimacy was broken, smashed in small bits. There was no more communion, lighted by a small star out of the past. All that remained was the word Murder. She gasped. Then she began to laugh, rather hysterically.

"So it's out! The lurid secret's out. Jeff, this is too good!"

I had not prepared for any such jarring crash. Her laughter turned to a cough as she swallowed smoke the wrong way. . . .

"You *know about* it, Jinny?"

"Know about it? Oh, my God, do I know about it? Well, I ought to. It's started all the trouble." She glared at me. "It's given mother melancholia, so bad she hardly ever speaks, and made father a wild man. It's——"

"But what is it?"

"I don't know. Father says," almost a sneer, "it's a white marble hand."

Chapter 5

Our Jesting Poisoner

AT LEAST," she amended, speaking very fast, "I know he *thinks* that's what it is. But, of course, he never mentions it. It would be better if he did."

She saw me looking over at Caligula's statue. She nodded, and went on fiercely:

"Yes. I know. It's crazy, isn't it? I know he's a little touched in the head, but that doesn't make it any better for the rest of us. If he has these spells, and imagines he sees a white marble hand crawling about, we're the ones who suffer. Because we know it's all imagination doesn't help us when he wakes up screaming in the night——"

"Jinny," I interrupted, not sure of my voice, "are you certain it's all imagination?"

You got an impression that the room had grown immense, somehow; that the smallest whisper would echo in it, and that the ticking of the clock came from a gulf. Or perhaps it was the way she seemed to shrink within herself. Only her eyes were enormous.

"Because," I said, "it wasn't your father who told me. It was Mary. She saw it."

"I—I've wondered. Yes, I've wondered about that." She spoke in a curious way, as though she were walking in her sleep, and stared at the cigarette. "But that would make it much worse, wouldn't it?"

"Worse?"

"I mean, if he really has seen it—in these last years; well, if he really *has* seen it, that means somebody around here is playing a horrible joke. Somebody is patiently scaring him, like a crazy child. He believes in it. And that's much worse than as though he imagined things, isn't it?"

Her voice had a note of eager hopefulness, a small girl answering questions in a schoolroom. The burnished hair strayed down in her eyes, and she pushed it back in that strange somnambulistic fashion.

"Of course, we know there's nothing supernatural, Jeff. And I'd much rather believe father was seeing things than that somebody here was . . ." She shuddered. "No ghost, nothing, is so bad as thinking one of the people you eat dinner with could get up in the middle of the night and keep on horribly, night after night—scaring your father . . ."

This wouldn't do. I had to get a grip on common sense. Steady! I said:

"Now, look here. Let's be sensible, old girl. Your father is the solidest, most practical man in the world. He wouldn't shy at a bed-sheet. Why should he be frightened by——"

"I don't know," she answered despondently. "I don't know."

"Well, then!"

She said in a flat voice: "There's no use arguing, Jeff. He's been like this ever since Tom went away." Her eyes seemed to be turned inwards; the wrinkle was again between her brows. "It would be just like Tom. Only we know Tom isn't here."

"Suppose you tell me the whole thing."

"All right. All right. Maybe *somebody*——?"

A gesture of despair. She flung her cigarette across the room towards the fireplace. "Well, you know how we used to be around here. We did anything we liked, and father was too absorbed in his work, or his books, or something, to pay much attention to us. Mother never interfered either —remember? She just smiled, as though she didn't know we were there; Tom was the only one she cared anything about. 'Her baby' she'd always call him. It used to humiliate him to death.

"Tom started the trouble. You never knew Tom in the last days, did you? I mean, after we started to get uneasy about what we'd do when we left college?"

I shook my head. "He was always," Jinny muttered, "a morose little devil. And it got worse."

(Yes. A full moon over the cobweb mist in the trees, and

the swimming pool silver light. Screams, yelling, and breath-lessness. Clarissa had had some football star visiting her then, and how Tom hated him! He hated all athletes, be-cause he wanted to be an athlete himself, and couldn't. I saw him in a wet bathing suit, hugging his dark knees on the edge of the pool. The silver light was split like a mirror in the crash of diving, and two white-armed figures, Clarissa and her guest, foamed across in a race. Swift chop of the crawl, gasping mouths twitched up for breath, the poplars tall against a moonlit sky. "Damned ass," Tom growled. The orange and yellow Japanese lanterns gleamed among those trees, swaying gently. A Victrola on the veranda was playing "Nobody Lied.")

"He had a nasty tongue," Jinny murmured thoughtfully. "Even when he was a kid, and had that robbers' den out in the carriage-house, the other kids used to hate him. But anyway!—I remember now: you went abroad, and stayed there. The rest of our crowd just vegetated. We danced, and we drank a little—just enough to make us feel devilish—and we went eternally on with those silly affairs where a few kisses made you think you were in love. Vegetated. That's a good word."

Her face looked old and bitter. She said:

"But Tom had only one interest. Did you know it?"

"He used to want to be an actor."

"That's it. And I think he kept on not so much because of that as because he wanted to oppose father. Father was determined on his studying law. Tom hated it. They never got along; but I don't believe father ever really believed Tom would keep on fighting him. . . . Even then, it wouldn't have been so bad if Tom hadn't kept insulting father's house-hold gods. Booth and Barrett and Irving were all ranting hams. Shakespeare was drivel. And so on. . . .

"Honestly, Jeff, I didn't know how bad it was until the last night. That was five years ago, during Easter vacation, and a March snowstorm. I never knew just what happened; father wouldn't talk of it. I was upstairs, dressing to go out, and I heard the most awful row in the library. You could hear them yelling even up in my room. From what happened, I think dad hit Tom. All I know is that when I came running downstairs, Tom rushed out of the library with blood coming out of his mouth. He was screaming, 'I'll kill the old devil!' and he was going upstairs after his gun. (You know he got three medals for pistol shooting?) Well, mother was crying, and she threw her arms around his neck, and she turned and shrieked at dad something melodramatic like, 'You'd strike a child, would you? You'd strike a child?' Dad was absolutely grey in the face, leaning on the table in the hall. They were all screaming something frightful.

"Tom was quieted, but he took dad seriously: and he *did* leave. He stuffed a lot of things in a bag, and Mary was crying, 'We've got guests; oh, please don't make a scene.' Clarissa said to let him go and make a fool of himself, if he wanted to. Mother was trying to hang to Tom's coat-tails when he went out the door. I remember the funny way he had his hat stuck over his eye. He said to dad, who was sitting in a chair with his hands over his eyes; he said, 'Well, I told you. It's going to get you in the middle of the night, you'll see.' Then he went out, and walked to town. We've never seen him since."

Jinny fumbled in the pocket of the coat and drew out a pack of cigarettes. Her eyes were bewildered; she swallowed hard, and fumbled a long time before she got out a cigarette.

"We telephoned everywhere. Dad was frantic. Mother just gave him a look and walked up to her room. That night she tried to kill herself with veronal, but there wasn't enough . . ."

"Where did he go?"

"We don't know. I think he went in to see that old lawyer in town who'd been such a friend of his—the one who taught him Latin before he went to school—and got some money. But Marlowe wouldn't tell. Dad never forgave him. And I knew Tom wouldn't come back. He was too hard; he was as hard as nails. He never forgave anybody anything."

I held out a match for her cigarette; over its flame she

gave me an oblique glance from which much of the bewilderment had cleared, and which remained very steady.

"The rest sounds like a nightmare. In the middle of the night——"

"The same one?"

"Yes. We were late getting to bed, because we had caught mother . . ." She shuddered. "Anyhow, she didn't kill herself. As I was saying, in the middle of the night we heard a scream. I thought it was mother again; I was sleeping with her; but when I opened my eyes she was asleep. I ran out into the upper hall. There was a bright moon, and I saw dad standing in the middle of the hall in his nightshirt. Matt came out of his room, and afterwards Mary; by that time he said he was all right—dad, I mean—but he was trembling. He said something about . . ."

She paused, so unsteady that I cut in:

"Where had he been sleeping?"

"Downstairs, in the library. Mother refused to occupy the same room with him. He had run out of there and rushed upstairs. . . . Jeff, I've got to tell you. All he could talk about was something—'*something white, with fingers,*' that had run across the library table in the moonlight."

The windows banged and rattled; Jinny glanced towards them, and flung her cigarette into the fireplace. The emotion in that room was strung so high that nobody could have failed to notice it. It beat about us like bat's wings against your forehead. Matt Quayle, entering then, could not fail to understand. He slammed the door.

"Jinny," he snapped, "you've been talking."

She asked leisurely, "Business of yours?"

"Airing dirty linen in public——"

"Matt, you're positively poetical. Hearing a metaphor from you——"

"I think I told you not to do it." He was trying to impress her with what I believe he fancied to be Dangerous Calm. "I suppose you want this spread all over town?"

Jinny put her hand on my arm and advised thoughtfully: "Don't, Jeff. It would be like hitting a tub of butter. Matt, how *do* you get any clients?"

Matt did not answer. He regarded us stupidly for a moment; then he sat down in a chair, and, grotesquely, the man began to sob.

"Don't pay any attention," he muttered jerkily. "I'm no good at this kind of thing. I'm no good at anything, I guess. I'm afraid I'm going to be the next one. I've just been talking to Twills. There was a load of arsenic in mother's milk-toast, and if she'd eaten it all . . . Stop picking on me!" he cried querulously. "I haven't done anything."

Jinny looked embarrassed. "Oh, well," she said, "*oh well!* . . . Buck up, Matt. We're for you." She rose, and patted his back awkwardly. I was afraid she would break out sobbing also, for her eyes looked strained. I knew then the depth of the nervousness, the uncertainty and dread in all their hearts.

"Do you know what Twills said to me?" Matt burst out. "He looked cool, and his eyes sort of glittered. He said, 'Now, then, I'm in charge here for once. Your lives depend on me.' And he showed me some sort of funnylooking milky stuff in a test tube. He said, 'That's arsenic,' he said, 'and, what's more, I know who put it in the milk-toast. . . .'

"Oh, hell, Jeff. Forget what I said. You take charge. I'm afraid that little rat in the glasses thinks *I* did it. 'And,'— this is what he was telling me—'I know who put the hyposomething, whatever it was, in the syphon.' You take charge, and *do* something."

So apparently Twills also suspected the syphon! This was a comedown. "Very well," I said. "Jinny was telling me something—about a change in the household after Tom left."

"There isn't much. Much that's definite, I mean," Jinny explained. "From that day on, though, everything was changed. Dad used to shut himself up in the library and drink, and we'd hear him pacing up and down. Mother began to get fits of moodiness. All the same, I thought it would blow over. The first intimation I had that there was a horrible change was one night a few months later. I was sitting with a chap named . . . it doesn't matter . . . I was sitting with him in a dark part of the porch under the library window towards the front; see?"

She indicated it. It was at right angles to the three windows facing the mountains.

"We were sitting in a swing, smoking. It was summer, as I told you, and the window was open—blinds down. He must have heard us; he was in the library. All of a sudden he came out with the fiercest kind of expression in his eyes. He roared, 'Take that cigarette out of your mouth! Act like a common slut, will you?' Then he pitched into Dal; Dal had his arm around me. Finally he ordered me in the house. Then I got the first of the lectures, while he paced around with his face all puffed up. I'd been getting too much liberty, it seemed. I'd been doing everything; I had no respect for my parents or my God, or anything. Too much liberty was what had ruined my brother Tom, it seemed . . . Too much liberty, too much staying out late at night, and no telling where I'd been . . .

"That was only the beginning of it. He had a fiendish row with Clarissa; she went to a dance at the Country Club, and came home a little wobbly. He retired from the bench that autumn, to work on his book and keep an eye on us, he said. It was no good appealing to mother; she just took all Tom's things, books, and pictures, and even clothes, to her own room; she wouldn't let anybody touch them."

"Say, listen!" Matt raised his head, thrusting forward a truculent jaw. "You're making him out—a—a tyrant, or something. He wasn't, Jeff. She's just got an axe to grind."

"Oh, I suppose he wasn't," Jinny admitted despondently. She shrugged. "Not according to his code, anyhow. . . . But it never bothered you, Matt. You were always the little whitehaired boy. You creased your hat in the proper way, you went to the right school, you played golf well enough to be considered a successful business man. An artist could paint your soul impressionistically, and call it A Crowd."

"That's *simple* talk," said Matt. "I never made a freak of myself, if that's what you mean. Like Tom. Or like that fool Englishman you were so crazy about. . . ."

"Oh, cut it *out*!" Jinny was pressing her hands together; she rose suddenly and walked to the window.

Matt was enjoying himself. He appealed to me.

"Fellow's name was Rossiter. He'd been kicked out of every job he ever had. Worked up at the Summit as a bell-hop or something. . . ."

"He went away. They all do!" cried Jinny, whirling from the window. Her lip trembled. "They all grow up, and go away. Dad sent *him* away. They all go away. Except me."

"Nobody's stopping you," Matt pointed out. "Do what Tom did, if you want to."

Jinny looked at the fireplace, at a corner of the ceiling, everywhere, as though she were searching for a door. Over her flushed face crept an expression of futility and cynicism.

"Oh, I admit it. I'm a Quayle. I'm spineless." She put her hand against the back of the chair, squeezing hard, and closed her eyes. "I don't go away because I don't dare. I'm afraid to strike out for myself, or I would. So I'm not one to talk. We'll all be here until father . . ."

"Gets poisoned, for instance?" demanded Matt.

A voice intruded on the hatred which had sprung up murkily between them. A voice from the doorway cried:

"What on earth is all this fuss about?"

The voice was drawling and petulant; it had what can only be described as an arrogant whine. Somehow you knew that it was the voice of a beauty whose charms have long since ceased to be fully appreciated, and knows it. Clarissa Quayle stood with her hand on the knob of the library door, her head thrown back and her eyebrows raised. It was an Entrance, requiring only a clock striking midnight to make it complete. It would have been almost comical had the situation been otherwise, or had she not still retained vestiges of her charm. The dark hair, parted and curled into lustrous wheels over her ears; the high cheek-bones; the madonna's eyes, blue and dark-fringed. There was a plump fold below her chin now. She looked hard, and faintly lined. Her head, tilted up, was bold against the white fur collar. . . .

A dozen years ago I always thought of her, when reading

fiction, as the Exotic Adventuress, and it is not improbable that she thought so too. I rescued her from any number of titled villains. *Les dieux vont vite.* She looked like a discomfited opera singer. Queer. . . .

"What on earth!" she repeated. "Do tell me——?"

She was stripping off long white gloves with the gesture of somebody genteelly pitching pennies. Some dark foreboding told me that she was probably a member of a Literary Society, and had just come from there. Her glazed, incurious eyes moved over us. Something of the judge there. . . .

"Listen, Clarissa," said Matt. "Listen . . ." He hesitated, wetting his lips. She was obviously his favourite of them all. "It's—it's terrible, but—somebody tried to poison dad."

Then it seemed that Mary ran in behind her, and both Mary and Matt began talking excitedly at once. Clarissa did not lose her pose, though the sentence banged at her from all directions. She was obviously very much alarmed, and she backed away from them as though they were attacking her; none the less, when she spoke it was in the same tone:

"Poison father! But that's dreadful, isn't it!"

"Oh, God," said Jinny. Clarissa gave her a nasty look.

"So sorry if I've offended you, dear," she observed, with viciousness.

"Not at all," said Jinny.

"Let her alone!" growled Matt. He took Clarissa's hands with a kind of elephantine gentleness. "Now, it's all right, dear. Get that! It's all right. He's in no danger. Walter pulled him through."

"Why, of course, Matt! Of course. He—he drank something by mistake, I suppose?"

Jinny was now the coolest one present. She leaned back in the chair, tossing her shining hair over the back of it, and her eyes were almost closed. She replied clearly:

"It looks very much like attempted murder, with a poison one doesn't take by mistake."

The word "murder" jarred. It was the first time one of the Quayles had used it; there was an ugly, obscene sound to the nasal syllables, and everyone flinched from its blatancy. Matt glanced at Mary, then at Clarissa, then back at me.

His forehead was moist again. Again I could hear the clock ticking . . .

"Don't—*say* that, will you?" Matt rasped querulously. By some trick of imagination or the lights, every face seemed to be more brilliant in the dingy room. Mary's was a sort of Rembrandt brown, the skin wrinkling into shadows. She was taking off Clarissa's wrap, and the face showed weirdly over its white fur collar. *Tick-tick, tick-tick* . . .

"I don't feel any better about it than you do," responded Jinny in a monotonous voice. "But we've got to admit it. We've got to drag it into the open. If this keeps on, we'll all go crazy."

"If it was anybody," said Matt, spilling his handkerchief as he pulled it out, "it was Joanna. Or somebody who sneaked in the house—"

"Nonsense," said Jinny clearly; "you know it wasn't."

Tick-tick, tick-tick . . .

During all this, Clarissa had remained motionless, her nostrils dilated and her eyes wide open. Now she blurted out an extraordinary thing, for which nobody was prepared.

"It wasn't—it wasn't the morphine, was it?" she asked.

Matt whirled on her. "What morphine?"

She had made a mistake, and knew it. "Why—why," she stammered, "I—that is, you said something that wasn't taken by mistake. I knew Walter had been giving mother morphine to quiet her, and naturally I thought he might have given daddy some." She uttered a nervous laugh. "Oh, come, darlings! You can't scare me, you know. You positively can't. Why, the minute you began telling me about it, I knew it *wasn't* serious."

Three poisons, Twills had said. Three poisons. And, in addition to hyoscin and arsenic, we heard of morphine. Clarissa's explanation was a lie, of course; she was fingering a bracelet, twirling it round her wrist, and looked at us deprecatingly. Matt spoke with an effort.

"What do you mean," he said, "you knew it wasn't serious?"

"Why, I saw him! I saw daddy standing at the window when I came in just now."

Chapter 6

Skull and Cross Bones

HER FOREHEAD wrinkled angrily. She cried: "After all, you needn't look at me like that! I'm telling the truth. I saw him—really. It was dark in the room, but I could see him in the moonlight when I took the car up the drive to the garage."

"What window?" demanded Jinny.

The arrogant whine grew louder, to conceal fear. "The surgery window. I—I thought it looked queer. His eyes were wide open, and his hands were on either side of the window frame. I waved to him, but he didn't wave back."

"He must have gotten up," Mary wailed. "He was lying down in there. Oh, Matt, please go and see about it, *please*! Oh, if he falls and hurts himself, I'll never forgive myself—"

Mary was aimlessly smoothing the fur collar, and seemed in some fashion to think that the wrap in her hands prevented her from motion. Matt hurried out.

"You see, my dears," Clarissa remarked, taking the whole thing as a personal affront, "you can't scare me, no matter how hard you try. I knew there wasn't much wrong with him. Try to control yourselves in the future."

Having administered this rebuke, she stalked across the room in a manner strongly suggestive of the motion pictures. She saw Jinny's coat and scarf thrown across the back of one chair; she lifted them daintily, as though she were lifting a fishing-worm, and sat down.

"Do you know," she exclaimed, looking at me, "there's something dreadfully familiar about your face. . . ! I wonder!"

I explained the dreadful familiarity of the face. Jinny giggled.

"But of course!" Clarissa cried. "How *do* you do?" She smiled brightly, and extended an arm at full length with a curving gesture of the wrist, as though she were pitching a slow inshoot. I restrained an impulse to bow over it. She continued: "How delightful to see you! I knew you when you were a child. It's dreadful that you had to come when the house is so upset. . . ."

Despite her evident terror, Mary's dark face glowed a little, and she drew her thin figure up as though to say proudly, "There! Now you've met the proper welcoming committee! *I* could never do that." All she achieved was a self-conscious smile. Anything was a relief from the uneasy weight of suspicion and dread. But Clarissa's loquaciousness was interrupted by the return of Dr. Twills, who came hurrying in with Matt at his elbow.

"We—oh, hello, dear," said the doctor, checking himself.

His wife took one look at the stud of his missing collar, at his baggy suit and rumpled short hair. She stiffened, and then fought down the remark which appeared in her eyes. "Oh . . . hello, Walter," she replied. Her glance at the mantelpiece snubbed the clock effectually.

The doctor's face was sardonic as he went on:

"There must be some mistake about what you saw. Judge Quayle is asleep on the couch in my room. Are you sure you didn't see somebody else, my dear?"

Clarissa shrugged.

"I think, Walter, that I am acquainted with my own father. Of course, if you insist—"

"Wait a moment, please," the doctor said in a hard voice. It was such an abrupt change of tone from his usual mild and harassed speech that everyone looked at him sharply. "It seems to me that it's about time for a show-down on this thing. Personally, I've put up with the parlor tricks around this house for just about long enough. If anybody can get any fun out of acting the fool with a white hand, all right! But—"

Everybody had stiffened. The mention of that taboo subject took them like a blow in the face; it was worse, you felt, than mention of poison.

Clarissa said with low-voiced fury: "Walter, if you have no better sense than to speak before strangers—"

"That's exactly why I'm speaking before a stranger, my dear," Twills told her coldly. His look had become malevolent. "So that somebody will be able to look at it calmly. You won't speak of it. You'd rather pretend you don't know anything about it, and have your father scared out of his wits. You'd rather pretend you think he's just seeing things, than try to help him out of his trouble. And you've let him be there alone . . ."

Matt said heavily: "I don't know what you're talking about."

"Oh, yes, you do! And I tell you this matter has got to be thrashed out now. Among ourselves. If it were only a question of a person playing a joke—why, keep your attitude if you like, and be damned to you. But it's become different. This is *murder*, do you hear?" Twills spoke the words through stiff jaws, with terrible intentness, and rapped his knuckles against the table. "It's murder. They send you to the electric chair for it. If there's somebody like that among us, we want to know it. Can't you realize that?"

A pause. In the enormous silence Mary whispered:

"But what are we going to do?"

"Well, I think it's agreed," he glanced sardonically at Matt, "I think it's agreed that we don't want to call in the police?"

"Oh, my God, no!" exclaimed Matt.

"Very well. Then let's put it in the hands of a stranger, who will be unprejudiced. Mr. Marle, will you see what you can do with it?"

There was another silence as he turned to me sharply. Then Matt said:

"You mean," very heavily, "you mean to be questioned as though we—"

"Yes."

"But I tell you, that *maid*—Joanna—!"

Over the same old ground, fighting in the same steps; desperate, rather pitiful. Twills regarded him with wrinkled brows. "She's been here only a couple of months. She came considerably after the marble hand got to work. And burglars don't indulge in such pleasantries. Will you go ahead, Mr. Marle?"

I looked round at the circle of faces, all trying to appear unconcerned, and yet, I thought, all shakily relieved that some expected catastrophe at last had happened. There was a tightening of jaws, a tense watchfulness, about each. Jinny had seated herself on the edge of the table, and was playing with a penholder; the thick bronze-coloured hair, which had fallen on her cheek and obscured the side of her face, glowed richly under the lights. Matt leaned against the mantelpiece, his chin lifted as though he were sitting in a witness-chair. Mary tried to bustle about the room, smiling at everybody, but she found nothing to do, and so she stopped. Twills took up a position behind the chair of his wife, who was unconcernedly lighting a cigarette.

"First," I said, "is there any arsenic in the house?"

"Oh, yes!" Mary cried, with such suddenness that we all jumped. "Lots of it, Jeff. For the rats. You put it into their holes, and they die."

"Who bought it?"

"Well," said Twills smiling, "as a matter of fact, I did: at Lock's drug store in town. Mary asked me to. She seemed to have the idea that it was the province of a medical man to do such things."

"But it *was*, Walter! Why, imagine—*me* going in there and asking the man for a *poison!*"

"Where," I asked, "is it kept?"

"In the pantry. But nobody could get it by mistake. It had a big skull and cross bones on the tin, and 'poison' written on it."

"However, anybody could get at it deliberately? Now, please don't get excited! We've got to go into this thing."

"If," Mary replied, very stiffly, "anybody wanted to, yes."

After that little outburst, everybody looked at everybody else. Jinny threw the penholder on the desk. "Well, I'm certain *I* didn't know there was any such dangerous junk lying around," she observed. "This place sounds like a poison-house. Everybody's wandering in and out of the kitchen all the time."

"Who buys the household supplies?" I asked. "You know —groceries, and things like that?"

They all looked at Mary, who seemed again uncomfortable at being in the limelight. She brushed back her sleek dark hair nervously.

"I do, Jeff. I mean, I order them from town, and the delivery wagon brings them out. But since yesterday—"

"What about, since yesterday?"

"Why, the delivery wagon from Sayles'—that's where we always deal—has been out of order. I'd have gone into town and gotten them, of course, only I can't drive the car. Clarissa went in today and brought them out."

Clarissa got up and went over to squash out her cigarette in the ashtray. A corner of her broad mouth was turned down.

"I got them, yes," she informed us. "Car full of stuff, like a silly little errand-girl! And I was all dressed to go out to tea—"

"You went late in the afternoon?"

"Yes. So I could get there before the stores closed. Really, Jeff, what on earth are you trying to prove?"

"Did you get this syphon, for instance?"

"Syphon?" She looked at me blankly. For a moment she had forgotten her poise, and the black frock drooped on her shoulders. "Oh! You mean the soda-water? Yes, I remember, because I had to take a lot of empty ones back. You get a rebate on the ones you return."

"You're sure it was this particular one you bought?"

"Oh, Lord, Jeff! Yes, I suppose so. Wasn't it, Mary?"

Mary nodded. "Yes. I remember, as soon as you gave it to me, I took it in and put it on the table here, because papa had been wanting it, and he won't drink anything without soda. He was waiting for it, and he had a bottle of whisky on the table. . . . Please understand!" she broke off earnestly. "Papa wasn't a drinking man. Really he wasn't! I *never* saw him drunk in my life."

"Better sometimes," put in Jinny gloomily, "if he had been."

"Wait a minute, please!" I said. "You brought the syphon in here, Mary. Did he take a drink then?"

"Yes. I saw him pour it out and drink it, because I waited

a while to talk to him. He seemed in such an awfully good humour, and"—her dark face was full of pride as she looked at all of us—"he patted my cheek, and said he didn't know how he'd get along without me."

"And at what time was this?"

"Time? I don't know . . . Wait; yes, I do, too! It was about a quarter after five, because that's when Clarissa came back. I took the soda-water in to him right away, because I knew he wanted it."

"Stay long?"

"I stayed till about half-past five." She was pathetically eager to help, so that her words were hurried and jumbled. "Then I had to go and get ready for supper. Joanna needs all kinds of watching when she cooks."

The poison, then—if my surmise were correct—had been introduced into the syphon between half-past five and about eight o'clock, the time I arrived. I saw that the others were getting restless, so I continued:

"Did he stay in the library after that?"

"No, he didn't," Matt answered. "I was coming home from the office about half-past five, and I saw him go in the direction of the kitchen. I hung up my hat, and he said something about his book being ready, and slapped me on the back. Then he went to the kitchen. I went upstairs to wash——"

"He went to the cellar," supplemented Mary. "I was in the kitchen, and I heard him going down the cellar stairs."

"To bring up a bottle of brandy?"

They all shook their heads and said they didn't know. Mary had heard him returning, but she had been busy with the meal and had not seen him.

"Just one more thing, then. Would all of you mind telling me where you were between about half-past five and, say, eight o'clock?"

At first there was a chorus of protest. Then Matt, nodding profoundly, said, "That's all right. That ought to help. They always want to know it; I've read that much. Shoot, Jeff.— Oh, you want me to begin?"

"Please."

"There isn't much. I got back from the office about five-thirty, as I told you. Went upstairs and looked in on mother; she wasn't feeling well, but she hadn't taken sick. She was sitting in a chair by the window, wrapped up in a quilt. After that I went to my room and washed up; then I sat down and had a look at the paper I'd brought home, before the rest of them could get at it. The gong rang for supper at six o'clock . . ."

"Just a minute, please. I understood Mary to tell me you were in the kitchen, and that you carried up your mother's supper-tray."

Matt snapped his fingers. His ruddy face became more red, and he laughed in a confused way. "Judas, that's *right!* You know, I never thought before how a witness on the stand could get so mixed up that . . . Well! Yes, I did go down, just before the supper-gong. The tray was prepared, and I took it up . . ."

"Did you pass anybody?"

"Nobody but father, who was coming down from upstairs. He lifted the cover and looked at what I was carrying. Then he said that ought to fix her up, and went on to the dining room."

"So you were the only one—"

Quite abruptly the significance of it entered Matt's mind. His boiled blue eyes almost protruded, and he made gestures as though he were shaking somebody fiercely by the neck. "I did not! Honest to God! You're trying to tell me I poisoned my mother, and—"

His voice was growing hysterically high. I said, "Not at all! Please go on. Did you take the tray to her and stay while she ate?"

"No! No! I opened the door, and she was dozing in the chair. She gets so little sleep that I didn't want to wake her, so I put down the tray on the table and left—I knew she wouldn't sleep long—"

"Why, Matt!" Mary protested in a rising wail. "That nice hot milk-toast! You let it get cold! Oh, won't *anybody* in this house do anything right?" she demanded, wringing her hands.

Matt turned to her, lowering his head to cool it for a moment. Then he announced gently: "Listen, dear. Listen to me. Somebody went in that room while mother was asleep and filled your nice hot milk-toast with arsenic. I don't see that it matters a damn whether it was hot or cold or medium, do you? Try to be sensible. Now, go ahead, Jeff."

"So anybody could have gone in there after you without waking your mother?"

"Uh-huh. We didn't start to eat for ten minutes or so, because Jinny was out, and only dad and I were in the dining-room. Where were you, Mary?"

"Why, I went up to see mother about—oh, I don't know! —quite a while after you'd taken the tray up. She'd just wakened up; I watched her start to eat, and then I came down to the dining-room. Jinny had just come in, and Clarissa was there, so we started to eat."

"I also," interposed Dr. Twills smoothly, "was there."

Mary jumped, and looked at him deprecatingly. "Why, of course, Walter! That's what I meant. You, too, of course. You were late getting there."

"I was in my office, working all afternoon. That was when I discovered . . . Never mind," said Twills curtly. "The rest of you?"

"I've already told you I went after the groceries," answered Clarissa. "After that—I mean, after I came back— Jinny borrowed the car to go into town. I went upstairs and lay down; I didn't leave my room until I came down to the dining-room. That's all *I* can tell you."

"I went to the lending library to get a book," Jinny said. "That accounts for *my* movements."

Dr. Twills came out from behind his wife's chair.

"Let me tell the rest of it. After dinner the judge went to his study and didn't leave it. The hyoscin had been put in before that time, and the arsenic had been put in the milk-toast before that time; so I don't think our subsequent movements count for anything. Mrs. Quayle was taken ill about seven-thirty—"

"Does arsenic act so rapidly, doctor?"

"The dose given *her* does," he responded. "It would have killed her if I hadn't suspected it, and treated her for arsenic poisoning instead of peripheral neuritis, as I told the rest of you. It was a terrific quantity, even considering that arsenic is a slow poison."

"You knew about this?" demanded Jinny.

"Yes. Now then. What it amounts to is this: considering that the judge went to the library immediately after dinner, at about six-forty-five, we know that the hyoscin was put into the syphon at some time between five-thirty and six-forty-five. A little over an hour. What we want to know is *when* during that time the judge was out of the library, so that the—the person had access to it. Mary heard him go to the cellar at five-thirty, and Matt saw him coming downstairs shortly after six, but did anybody see him in the meantime?"

I looked round, and saw blankness on all their faces.

"We shall have to wait and ask him what happened during that half-hour," I said.

"The point being," murmured Twills, "that anybody had access to the library before we ate dinner—"

"Except me," said Jinny. "I was in town."

"Except you, then. Now, about the tray. In that ten-minute interval after Matt took up the tray and left it in Mrs. Quayle's room, anybody had access to it. Any of us."

Matt drew a deep breath. Again his hand moved up and down his coat lapel.

"You're forgetting, Walter, that I came downstairs just after I'd left the tray on the table. And father will testify to my being in the dining-room before we ate."

In the pause that followed, Jinny slid off the table. She stood, hands on hips, watching her brother with eyes of amusement.

"What a lawyer; Oh, Matt dear, what a lawyer you are! —You were the one who carried the tray, you know. You were the one with the real opportunity to put the poison in. So you say now, 'I must be innocent; I have a perfect alibi *after* the thing was done.' "

Matt was not angry. He was just aghast and helpless.

"My God," he shouted, "do you think I'd poison my own mother?"

"Well, do you think any of the rest of us would?"

The diminutive figure of Dr. Twills expanded, and his stride to the middle of the group—which had begun to cluster about Matt and shout also—gave the impression that he hopped like a monkey.

"Wait a minute!" he shrilled. "Quiet down, damn it!"

They moved back under the furious blinking of his eyes; the babble died. Twills was very stern in his five-feet-three inches. He wiggled his cropped hair backwards and forwards, glaring determinedly.

"That sort of business won't get you anywhere," he said, more calmly. "This is a problem for Mr. Marle and me, and we're going to solve it. That is, unless you want the police in. Personally, I don't care; it would take a load off my mind . . ."

For a moment I thought Jinny was going to cry.

"I'm sorry, Matt," she muttered; "I didn't mean it. You know that. . . . But, Walter," she made an aimless gesture, "this thing isn't *real*. I can't imagine we're actually standing here and . . . It's like that game called Murder, and Jeff is the district attorney asking questions; and sooner or later it seems he'll say to somebody, 'Are you guilty?' and the person will say, 'Yes,' and then the game will be over. . . . Only I know it *isn't* a game, and it's so damned ghastly—!"

Her voice was rising in a hysterical way. Twills fidgeted.

"Well," he mumbled, seeming to regret his outburst, "well, you see, in a way it is a game, Jinny. That is, your mother and father are safe. The nurse is with your mother, and your father's locked in the surgery; there's no danger. But for everybody's peace of mind, it's got to be thrashed out." He became hard again, and went on aggressively: "Now get this, all of you! You're going to bed, do you hear? Mr. Marle and I will take care of this. You're going to *bed* . . ."

I have never yet been able to puzzle out just how Twills shook the whip over them. He, of course, was not worried; the near-tragedies did not upset him in the least; and the others were so distracted that anybody who showed firmness could cow them into submission. They protested. Clarissa in particular was haughty and vehement; she kept lifting up her string of beads and dropping them—plop—back on her breast again; and she said, "Walter, you're positively too masterful!" very ironically. But he just glared at her, and she shut up considerably alarmed. Matt continued to boom out that he was a lawyer, and that he was not going to be excluded from any councils. . . .

Somehow, the room was cleared presently. It had been decided that I should stay the night, though I insisted on a couch in the library; it seemed that there would probably be little enough sleep that night anyway.

The last I saw of them, they were all hesitating in the hallway. Mary was afraid to go upstairs alone, and Matt went up with her, his arm around her shoulder, hooting loudly at bogeys. Clarissa said no word to her husband, but stalked out and hurried to join the other two. Everybody talked loudly and affectionately to everybody else—loudly, affectionately and defiantly. Only Jinny was silent and pale. Sweet affection jarred. . . .

Darkness, and the things of darkness, came to take possession of the house when the lights were extinguished. I do not know why I shivered, standing in the middle of the hallway, because everything was familiar. Or was it? From minds that decay, there may be some chemical exhalation which shrivels with dust and mould the furnishings that surround them, as the decay of bodies makes grisly the atmosphere of a vault. Inside the separate heads of these people there beat small hammers of rage or hate or disappointment—their faces floated before me now—and, in the case of one of them, the hammer cracked through. They went on leading their regular lives. But the corrosion of unspoken things had crept through this house, making it cold and damp. A fist clenched secretly, the glare of an eye over a sedate coffee-cup, were the only outward signs, yet they were the signs of a killer. A killer who took the most evil way, which is the smiling relentlessness of the poisoner.

The only light now was a dim yellow glow from a ground-glass lamp on the second floor. It threw on the lower wall a silhouette of the stair balustrades; it outlined with sinister humps the hats and coats on the hall-tree. A series of creaks came from the staircase, and you looked for another silhouette descending, but there was nothing. A glitter of gold touched the frame of a portrait. The night wind, winging past, made the portrait tremble slightly, and the whole hall creaked. With my back to the front door, I stared about. In the library I could hear Twills trundling something heavy and dropping it into the fireplace; he seemed to be making up the fire. Again the wind drove seething across the lawn outside. . . .

Over my shoulder, quick and sharp and rattling, there was a knock at the front door.

Chapter 7

The Second Stroke

TWILLS popped out of the library door, almost as though he had been expecting that knock. He drew the bolts and opened the door; a blast of wind blew through the vestibule, and we saw a very sullen messenger-boy holding out a yellow envelope.

"Hell of a time of night——" said the boy. "Sign here."

Twills scribbled on the receipt and gave the boy a dollar. After he had shut the door he beckoned me to the library, still examining the telegram.

"It's for Jinny," he announced, and coolly tore it open.

"Look here!" I said. "What the devil are you doing?"

"Good reason, rest assured. H'm. That's what she did this afternoon when she said she went to town to get a book from the lending library. She didn't come back with a book. She sent a telegram. Here's the answer. Look at it."

"Is it any of our bus——?"

"I'll read it to you then," the doctor interposed calmly. "It says: *'Will come at once what do you mean all our troubles will be over in a few days has the old man given in all love.'* It's signed *'Pat.'* "

"Who's Pat?"

"Pat Rossiter. Two hearts that beat as one." He winked his eye slowly and inserted a hand beneath his coat, which he wiggled against the chest to illustrate the two hearts. I said:

"Don't you think you could play Cupid better if you didn't——"

"I'm not playing Cupid! God damn it!" said the doctor, giving another hop. "Here, I'm going to take care of this myself. Wait a minute."

I waited while he lighted the small sticks under the logs

in the fireplace, and then worked the bellows like a bespectacled gnome.

"What you're thinking," I protested, "is absurd."

"How do you know what I'm thinking?"

"Well—"

"You don't. You jump at conclusions. Ah-ha!" cried the doctor, jumping round and pointing his finger at me with a curiously malevolent expression. "That's exactly what you do. Look."

The fire had begun to crackle. He took the yellow sheet and thrust it into the flames.

"There! I was afraid the young fool was going to send a wire like that, and I knew she'd get a crazy reply. How would that look if the rest of those hyenas got hold of it? How did it look to *you*?"

"Doctor," I said, "I still don't understand your mental processes. But I can never anticipate them; so go ahead."

Twills sat down, smiling obscurely, and took out a pipe, which he began to fill with the leisureliness of one on the verge of a discourse.

"There are points," he mused, "that I want to discuss. Or one point in particular. The glaring one. The strangest feature of the whole affair."

"That hand?"

"Oh, nonsense! Not the hand; that's stage-play. But don't you see the oddest angle of all? Why, man, it's the attitude of the family."

"How so?"

Still stuffing tobacco into his pipe, Twills frowned. "Have you got any brothers or sisters?"

"No."

"Ah, I thought not. Then you're not quite capable of seeing it. Families fight; they may not like each other; they may be at swords' points. But in a crisis, a real crisis, do you know what they do? Yes, that's it. They stick together. And that's precisely what this gang isn't doing."

"Still I don't follow you."

"Why, hang it, look here! Don't you see that they accepted too easily the statement that *one of them* had poisoned their father and mother? What would a normal group do? They'd search the house for outsiders. They'd thrash over what enemies from town—from anywhere—might have done the thing. And first off they'd have had the maid on the carpet, absolutely convinced it was she. They'd have been willing to suspect anybody except one of themselves!"

"That sounds reasonable . . ."

"Of course, it is. Instead they accept our accusations impassively, and are even on the verge of accusing each other. Find out why, and you've got the case solved." Having lighted his pipe, he surveyed me triumphantly. "Man, they didn't even inquire whether all the doors were bolted, and all the windows locked. Enemies? Of course, the judge has 'em, and they might have been hiding here. But they never mentioned that, the clear and obvious angle. It isn't natural."

"But the idea of an outsider is rather far-fetched, isn't it?"

"You still don't see my point!" The doctor made helpless gestures. "Certainly it's far-fetched—to us. But it isn't to them. That's the first thing they would insist on, don't you see? They'd band together against all hell, swearing that somebody hidden in the hall closet, or something, had done the dirty work; they'd at least go after the maid. Not a one of them did."

"Matt mentioned it. But he didn't really believe it, I think."

Meditatively the doctor said: "They took the wrong tack. If they'd had time to collect themselves, they'd have created a straw man of an outsider and lambasted it mercilessly. Never occurred to them, I suppose. They must have realized . . ."

"Remember," I pointed out, "that for some years they've all been living in fear of an outburst. They know somebody is behind this white-marble-hand business, and, when the threatened break came, the family alliance had grown very strained."

"Poisoning, though! Poisoning is very different from play-acting with a hand, however ghastly. They might be willing to think that one of their number had tried to scare the old man—but hyoscin! No, no, Mr. Marle." He regarded me whimsically. "I see you don't agree with me. But I tell you this: when you understand why they're acting as they do, you'll have the whole truth."

"Do you know it now?"

He took a reflective draw at his pipe. "I think so. And, hang me, I'm afraid to mention it! Tonight, maybe—"

"What about tonight?"

"Somebody may see me voluntarily, and tell me the truth. My door is always open."

The fire was high now, crackling, snapping, lighting up the lenses of the doctor's spectacles. He looked very small in the big chair, smiling, and rubbing his button nose with the stem of his pipe.

"You've let the—person know you suspect?"

"Yes."

"Pretty dangerous, isn't it?"

Again he smiled. "I doubt it. Anyway, I'll take the risk. At first, I admit, my suspicions were in the wrong direction. But tonight, when I heard them all together, I changed my mind." Yawning, he rose. "Got to turn in now. They rout you out early."

Still absorbed in his meditations, still with the ghost of a smile, he went over and took the syphon from the table. The pipe was stuck at an absurd angle in his mouth as he put his hand on the knob of the door.

"Well," I said, "I'm sleeping here. Look sharp tonight!"

"Oh . . . *that*?" He waved his hand. "I don't mind that. I was thinking about getting up in the morning. In Vienna, in the old days, I used to be waked up by a grind-organ. It came under my window just at eight o'clock. I'd poke my head out the window and exchange that doleful Viennese 'Guten morgen' with the grinder, and he'd take off his cap and play that song out of *The Pink Lady*, because he knew I liked it. . . ."

The pipe stuck at an angle in his mouth, he tried to whistle a few bars of "Beautiful Lady." His hands were dug so deeply in the pockets of his baggy grey coat that it seemed to come down almost to his knees, and the syphon was tucked under his arm. One eye, dreamily pleased, was cocked at the ceiling.

"You could smell the linden trees," he continued, squinting, "and hear the housemaids opening windows, and slapping pillows out to air them, and see the sun on the weathervanes. . . . Y'know, that's what I dream about. Listening to the grind-organ. That fellow won't come around again, though. He stopped a bullet in the war."

Twills adjusted his thick-lensed glasses rather apologetically. His smile was a little shamefaced. "Well . . . can't stand here gassing all night, can I? G'night, Mr. Marle. Sleep well."

Left to myself, I lighted a cigarette and settled down before the fire. Yes, Twills would dream of that. Then why didn't he go? For the second time that night the thought occurred to me. In some vague, baffling manner it seemed to be connected with these events, but I could not give any reason for thinking so. A hunch, probably unimportant; but why didn't he go? Clarissa must be willing to preen her hats on the Ringstrasse. The Ringstrasse: trees like green lace, sun on the top-hats of coachmen, a clop of hoofs, and music . . .

A nostalgia for more gracious streets was stealing over me too, in this cold house by the mountains. But I must not think of that yet. It had begun to snow; a few white flakes stole past the windows, and one clung to the pane. Wind rattled faintly. I rose and began to pace about, examining the ugly puzzle. There were sinister echoes and tinglings of my footsteps . . .

I looked up at the portraits above the bookcases. They were dark daubs of the kind which have a sketchy look, as though the artist had tried to paint a ghost. The eyes are never right, either, so that faces look either witless or wall-eyed. There was Judge Quayle's father, in a high collar and string tie. He had built this gimcrack house in the early eighteen-seventies, on the precise spot where his own father's old stone place had stood. There was Judge Quayle's mother, with a flat face and a lace cap, like Queen Victoria. Beside them was another portrait which had always intrigued my interest, for I had heard legends of this Jane McGregor. She was a fierce old Scotswoman, a nurse who had become one of the family at the time the judge's parents lived here; she had ruled tyrannically, with lash and brimstone, and died in the garret, at an incredible age, with hot bricks at her feet and her bony nose still thrust out aggressively at death.

Mary Quayle once told me that she vaguely remembered Jane McGregor on her attic deathbed, in a smelly room with a low ceiling. There had been an oil lamp burning, and a huge Bible. Jane McGregor had snarled and cackled and prayed, and then had gone up hobbling to meet her inflexible Calvinistic God. Mary had remembered only flashes —Jane McGregor going, with grim delight, to every funeral, where she was indispensable in helping the undertaker; Jane McGregor giving long lectures on the horrors of death. She was reputed to have known worse and more terrifying ghost stories than any woman in western Pennsylvania. Not a pleasant person to have been Judge Quayle's nurse, and to have ruled him even after his marriage. When he brought Mrs. Quayle, as a bride, to this house, the domination of the old virago must have scared the house's new mistress out of her wits. . . .

Looking down from the canvas, mannish and domineering in her black dress of the eighteen-sixties, Jane outlived even the brush of a bad artist. She had a half-cracked brother, I remembered, who had served as man-of-all-work before his death in the Civil War. Yes! It was the brother who had made that statue of Caligula in the corner. He had ambitions at being a sculptor, they said, and Judge Quayle's father— old Judge Anthony Quayle, of the Superior Court—had indulged him. He had a studio in an abandoned smoke-house, where Jane used to shriek at him for making heathen images. But Jane—according to Tom, I remembered—was secretly fascinated by the depravity of the Roman emperors, whose busts her brother persisted in making. She had listened, with comments and grim pulpit-whacks on the table, to Duncan McGregor's accounts of his favourite subjects. Once she broke a head of Tiberius with a mallet, but she would allow nobody else to touch her brother's masterpieces. And then cracked Duncan stuck a feather in his hat, joined the Ring-gold Cavalry, and got a rifle-ball through his heart at Antietam. So he became deified to Jane. She insisted on bringing Caligula into the parlour of the old stone house, and he had remained in the library of the new. Tom Quayle used to tell me how, years afterwards (according to his mother), Jane McGregor made the abandoned smoke-house a place of terror for every child in the neighborhood. She pictured Duncan's ghost still at work, on moonlight nights, whistling over the tap of his mallet and chisel.

Ghost stories—some queer strain, from the nurse to the father, and then to Tom Quayle. Some dark floating bit in the mind, which I tried to dismiss, but without much success. In a corner between two bookcases, I discovered a radio. It seemed apologetic about being there; it was a radio of such antiquated style that it seemed as old as the room. Trying to dismiss the phantoms, I turned it on. Faint bell-notes trembled in the library, followed by a dim, buzzing voice announcing that it was one o'clock. Then dance-music began to flow, sounding thin and incongruous. That would be another thing Judge Quayle would not understand. . . .

I switched off the radio, but the saccharine music still seemed to jingle. The judge was like his fathers, trained in a school of Jane McGregor patriarchs. They reared large families, and the families loved them. They ate pie for breakfast, and administered sternness to their children, like sulphur and molasses, for the good of their stomachs. I could imagine Judge Quayle with black stock, and seals on his watch-chain, disdaining spittoons and damning Nick Biddle in a tavern. But now the squirrel-gun decaying in the attic, and his lonely ghost was watching, puzzled, a world of tea and bridge-tables, where women drink a little bad gin and get sick, and men solemnly pursue the athletic activities of ping-pong and miniature golf.

He had spoken well of Matt. But he must know Matt; he must know Matt's mean caution, his mincing steps in the right direction. And even though Matt had taken up the practice of law, his father must despise such a son in the profession of Luther Martin and John Marshall. Tom—yes. Tom had possessed the fire and power he wanted to see in a son; but Tom had slammed the door of his house forever. So that was why, perhaps, the old ghost's heart was broken . . .

What was that noise?

The heart rose up in my chest. Dreaming made a bad background when you were suddenly jerked out of it by some faint sound from the house. . . .

I listened. There were the usual night-creakings. There was the wind. There was the hissing of the gas. A brand stirred uneasily in the fireplace; rustled, and fell. Nothing more. But it had sounded like slow, cautious, shuffling footfalls somewhere upstairs.

Crazy Work. Was the crazy work to begin again? Here in this room, at one in the morning, you were in a different world; you could really believe that one of your old friends possessed a mad, smiling devil, and would crawl about the halls to—what? Walking softly, I went over to the library door. The electric-switch was beside it; I pressed the switch, but the room did not go dark. Three nervous, pale gasmantles fluttered in a bluish dusk, more terrifying than darkness. There was no time to turn them off. I opened the door quietly, slid through into the hall, and closed it again.

Silence. It was so dark that patterns of the library lights wove dazzlingly in my eyes until I grew accustomed to it. . . . Then a creak. The hall was very cold. Somebody *was* shuffling upstairs.

I took a step forward, and a whole succession of squeaks ran along the boards under me. Another, with the same result. Trying to follow anybody in this house was impossible. I waited, and the shuffling upstairs ceased. A door clicked shut somewhere; but what door I could not tell.

Then I realized the absurdity of what I had been thinking. Twills had gone upstairs only fifteen or twenty minutes ago; he could hardly be asleep yet. The nurse was sitting up with Mrs. Quayle, her door probably standing open. The whole house was watched; it was insane to suppose that the poisoner would be up to any tricks this night. Besides, I could not take a step unheard on these creaking floors. Instead I would go back to the library, leave the door open and the lights on, and keep the radio playing softly. If there was anybody with a purpose that was not innocent, he would be mad to venture out with somebody on the watch all night.

The library was very dim, washed only by that weird yellow-blue light from the gas. It fluttered and shrank on the portraits; it threw a big shadow of Caligula on the farther wall. I drew up a chair beside the radio, and sat down facing that statue, because it was not pleasant to think of its arm extended behind me. Colder yet; I pulled up the collar of my coat. The radio stirred with faint music, in that dreamiest of all sounds by night. Throbbing dimly, suggesting the glare and clang of cities far from this bleak house by the mountains . . .

"To thee, beautiful lady, I raise my eyes—"

Snow ticked against the window-panes, the fire fell with a collapsing rattle. A smell of dust, and old books, and blistered paint. By what caprice was the radio thinly swelling that song of which Twills had spoken?

I had not realized how tired I was. "To thee, beautiful lady—" A hand-organ tinkling on an ordered Vienna street in spring. The tip of my cigarette was glowing brightly in yellow-blue gloom. "They all go away!" Jinny Quayle had cried desperately; "they all go away, except me." I saw her wry face, her clenched fists. Dr. Twills spoke also, the syphon under his arm, squinting at the ceiling, dreaming in a lonely house of apple-blossoms, and the muddy Danube, and the witchery of the waltz-kings. "To thee, beautiful lady, I raise my eyes . . ."

"Jeff!" said the voice of Mary Quayle.

I did not know that I had been asleep. I started up painfully, to a cold room, full of stale smoke, the gas still burning. Murky daylight was in the library.

"—but why on earth," she was saying, "didn't you go to *bed*? Sitting up all night! Jeff, you'll *ruin* your health! Come out and have some coffee."

"Aren't you up early?" I asked, still struggling with my wits.

"Oh, I've been up all night," she explained; "sitting in with mother and the nurse. I was afraid the nurse might go to sleep, and mother might want something. But it's nearly eight o'clock." She looked haggard and weary enough, though her eyes were bright. "Come on, like a good boy, and have some coffee! The rest of them are up."

I shivered, feeling begrimed and rumpled and unshaven. Getting up stiffly, I said:

"Is everything——?"

"All right? Oh, yes! Jeff, I'm so glad I could cry! Mother's much stronger. I was in to see dad just a minute ago. He's still sleeping, but his colour's all right, and I took his pulse; it's normal. Come on!"

I crossed the hall to the dining-room. The sober day was brightening out of greyness, and the wind rising to a halloo. In the long and dusky dining-room, Jinny alone was seated at the table, staring moodily at a cup of coffee. She only said:

"It's so cold in this damn' place! Haven't you got the furnace on, Mary?"

"Joanna just fixed it up, dear," Mary answered soothingly. "You just drink your good coffee. Where is Matt?"

"Gone out for a walk. Health fiend. H'lo, Jeff; see anything last night?"

There was a sudden bang of footsteps on the front steps. Jinny jumped and stared at me with tired eyes. The steps ran up, crossed the porch, and the front door was thrown open. Momentarily a whiff of damp air and woodsmoke blew through the hallway, belling the heavy draperies at the dining-room door. Matt appeared there. I could not see his face clearly in the gloom, but he seemed nervous. He said:

"Is Walter down yet?"

Jinny's cup rattled on her saucer. Mary shook her head.

"Well," Matt said, wetting his lips, "the light's still burning in his room."

I felt a hot terror rising in my throat. "He might have turned it on to dress," I remarked. The words sounded unnaturally loud.

"I knocked at his door when I came down," Jinny said slowly. "He didn't answer. I thought he was still asleep."

Mary's hands were shaking so that she had to put down the plate of toast she was offering to Jinny. In a shrill voice Matt said:

"Come on upstairs, Jeff."

We began to walk rapidly when we had left the dining-room door. By the time we reached the top of the stairs we were almost at a run, and Matt was panting. His eyes had a boiled and fishlike rigidity. I said, "Steady, now! He's probably just dressing," and Matt mumbled something under his breath. My knocking at the door Matt indicated rattled in hollow echoes, unanswered. . . .

I opened the door. Every light was burning brightly, so that the mahogany of the furniture gleamed, and there were blurred yellow reflections in the glass of the window. A rumpled bed stood against the right-hand wall, just opposite a big bureau with its mirror tilted slightly outwards at the top. Matt called, "Walter!" but there was no answer in a quiet whose sinister suggestion was emphasized by the bright lights. A yellow leaf had been plastered against one of the windows, and beyond it the trees swam in a grey twilight. Then, in the tilted mirror, I caught sight of a red-and-white striped pajama leg. . . .

Twills lay doubled up on the floor at the other side of the bed, his head under it and one leg drawn up towards the abdomen. When I touched the little figure in the red-and-white pajamas, I found that it was cold.

Chapter 8

A Bromide in the Bathroom

I HAVE BEEN asked to prepare this record in justice to certain members of the Quayle household who, long after the case is closed, remain under some lurking suspicion which will not be fully lifted until the whole truth becomes known. But I do not think it will serve any good purpose to go into details of this ghastly morning, up until the time the police arrived. That hysterical interval remains in my memory as one of the worst hours I have ever spent. Clarissa had hysterics, as anybody could have foretold. In her superior and patronizing fashion, I think she was as genuinely fond of her husband as it was possible for her to be fond of anyone—though, of course, she dramatized the thing until it was almost unbearable. Her room communicated with Twills' by way of the bath. She walked in just as Matt and I were bending over the little figure in the red-and-white pajamas, and her shriek gave the news to the whole house.

Mary was little better, though less voluble, and the way she kept fluttering her hands would have put anybody's nerves on edge. Each of them, in fact, had some mannerism which sawed the others' temper. Jinny afterwards confessed to me that the worst of it was the way Matt kept wandering from room to room in the house, mumbling to himself; appearing suddenly at doors, saying, "Oh God I'm sorry," all in one breath, and wandering out again. The only two cool persons were the nurse and the Slavish maid, the latter of whom continued stolidly to roll dough in the kitchen. It was not the death of Dr. Twills which had so shaken everybody; it was the knowledge—now horribly clear and beyond any doubt—that some one was a murderer.

Let me, then, merely narrate the circumstances of Twills' murder, as I saw them that morning before the police arrived, and as they were afterwards confirmed.

That Twills had died of hyoscin poisoning I did not doubt

84

from the first. The face was cyanosed, the pupils of the eyes dilated, and there were indications of convulsions preceding the coma in which he had died. He lay (as has been already indicated) on the floor with his head partly under the bed, on the side nearest the only window in the room. He was still wearing his glasses, though they had come loose from one ear and fallen across his nose; the body, lying partly on its left side, was just touching a table which stood at the head of the bed. The right arm was flung out against a leg of the table, the left doubled under him. On the side towards the window, in the same wall against which stood the head-board of the bed, was a door leading to the bathroom.

The bedclothes were much rumpled. They had been flung back and pulled partly over the side on which the doctor lay. Among them, squashed face down, lay a copy of the poems of Heinrich Heine. Two pillows, placed upright at the head of the bed, had sagged sideways, and bore the imprint of a head. On the bedside table, a goose-neck lamp was still burning. Beside it stood a tin of tobacco and a glass ashtray into which ashes had been spilled from an inverted pipe. There was a paper of matches in the pocket of Twills' pajamas.

It was clear, then, that he had been reading and smoking in bed when the poison caught him. Probably he had already knocked out his pipe but he had not intended to go to sleep for some time, as witness the matches in his pocket and the fact that he had not opened the window. He felt the poison overcoming him. He made a desperate effort to get up, towards the bathroom; then he either slipped, or grew giddy and fell, where we found him; and he was no more able to cry out than Judge Quayle had been. Or possibly he had been able to cry out, and didn't. I could not be sure.

There was only one receptacle from which poison could have been drunk. A tumbler, containing the dregs of a bromide, stood on the glass shelf over the wash-bowl in the bathroom. Beside it I saw a bottle containing white bromide powder, a smaller bottle of aromatic spirits of ammonia, and a spoon with traces of the powder clinging to it. A large blue bottle of eye-wash, its eyecup-lid slightly askew, leaned against one of the faucets. Everything else was in its place.

The dead man's clothes were thrown carelessly across a cane chair in the middle of the room, the shoes kicked into different corners. A frayed dressing-gown hung from the top of a partly opened closet door. The bureau was a litter of brushes, ties, collar-buttons, notebooks, and pencils, over which had been spilled a tin of talcum powder. A large cabinet photograph of Clarissa stood on top of several issues of the *American Mercury*. Into the mirror was stuck a snapshot showing Twills sitting at a sidewalk café, with a pleased grin, and holding up a seidel of beer.

That last homely detail brought home the tragedy with a sharpness I had not felt before. I remember looking round the bright, bleak, dishevelled room, at the shining mahogany of the furniture and the grey daylight outside, and then back to the naïve pathos of that Vienna snapshot in the mirror. . . . For, in the same tilted mirror, I could see Twills' body reflected on the floor, and the rumpled bed from which he had fallen.

There was an unholy quiet in the room, and a lingering scent of pipe-smoke gone stale. He had come in here, put the syphon on the upper shelf of the closet (where it stood now), and undressed. He had gone into the bathroom, bathed his eyes with the lotion, and mixed himself the bromide. Then—death.

I wished Bencolin were here. Nothing cried out a clue, nothing gave a lead, though you stared at the room till your eyes ached. One fact alone was manifest. To begin with, it was physically possible for this death to be suicide. It had not occurred to the others, because their minds were so set on the poisonings last night that they jumped instantly to a belief in murder. And I knew that they were entirely correct. Suicides do not prop themselves up in bed to smoke and read Heine while they wait for the end; suicides do not carefully bathe their eyes before drinking a poisoned draught. It might be argued, entirely within the physical facts, that it was Twills who had attempted to kill the judge and Mr. Quayle; that he had the poison and knew how to use it; and, failing in his effort, he had killed himself. Superficial minds might even be able to construct a motive which would sound plausible to the equally superficial. It might even be said that a belated attack of remorse caused him to save the judge's life after he had poisoned the syphon. Then despair, and the hyoscin cup for himself. But this is not, and in the whole history of crime has never been, the way of the poisoner; in particular, it was not the way of Twills. It was a reasonable explanation. But I knew that it wasn't true.

Nevertheless, it offered a plausible enough way out of scandal for the family, if only they had possessed sense enough to realize it at the beginning. But, as usual, the very thing they wanted to avoid was the very thing they blundered into. Before I knew where she was, Mary had run down wildly to the telephone and called their old family physician, Dr. Reed, who was also, unfortunately, the county coroner. She had blurted out something about "murder," and "you must get the police," before Matt yanked the phone out of her hands. The damage was done. Then Matt had made matters worse by immediately telephoning all three newspapers, asking to speak to the editors, and blurting out some incoherent words to the effect that they must promise not to print anything they heard about the business. Now, small-town newspapers are run on a highly co-operative basis; it was likely, considering the prominence of the Quayles, that it could be hushed up entirely. But the rumours had begun.

A suicide verdict, if it could be obtained, was the way out of publicity. Despite the indiscreet remarks of Mary and Matt, we might get it put down as such on a death-certificate, and have no police interference. Twills *might* have killed himself, after all.

It was too much of a muddle. I was still upstairs when I heard the front doorbell ring, and I hurried down to see Matt admitting Dr. Reed and (oh, yes, it was inevitable!) the county detective. The latter I knew only slightly, but well enough to know that he was more than ordinarily shrewd.

The title "county detective" means little in communities like ours. The office is political, and it is this official's business, generally, to make a dignified show of maintaining the public peace. As a rule he is brisk and easy-going; occasionally he raids a suspicious house and triumphantly finds whisky; and he is pictured in the newspapers as "investigating" when some Slav or Pole goes berserk with a razor. Joe Sargent, who wore the badge now, was a hearty, well-meaning soul with a conscience. Also, he was intelligent in a business man's way; and he looked, dressed, and acted like a slightly embarrassed lawyer. He was shifting his bulk with an uneasy smile in the lower hallway now, and shaking hands with Matt. Joe Sargent had grey hair combed in a high pompadour, politician's eyes, and a wrinkled, sympathetic face; he exuded that well-brushed, property-owning air peculiar to what is known as the Good Family Man, and always seemed to have just stepped out of the house in his slippers. Dr. Reed was small, wearing whiskers and glasses according to the ancient fashion, and he barked like a terrier.

The four of us went into the library, while Dr. Reed worried at Matt's heels with questions. Matt, faced with the situation at last, was surprisingly calm. His moist, red face was persuasive and deprecating; he talked like a salesman, and urged on them that an accident had occurred, but nothing more. Dr. Reed said, "Bosh!" and everybody looked awkward except the terrier. He also said, testily:

"Don't try any such song and dance on me, young man. I know your father too well, and I know you too well. Now, then: who's sick, or who's dead, or what is it? Out with it!"

"You see, Mr. Quayle," Sargent interposed, in his large and benevolent way, "we only want to help, that's all. Doc tells me your sister was a little upset, but I thought I'd come on out, just in case—eh?"

Matt looked from one to the other. "I guess," he muttered, "I guess it'll have to come out. Oh, go on, Jeff! You tell them; you saw it. Tell them!"

I do not think that either of them had honestly believed much was amiss at the Quayle house. When I began my story, Sargent's big wrinkled face wore an expression of mild and judicial attention, and the doctor looked impatient. As I continued, the county detective's mouth grew loose, and he began nervously to jingle coins in his pocket. Matt winced at each detail. It sounded incredible, as I was well aware. The doctor snuffled and snorted at the conclusion. He started to say, "Stuff and—!" but he looked from Matt's face to mine, and he was suddenly silent.

"You might as well go up and look at him," I said. "He's in the back room on the second floor. It's very possible, even probable, that he committed suicide . . ." Dr. Reed caught my look, and pursed his lips as though he were whistling. "If so, doctor, I think you're an old enough friend of the family to spare them any unpleasantness."

"H'm," said the doctor. "I see. Hyoscin. By God!"

Sargent rubbed his forehead. "I don't know exactly what to say, Mr. Marle——"

"Say?" snapped the doctor. "Don't say anything. Young man, if this were any other house, *I'd* say you were a pack of liars. But old Matt Quayle—h'm. Maybe. Come along, Joe; let's go up and look at him. Wait for us here, will you?"

When they had gone, Matt laid his hand on my arm eagerly. Throughout my recital, there had been a sort of troubled hope struggling in his face.

"Did you mean that?" he demanded. "About Walter's committing suicide? Great God, why didn't I think of it before! That's it. Walter——"

He paused as Jinny opened the door cautiously and came in. I knew she had overheard it also. He continued hurriedly:

"Shut the door, Jinny. . . . Listen, old man. I never liked Walter anyway. He'd be just the sort to do a thing like that. You know it!"

He had taken hold of my lapels to shake them, and he was almost drooling with the intensity of his gaze. Jinny said:

"No. I'd like to think so, but he wasn't." She spoke dully, with a white face. "I don't think he did anything of the kind."

"Neither do I. I was trying to shield everybody, Matt. They'll know better."

"But——!"

"How long," I asked, "has the hand been working? Five years, Jinny said. And Twills has been here only in the last three; isn't that so?"

"But the hand is just dad's imagination——"

"Oh, for God's sake, let's not go over all that again?" cried Jinny. "We just keep going round in circles. Sit down, Matt, and stop pacing around like that! I never knew anybody could get on a person's nerves so much."

"Is that so? Well, you're not any tonic yourself. Maybe you can sit around and hear yourself being accused of murder——"

She flared. "Nobody's accused you of murder. But if you keep acting like a silly little kid, maybe they *will* accuse you of murder before you're much older. And if you haven't any more guts than to try to put the blame on the only decent person in the house . . ."

"Yeah?—The only decent person in the house? The only decent person in the house, eh?" Matt's wrath was bubbling up into a shrill squawk, and he was not pleasant to look at. "You would say so! Well, now, get this: I'll put the blame on him. That's exactly what I'll do!"

"Oh, you will?"

"Yes, I will. And——"

They were quieted only with difficulty; I had to shout myself, and then soothe until exhaustion settled down on the room. Jinny, her face half ugly with repressed tears, went over and sat down with her back to us. We were all trembling with the aftermath of that scene. All the naked little spites and faults were beginning to prickle out now. We sat down in different corners of the room, and Matt lit a cigarette shakily. Through the front windows I could see snow patching the dark earth on the lawn; the library was chill and grey-shadowed. We could hear people walking upstairs, during an interminable wait. Presently there was a noise of steps descending the stairs; and Reed came in hurriedly with Sargent following at a slower pace.

"We've seen it. . . . Oh. Hello, Virginia," the doctor

broke off. He looked at her sharply as she turned round. "How are you feeling, girl? No scenes, now. We want brains."

He had removed his overcoat; he stood wiry and belligerent, snuffling in his thin black beard. His dark suit fitted him too tightly, and his terrier eyes went roving and darting behind a pince-nez on a long black ribbon. I thought, absurdly, of those pictures which used to hang in my father's study, of dogs, playing poker round a table.

"We've decided on something," he said. "It's probably murder. Mind, I don't say it *is* murder; but I think it's probable."

"Well, now—" protested the county detective, mildly, and rubbed his chin. "Now, doc!" He looked at the rest of us with a slightly injured air, as though to say, "You see? What can I do about it?"

"Bosh!" said Reed. "Tell them what we thought."

"It's this way," Sargent explained. "Now, we're not a bit satisfied about this thing, the doc and I. Now, I know the judge, and I respect him, and I want to help you all I can. So you can give it out as suicide, if you want to. But it won't go down as that, I'm afraid. I'll have to investigate. And if I discover anything—well, I can't stall on that, you know." The wrinkles deepened in his big forehead. "Sorry. But that's the best I can do."

"You mean there won't be an inquest?" demanded Matt.

"H'm. Well. We're not sure yet. You needn't be afraid, Joe." Reed told him sourly; "the judge can't break you. He's the one we want to talk to, before we decide on anything definite. If I know him, he'll want it dragged out in the open. Is he still in the surgery? I want a look at him."

He bustled out again. Sargent remained standing by the door as though indecisive. Then he drew a deep breath; he brushed invisible crumbs off his suit, and became again the Good Family Man, as though every wrinkle in his face said, "I have loved ones, too." But you somehow felt that this attitude rode on him like a loose straw hat, liable to blow off at any minute, and show ugly temper.

"I'm afraid I'll have to ask you all a lot of questions," he informed us, smiling. "But it won't be any easier for me, you see?"

He paused, and narrowed his eyes. The thought struck me: God help everybody if this man suddenly gets delusions of grandeur, and tries to play the great detective. It was a chilling thought, for I had known this type of police official before, in Paris, and it had given Bencolin more trouble than the crime itself. If he gets an idea stuck in his head, right or wrong; if he sees his name in headlines as a great criminologist—SARGENT SOLVES QUAYLE MURDER, 110-point caps—then we were undone.

"I suppose," observed Matt, feigning indifference, "you'll want to know where we were last night. Well, I never left my room after I'd gone upstairs, and——"

Sargent jingled coins. He was complacent.

"Why, no, Mr. Quayle, I don't. It's easy to see what happened. He took the poison in a bromide, you understand? He seems to have drunk it as soon as he got up to his room. So, of course, nobody could have sneaked in and poisoned the bromide powder after you had all gone to bed; he was right there. It means that the poison had been in the bromide all evening, probably put in at the same time as it was put in the soda-water bottle . . . Provided," Sargent added hurriedly, "it *was* murder. No, your movements don't amount to anything."

A curious gleam had come into his look. He sighted at the chandelier, still more complacently. I coughed meekly and said:

"Maybe I didn't make it clear . . . Dr. Twills was down here with me at least fifteen or twenty minutes after the household had retired. You'll probably have to take that into consideration, if you decide it was murder."

"Oh!" said Sargent. "Oh—er—no; I didn't understand that. 'M. Fifteen minutes' time—h'm." He coughed. "You—you went right to bed, when you went upstairs, Mr. Quayle?"

"Yes, I did!" Matt stated. "We all went up together, didn't we, Jinny? You saw me."

Jinny nodded. She was standing up now, leaning against

the back of the chair, her eyes a blank. She looked at Matt curiously as he appealed to her. In a monotonous, very tired voice she replied:

"Yes, Matt. You were very exemplary. You went right into your room and closed the door. I saw you."

"Matt's is—second floor towards the front on the left-hand side," Jinny answered in the same indifferent voice. "Right opposite mother's. Mine is on the third floor, in the tower, over Matt's.

Sargent's expression, a thoughtful frown, said: "Now we're getting somewhere!" Aloud he inquired: "Was Mrs. Quayle's door open?"

"Yes, it was!" said Matt. "And the nurse was sitting so she could look out in the hall, and she'll tell you I didn't leave."

"And Miss—you're Miss Quayle, aren't you? Yes. How do you get up to the third floor?"

"Little staircase. It's beside the door to Matt's room."

"Oh! Then it can be seen from Mrs. Quayle's room?"

"Yes."

"And, of course," Sargent smiled heartily, "you didn't leave your room?"

"Yes, I did. Twice."

Her indifference seemed to rouse him. His eyes narrowed again.

"When did you do that, Miss Quayle?"

"Why, the first time was just after I'd gone to my room. I remembered . . ." She paused. A tired, quizzical gleam of humour quickened in the green eyes; she looked at us with eyebrows raised, and her lips twitched. Then she burst into what was half laugh and half giggle.

"This is a serious business, Jinny!" Matt announced haughtily, with one eye out for the approval of the county detective. "This is no time for—"

"But it's so damn' funny!" she cried, still with the impish look flickering between us. "They always go downstairs for a book in the detective stories. And that's just what I did. Clarissa had taken my *Aphrodite*—pinched it before I was halfway through, and pretended to be so terribly shocked.

I knew I couldn't sleep, and so I went down after it. At first she pretended she didn't have it, and she was very much outraged, but I said, 'Look here, darling, don't try any of that on *me*,' and she gave it up. . . . I'm sorry. It's a terribly stale situation, but I really did go down after a book."

"Clarissa—that is Mrs. Twills?"

Since everybody had accepted his statement about not leaving his room, and his skirts were unsmirched, Matt had been growing more and more judicial. He had followed with thoughtful approval every question of the county detective. "Here," he seemed to say, "is intelligence; watch it!" And the county detective was expanding under that approval, growing smoother and more judicial also.

"That's right, Mr. Sargent," nodded Matt. "You've hit it."

"I thought so," said Sargent. He put down his chin in his collar, hooked a thumb in the arm-hole of his vest, and looked sternly upon Jinny. "And Mrs. Twills' room connects with the doctor's by way of that bath. H'm. I see. How long did you stay there?"

The laughter had died out of Jinny's face.

"Only—only a few minutes."

"Had Dr. Twills come upstairs yet?"

"No."

"Where was Mrs. Twills when you left?"

Jinny's eyes were blank again. She did not reply.

"Pardon me, Miss Quayle." Sargent cleared his throat. "I asked you, where was she when you left?"

Jinny said in a low voice:

"She was mixing herself a bromide in the bathroom."

Chapter 9

Murder Misses a Chance

SARGENT remained motionless, his head slightly on one side and his eyes wide open. His mouth sagged a little, and the thumb slid down limply from the arm-hole in the vest. A silence in the grey-shadowed room.

"Ha!" said Sargent finally. "That is—ha!" He cleared his throat. "Did I understand you to say," he went on loudly, screwing up his face, "that you saw her mixing a *bromide* in the *bathroom*?"

"A bromide," affirmed Jinny, "in the bathroom." I felt that she was on the verge of another hysterical laugh.

"H'm," said Sargent. The breath whistled through his nostrils. "You mean—for herself?"

"Naturally. I suppose so."

Still the county detective's voice was unnaturally loud. "Was she mixing it when you went in?"

"No. It was when I was just about to leave. She was still talking to me; she went into the bathroom, took down the bottle from the medicine chest, and started to measure the powder in the glass. That was when I left."

"But did you see her drink it?"

"No. I tell you, I was just leaving."

Sargent began to make rather excited gestures. He ran a hand through his grey pompadour; and then he seemed to implore her for more time. "Wait, now! Wait a minute! —I want to ask you, Miss Quayle! Are you sure it was the same bottle? I mean, the same one as Dr. Twills used?"

"I don't know. I haven't even looked in the room." Jinny shuddered. "But there's only one bromide-bottle there, so far as I know."

"And it didn't affect *her*—" Sargent mused, half aloud.

He had closed his eyes, and was rumpling his mouth and

nose with long nervous fingers: in attitude of Concentrated Thought.

I shivered. Was he getting a glimmer of those headlines? SARGENT SOLVES . . .

"That's . . . that's crazy!" Matt suddenly boomed out. "Why, look here, Clarissa—why . . ." He darted a malevolent glare at Jinny. Sargent looked pained at this treachery from an ally.

"I haven't said anything, Mr. Quayle," he protested opening his eyes. "I'll be damned if I know what I do think."

"Yes, yes, of course. I—er—I know you have to do your duty," said Matt, with a flabby smile. "But, say! Clarissa! After all, she mightn't have drunk the bromide."

"Well, why do you mix up a bromide, anyway, unless you intend to drink it?" argued the county detective, not unreasonably.

"You people," I said, "seem to be very much put out because Clarissa wasn't poisoned. Why not ask her?"

"That's a very good suggestion, Mr. Marle. We—but wait! Everything in order, now; everything in order! There was something else," muttered Sargent, scowling. "Oh, yes. I almost forgot. Miss Quayle, you said you came down from your room twice last night. When was the second time?"

During the excitement attendant on the last sensation, they had forgotten Jinny entirely. She had regained the sombre and far-away look, and raised her head in a rather dazed fashion as Sargent spoke.

"Oh!—That was later, around one o'clock." She hesitated. "I was a little afraid to go down, because I had turned off the light in the second-floor hall when I left Clarissa, and it was dark."

"Why did you go down?"

"There is no bathroom on the third floor."

Sargent looked a little discomfited. "Oh. Yes. Is the bath between Mrs. Twills' and the doctor's rooms the only one in the house?"

"Naturally not. There is one at the extreme rear of the hall. Yes, and one between mother and father's rooms, for that matter."

"Did the nurse hear or see you at this time?"

"I don't know. Probably." She lifted her shoulders. "Every board in the hall squeaks. I made a lot of noise."

This, then, must have been what I heard last night, and mistook for a prowler. One o'clock; that would have been about right.

"I see. Had Dr. Twills come upstairs yet?"

"Yes, I think he had. Anyway, there was a light through the transom of his door, and it had been dark before." Again she hesitated. "Yes, and I heard somebody talking in the room, not very loud. I was so nervous that I thought of going in and talking to Walter for a while, but I decided not to."

"Somebody talking!" repeated Sargent, beginning to rub his jaw vigorously. "H'm! That sounds very important, Miss Quayle. What was it?"

"I couldn't tell. Walter, probably. It was just a mumble, and I didn't catch any words."

She seemed about to continue when Dr. Reed bustled in again. He looked at us all sharply, with jerky motions of his head.

"Well!" he said. "Well—that's something. The judge is awake. Not feeling well, but he'll talk to us before long." A grudging sniff. "That fellow Twills knew his business. H'mf. Damned shame. Virginia! Suppose you run out to the kitchen and get him a little something to eat. Chicken soup, if you've got any; but make it with water, not milk. A little weak tea. Now, then!"

Sargent was obviously bursting with his news. But he teetered back and forth, frowning, until Jinny had left. Then he recounted it with the modest air of one who had made great discoveries, and wishes to deprecate them. Reed swore under his breath.

"Don't like this a little bit," he growled. "Where is Mrs. Twills now?"

"In bed in Jinny's room," Matt volunteered. "She said she wouldn't stay in her own. Mary's with her."

"Let's go up and see her. No, young man!" as Matt moved forward, "you stay here. Much better." He looked me over, as though he were sniffing at me, and added: "Maybe you'd like to come along, Mr.—Marle? Help us some. Know what you've been up to, a little. Ready, Joe?"

Matt was outraged, but he said nothing. The three of us went out into the hall, where dim light fell through the red-and-white panes of the front door. Reed carefully closed the door to the library.

"Now, then," he said, "straight out! Who's doing all this? Have you any idea?"

I shook my head. "But Mr. Sargent's original idea seems to be right. That is, the poison must have been put into the bromide-bottle early last night, and not after the members of the household had gone to bed. If Clarissa had gone to bed as soon as she went upstairs, somebody might have gone into the bathroom and done the work unobserved. But, according to Jinny, she didn't. And she couldn't have failed to hear——"

"But she was mixing that bromide!" interrupted Sargent. "That's what I can't get through my head."

"Well, well, we've just got to ask her," the doctor said impatiently. He began to whistle between his teeth. "Look here. What strikes you right away about this business? I'll tell you. It's the slap-dash, hit-or-miss methods of whoever it is. No matter when the hyoscin was put in the bottle, look at it! This person just goes in and casually poisons a bromide in a bathroom both Mr. and Mrs. Twills used. How did he know Twills was going to take a bromide? Did Twills usually take one? Or did this person slap in his poison on the off-chance that Twills *would* drink it?—What the hell! It looks as though this fellow is taking a crack at everybody in the house, and not caring who he gets. Or else . . ."

He paused, snuffling again.

"Suicide! It looks more and more like suicide. That's the only other explanation. H'm. Mrs. Twills drinks a bromide —or mixes one, anyway—and she's all right. Her husband drinks out of the same bottle, and dies. Suicide. How about letting it go at that, Joe?"

I looked at the little doctor in some surprise. His terrier

eyes were worrying at the county dective's face; he seemed intense, and somewhat nervous. Obviously there had been something in his brief conversation with the judge which had changed his attitude, if not his mind, on the matter. Half an hour earlier, Sargent would in all likelihood have assented. But something was revolving in Sargent's brain; he seemed suddenly conscious of his official position. He frowned, and straightened up rather pompously.

"We'll see," he promised. "Let's go and talk to Mrs. Twills."

Reed regarded him steadily for a long time. . . .

According to the weird architecture of the house, the third floor was reached by a narrow enclosed staircase going up between Clarissa's room and Matt's room. There were several finished rooms here, including Jinny's room in the lower part of one tower (right-hand side as you faced the house) and Mary's room in the other tower. A line of windows at the front opened on a scrollwork balcony; they were of stained glass, and the light fell weirdly dappled into the upper hallway. There was a stuffy smell of dust, and old wood, and paint. Dingy gas-brackets were set into the wall, and your feet creaked on ragged straw matting. Draughts stirred under doors, icily damp; and there was that sound, common to bleak attics, of papers rustling in the shadows. It had begun to snow again; we stood a moment looking round in a moving and changing flicker of coloured light before Reed knocked at Jinny's door.

The tower room was octagonal, with narrow windows on every side except that by which we entered. Under the windows were low bookcases painted white; a couple of good etchings hung on blue walls; and the furniture was wicker covered with chintz. A gas fire was burning, sharp in contrast to the falling snow, and Mary Quayle sat huddled before the low grate. Propped up in a brass bed, the gaslight above it shining on her tense face, Clarissa stared at us. She had not forgotten to wear black négligé even at this time. But her eyes were red and puffy; and she was acutely conscious of the harsh light on her oily, faintly lined face. She was the stout matron, and knew it. Suddenly she shivered. The fine, dark-blue eyes winked in their intent gaze on us; a couple of tears trickled down plump cheeks.

There was no sound but the singing of the gas. Sargent shifted on his feet, embarrassed and somewhat alarmed.

"Dr. Reed!" she cried. "I—I don't need you, I'm all right."

The doctor became cheerful and sympathetic. He went over and took her hand; amiable growlings came from his throat, and he leered through his pince-nez. "Hah!" he said. "Feel better now? Ah, that's good. Chin up, or I'll give you castor oil the way I used to. *Eh*?" He achieved a terrifying grin. "You know how I feel, my dear. Eh? Bad, very bad, this is. You're strong enough to talk, aren't you? Certainly you are. Weakness—stuff and nonsense!"

He leered over at Mary, who jumped nervously.

"Now, here it is, my dear," Reed went on in an argumentative way; "got to make you talk, you see? Want you to meet Mr. Sargent. He's the county detective, and . . ."

A convulsion agitated the bedclothes. She threw out an arm. "That's dreadful! Oh, doctor, how horrible! I won't see any detective . . ." Then the stateliness deserted her. She said, low and tearfully: "Please go 'way."

"Bosh!" said the doctor genially. He would have said "Bosh!" to a dying man. He patted her hand again. "Not going to hurt you, my dear. Do you good. Shakes off the jim-jams, that's what it does."

I looked at the county detective. Sargent had a soft heart. He had come up here grimly and pompously, determined to be the great detective; the calm and analytic weigher of evidence—and so on, after the fashion of the magazines. I think he had more than half suspected Clarissa of poisoning her husband. Now he looked as though he felt collapsed and foolish. He mumbled something to the effect that they didn't *need* to question Mrs. Twills now, after all, and she gave him a grateful schoolgirl glance which won him over completely.

"Bosh! Utter tommyrot!" chirped the doctor, his voice rising querulously. "She's in fine shape, a'n't you, my dear? I'll do it myself, then."

"No!" Sargent interposed hurriedly. "If it's got to be done, I'll attend to it. You see, Mrs Twills, I hate to do this . . ." He was rumbling and smiling, the eyes pleading in his big wrinkled face. He came blundering over to sit down at her bedside. "I won't be hard on you. Honest!"

Clarissa's suspicion and terror of him were obviously fading. He was different from her expectations. Here, it became clear, was an attentive follower. And I thought that Clarissa, even in perfectly sincere grief, was even now rehearsing drama behind her closed eyes. You could see it by the quicker breathing, and the raptness of her upturned face under yellow gaslight. Again we were silent, while the gas sang, and snow thickened beyond the grey windows.

"You—you know, ma'am," said Sargent, "how your husband came to . . ." He hesitated, and added, with some confused idea of sparing her feelings: "Pass on?"

"No. I—only looked in. I know they poisoned him. That's all."

She spoke in a trancelike voice. Sargent looked startled. Then he smiled guiltily, and went on with surprising deftness:

"Well, we'll spare you that right this minute, Mrs. Twills. Suppose you just tell us everything that happened from the time you went to your room last night until this morning."

Another silence. She was rehearsing.

"Very well. If you wish it. I saw Walter when he came upstairs . . ."

"Before that, my dear!" put in the doctor, shooting out his neck. "What happened before that? Everything."

"Before—? Oh, please!" She opened her eyes, and again looked appealingly at the county detective. "I don't know what you mean!"

"Just tell us everything, ma'am. Start at the time you went upstairs. You had a talk with Miss Quayle—you know, the little one. Didn't you?"

Clarissa sat up straighter in bed. Her black hair rippled in the light; and she thrust it behind her ears. From piteousness, her eyes took on a hard, suspicious glaze.

"Jinny?" she demanded in a suppressed voice. "Jinny? Has that little devil been saying anything against . . . ?"

"Bosh!" said the doctor. "It was about a book."

"Oh," said Clarissa, letting her eyelids droop and forcing a drawl. "Oh. I see. Of course, I do not understand what her fondness for erotic literature has to do with this, but if she *must* mention books of that sort even when her own father and mother and brother-in-law——!" She shrugged, viciously.

Sargent was still patient. "That wasn't the point, Mrs. Twills. Miss Quayle came down to see you. What happened then?"

"Why, we—we talked, that's all," said Clarissa, still suspicious. "What on earth has this to do with my husband?"

"When did she leave?"

"I don't know the time. She didn't stay long."

"What happened then?"

"I felt ghastly. I knew, Mr. Sargent, how utterly impossible it was for me to sleep . . ." She was clenching her hands, back into the swing of the drama now, and staring at us earnestly. "If you could only *conceive* of the torture! I paced my room, up and down, and then I remembered poor Walter's bromides. Poor Walter! . . ."

"Was he accustomed to taking them, Mrs. Twills?"

"Pardon?—Oh! Almost every night," Clarissa answered slowly. "He knew they were bad for him. But my husband was so—so high-strung, and nervous! . . . Poor Walter! He didn't like it here, Mr. Sargent. He said: 'It eases me up,' and he took them regularly, these past few months. I can see his face . . ." Her face wrinkled up. "But it doesn't matter now, does it?"

"Go on, Mrs. Twills!" urged Sargent, with an eagerness which would have made her wonder under ordinary circumstances. "You remember the bromides; and then what?"

"I thought one would ease me. I *never* take them ordinarily. I wouldn't touch one of them! I tried them once, and they made my face break out. It was horrible. . . . But last night I couldn't stand feeling the way I did, so . . ."

"So you took a bromide?"

She caught the strange expression in his voice, and drew herself up to look at him suddenly. "Why, no, Mr. Sargent, I didn't. I mixed one. And then I couldn't remember how much you put into the glass; I was afraid I might have put too much, and it might kill me, or something. So I poured it out in the washbowl. . . . But why on earth do you want to know all this?"

Sargent passed a hand over his forehead. My throat was dry, and my heart beating heavily. Death had brushed past Clarissa, as it had brushed past me when I refused soda-water in a glass of brandy. What we felt must have been apparent in all our faces, for she cried, "Oh, my God, it wasn't the bromide, was it?" and began to slap at the counterpane wildly. . . .

"Damn," said Dr. Reed. "Easy! Quit that!" He strode forward and seized her wrist when she started to whimper piteously. I was grateful for his presence then. Sargent kept moistening his lips nervously.

It took some time to quiet her down. At length she leaned back among the pillows.

"I see now why you asked me. Oh, sometimes I think I'll go mad! I—well, let me go on. Please. Yes, I'm all right. I was telling you: I thought I would wait for Walter to come up, and ask him to mix the bromide for me. So I left the light on in the bathroom, and my door open . . ."

"Nobody could have got in and poisoned the bottle then, could they? Eh?" demanded Reed.

"While I was there? Oh, no! Well," she swallowed hard, "Walter came upstairs not long afterwards. He was quite astonished to see me up. I told him, and he laughed, and said, 'That won't make you sleep, if it's sleep you want. It only quiets the nerves. Wait,' he said; 'wait, I'll get you something.' He went into his room and got me some sort of pill—I don't know what was in it. And I rinsed out the glass . . ." She stopped, as the horror returned; "I rinsed out the glass, and drank some water with it. He sat down by my bed, 'Don't be afraid; go to sleep. I'll sit here for a while.' He looked tired. Poor Walter! I tried to make him talk, but he said, 'Don't worry, they won't hurt you. If they're after anybody, it's me . . .' "

Again she broke off, fretfully. "Walter was so careless of his grammar, and he was *such* an educated man! Well, gradually I dozed off. He was sitting there making some marks in a book, or writing, or something, and he seemed worried. That was the last I saw of him. I slept all night."

Making some marks in a book! Was it, then, Heine's poems: the same book he had been reading before his death? A suicide note? Or, more likely, an outline of his theories on this case? Reed exchanged a glance with the county detective; whether or not they were thinking the same thing I could not tell. But I could have sworn that the same uneasy expression as I had noticed once before crept into Reed's face.

"H'm," he muttered. "Worried, hey? He was worried, was he? . . . Now don't you think, seriously, my dear, that he might have—eh?"

Clearly the question of suicide had never entered Clarissa's head. When it was made plain to her, she caught her breath with the same troubled hope which had come to Matt. But, though she started to speak, she could not say treasonable things; she only looked wretched and indecisive.

"F'rinstance, now," Reed was leading her, "if it had been your husband who—mind, I won't say he did!—but if it had been your husband who nearly killed the judge, maybe by mistake—er? And then he'd decided—eh?"

"Oh, *no*. You didn't know Walter, or you wouldn't even think that!" It was a cry of remorse. Remorse: why? "He was careless and untidy, but—oh, you don't know what you're saying!"

Tears had gathered in her eyes again. "As good as he was to everybody," she said jerkily, "and as hateful as— we've been—oh, no! When I think the way I've treated him sometimes, I pity myself all the more because he's dead. Why, he wanted us to go away from here. But we didn't, because I knew we had to stay; because he was practically supporting the whole lot of us . . . !"

She checked herself. The tears suddenly dried in her eyes as though they had been frozen there, and in a scared way she glanced across at Mary.

"What's that?" said Sargent. "Supporting the family, you say? What do you mean, Mrs. Twills? I thought the judge——"

It was the timid Mary who came clucking and bristling out of her chair then, in a sort of dry fury. On Mary's face the skin appeared to be as thin as brownish rubber, pulled into ugly wrinkles by the way she accented each word. She drew up her thin body. She looked as though she were trying to swallow a mouthful of teeth.

"Clarissa," she said, "I hope you live to regret what you've just said! Of all the awful, of all the low and mean things I ever heard, that is the worst. The idea! The very idea of—Haven't you got done driving us all crazy?" she demanded, whirling on the rest of us and making motions as though she were jabbing at us with a broom. "Isn't it enough, with poor papa suffering the way he is?" She began to whimper. "Oh, God, I'll never live through it!"

"Well, you're not going to run down Walter. I'll tell you that much," Clarissa informed her coldly. "He'll get credit for what he's done, even if he is dead."

"You're not going to tell them?"

"I'll only tell them what everybody in the house knows. Yes, and probably everybody in town," returned Clarissa, stung.

"Clarissa Quayle, I hope God will strike you dead!"

Mary turned and stalked out of the room, banging the door. She was so furious, so strangled and sincere that she spoke exactly in the style of the old-time melodrama. Then Clarissa began to blubber.

"Stuff and nonsense!" squeaked the doctor. "Quiet! What's all this fuss, anyway? Stop acting like a hysterical old woman, now, and sit up."

"I have my p-pride too," she blurted. "I'm just as proud as she is. But I won't have her saying things about Walter, now that he's dead and gone. Everybody knows it, except maybe mother, and we didn't dare tell . . . Father *was* wealthy. But he lost all his money in coal, and Walter's been supporting us all, and we were to pretend we didn't know anything about it, and just believe it was father's money. . . . It was all right when Walter was alive, but now that he's dead they shan't talk like that about him!"

"L-let's get out of here," said the county detective, mopping his forehead.

Even Reed was ill at ease. "All right," he growled. "Clarissa! Shut up, will you? We'll take care of everything. O Lord! We'll go downstairs now, and you rest yourself." He meant it; he was her defender now. We left her sniffling into a pillow.

Sargent rose with alacrity, and we made clumsy farewells, the county detective telling her to trust everything to him.

The cold and dimness of the hall took us gratefully after the emotional heat in that room. We stood in the light of the stained-glass window, listening to the prowling draughts and the creak of beams. So that was why Twills could never have his dream? They took him with a not even graceful selfishness; they made him a nonentity in his own house; they used his money and his skill and his poisons; and then one windy morning, they killed him. . . .

"Poor little devil," the doctor growled suddenly.

We tramped in silence down the creaking stairs. . . .

Chapter 10

The Yellow Book

Now, THEN," said Reed, when we stood again in the dead man's room, "there's a lot to be done. I'll call Kitson's——"

"Kitson's?" I asked.

"The undertaker; I think that'll be all right with the family. We'll get the basket out here, and have the body taken in for an autopsy. I've got to do that, anyhow. We can't swear even yet that he died from hyoscin poisoning. The bromide-bottle and that glass will have to go in for analysis. For all we know, there may not be hyoscin in them. Everything's guesswork, so far."

He stood pulling at his thin dark whiskers, frowning round the bright and disordered room. They had already laid Twills' body on the bed and covered it with a sheet. On the table lay that yellow-bound volume of Heine's poems.

"Doc," said the county detective. "I'm getting farther and farther away from the suicide idea every minute. According to what Mr. Marle told us, this fellow had some idea of—well, of what was going on. And Mrs. Twills said he was writing in a book before he died. Is that it?"

He pointed at the Heine, but he made no move to pick it up. Growling, Reed brushed past him and opened the book with a snap which almost broke its back. We looked over his shoulder as he ruffled the pages. The last thing he came to was the flyleaf, and on the flyleaf there was writing. . . .

Twills had been musing. First his pencil had run aimlessly; then he had drawn a number of thick "o's" such as children used to make as writing exercises; some horizontal dashes and squiggles, a crude figure of a bird, and an equally crude face with curly hair and sour features. Next appeared 12/10/31—the date of last night. Still with a musing pencil, he had written "Questions I must Answer," and scratched it out. Just below it, in a regular line, the handwriting became very firm.

Am I sure I know poisoner?
What was burned in the fireplace, and why? (O. K.)
Could personality have made such impression? Medically possible? Psychologically? (Yes. See Lambert, Grafstein.)
Was it hope of money, or growing canker?

The pencil trailed off, drew aimless lines, and then:

To hell with it——
Ship me somewhere east of Suez
. . . Helen, thy beauty is to me
Clarissa Twills Walter Willesden Twills, Jr. 12/10/31.
What about $C_{17} N_{19} NO_3 + H_2O$? Influence?

Sargent raised a puzzled face, and automatically he looked at the bulge under the sheet where Twills lay. "Am I sure I know poisoner?" That, in the dead man's own hand, disposed of suicide. But more revealing yet were those idle lines scribbled at the end. I could imagine Twills sitting beside the bed of his wife, staring at her as she dozed in the long night, and brooding over a racking and devilish problem. Oh, "to hell with it," said his rambling pencil. Let me drift in warmer climes, where there are no worries. The road to Mandalay, a symbol for those irkingly confined. But no, I can't; she's beautiful—I love her—my wife; Helen, queen of the wine-dark sea. "Walter Willesden Twills, Jr." Oh, dear God, if I only had a son!

From a great distance drifted the county detective's voice: "This shows it wasn't suicide. That's clear."

"I suppose so," Reed said gloomily. "It still looks funny, though." He put down the book with an irritated gesture. "Well, I warn you, Joe, you'll have a job on your hands. What does all that gibberish mean, anyway?"

For some reason, what he read seemed to have upset the

coroner more than he was willing to admit. He took a few bustling steps around the room.

"Burned in the fireplace? *What* was burned in the fireplace? H'mf. Do you know anything about this, Mr. Marle?"

"Nothing," I said. "There was no talk of anything being burned . . ." I was about to add, "Except for a telegram sent to Jinny Quayle, which Twills himself burned," but I caught myself in time. There was no use in dragging in more complications at this juncture. Besides, I still felt rather guilty about that telegram.

"What about that C-seventeen something, doc?" asked Sargent, taking up the book again. "Here it is. C-seventeen N-nineteen NO-three plus H-two-O. Looks like a chemical formula."

"It is," said the doctor, biting at his nails. "It's the formula for morphine. Damn. Isn't there anything but dope in this house?" He broke off in exasperation.

"Morphine? But that isn't the same stuff——?"

"No, no. Hyoscin. And it was arsenic they were giving Mrs. Quayle. I don't know anything about morphine. Unless . . . Well, *no*. It hasn't been used to poison anybody."

Sargent put his head on one side.

"Doc," he said, "you're not holding out on us, are you?"

"Holding out on you?" yelped Reed. "Me? Why, damn your pictures, Joe Sargent, you've got a nerve, you have! 'Holding out—' Think I don't know my business. Eh?"

"I didn't say that, doc. I only asked——"

"Asked? Asked? You would. Listen." The coroner took a few brisk turns around the room, and then turned sharply. "Here's your last chance, Joe. If you dig into this thing, I'm telling you, you may dig up more than you can handle."

"Well, doc, that's my business. Let's go down and talk to the judge."

Reed stared at him for a moment, and then nodded curtly. "All right. You've said it. . . . Wait! We'd better stop on the way and see that nurse. Does Mrs. Quayle know?" he asked me.

"I don't think so. There was a terrific row this morning, but I think she was in a stupor."

Miss Herries, the nurse, confirmed this statement when we knocked at Mrs. Quayle's door. She was a broad, unexcited woman with tired eyes and hair on her upper lip. Mrs. Quayle, she said, was awake now, and resting more easily, though she was very weak. The patient had spent a bad night, with occasional vomiting in which blood had appeared. In accordance with Dr. Twills' instructions, she had washed out the patient's stomach again, and used magnesia liberally, with the supporting measures of heat, alcohol and coffee.

"I'd better look in on her," said Reed, "just in case. Don't worry; I won't say anything. She'll probably think I've been called in to help Twills."

When he had slipped into the room and closed the door, Sargent said:

"Miss Herries, you were up all night, weren't you?"

She looked at him incuriously. "Of course. Why?"

"I just wondered if you heard anything—a fall, or a cry, or anything like that—from the direction of Dr. Twills' room?"

The nurse hesitated, nibbling at her lower lip. At last she answered:

"I didn't hear any fall or cry, Mr. Sargent. But there was something . . . I wonder whether I ought to mention it."

"Go on, please! Anything!"

"I heard some one laughing," said Miss Herries.

Perhaps it was the matter-of-fact way she spoke, with a restraint much more terrifying than loud protestations. Perhaps it was the dim narrow hallway, with its narrow brown doors and white porcelain knobs. But my flesh shrank in a crawling chill. With her white costume and expressionless face dull-lit in a light that was shadowed by snow, the nurse looked horribly like Caligula's statue. "I heard someone laughing . . ."

The county detective felt it too. "From the direction of the doctor's room?" he asked, looking over his shoulder.

"I think so. I am not sure."

"When did you hear it?"

"It was at precisely five minutes past three," she replied

in a monotonous voice. Her hands made rushing noises on her starched skirt. "I know, because I intended to administer ether hypodermically at three-fifteen. I had sent Miss Quayle —Miss Mary Quayle—downstairs to sterilize the needle again, and the door was partly open. That was when I heard some-one laughing. It wasn't a pleasant sound."

"What did you do?"

"I went to the door and listened. It was not repeated. I supposed it was somebody talking in his sleep, so I shut the door and came back again."

I fancied that laughter, bubbling up in a quiet house. It seemed to me, somehow, that the laughter had been high and giggling. Perhaps the poisoner had come to gloat. That thought was the most terrifying of all.

"Did you see anybody?" Sargent inquired, after a pause. His voice was low, and not easy.

"No."

"Or hear anything?"

"I may have heard footsteps," the nurse admitted, com-pressing her brows. "But I couldn't swear to it. If I did, I supposed they belonged to Miss Quayle downstairs, and thought nothing more of it."

"Three o'clock. That," Sargent said, "that was about the time Dr. Twills died."

We remained silent in the shadowy hall, each of us see-ing his own picture of what had happened. Dr. Reed re-joined us presently, nodding his satisfaction at the condition of the patient. The nurse went rustling back to the sick-room, and we continued on downstairs. Neither Sargent nor I mentioned this last piece of information to the coroner. Why, I do not know; unless it was because we knew he would squeak "Stuff and nonsense!" and both of us were rather tired of hearing "Stuff and nonsense!" by this time.

Matt met us in the downstairs hall, palpably ghoulish with curiosity, and joined us when we went to the surgery. The gaslamp with the green silk shade still burned on the centre table. Judge Quayle sat beside it in an easy chair, a blanket round his shoulders and a pillow behind his head. With unsteady fingers he was holding a cup of chicken-broth to his lips; his eyes, smeary and haggard, stared at us fixedly, and he started as we came in. He was unshaven, gaunt, with the long hair falling in greyish strands over his ears, like a woman's. There were blue veins in the thin, mottled-brown hands which held the cup. Mary, standing behind his chair, had been patting the pillow at his head when we knocked; but at our entrance she retreated to one of the glass cases at the other side of the room.

"Sit down, gentlemen," he rasped out of a dry throat. He indicated chairs with a trembling cup. "Sit down. I am better now."

"You be careful, papa!" said Mary, looking at us malevolently. "They've been deviling everybody, driving us all crazy, and I won't have you upset. I won't!"

The judge sucked in his lips noisily. The movement made his face even longer, and intensified jumping nerves. But he turned in a lordly way.

"Go out, Mary. Leave me." She hesitated, and he slapped the arm of his chair. "Did you hear what I said, young woman? Must I tell you again? Go!"

"Yes, papa. Yes. I'm going . . ."

He glared after her as she hurried out. Then his wandering eye moved back to us, and he continued to suck at bunched lips.

"You must tell me everything, gentlemen. Everything. I know that they tried to poison me. I am not surprised. If I were stronger"—the voice quavered, and then grew firm —"by God, sir, I would strangle the truth out of somebody. But I am weak. Very weak."

"They killed Twills, judge," said the doctor, leaning back in his chair. "And they tried to kill Mrs. Quayle."

"Yes. Yes. I didn't believe that, doctor, Walter told me so last night, just before I was—stricken. He came into the library; you remember?" Judge Quayle looked at me as though he were groping after a memory of years ago. "You remember? He told me Mrs. Quayle had hung to his arm, and said, 'Oh, please, I've got such cramps. I think I'm being . . .'"

The judge shaded his eyes with his hand, convulsively.

"And now Walter. Walter is dead. I can't believe it."

"Judge," the coroner said casually, "who did it?"

The other did not seem to hear. His head was lowered, and his red-rimmed eye wandered snakily along the floor.

"Why not speak out, judge? We know everything."

Slowly the head was lifting . . . Terror again, tensity, dynamite!

"I mean," Reed went on, still casually, "persecution. Somebody's been after you right here. Joe says he'll find out. Why not tell us?"

The judge stared at me. He spoke with sudden harshness: "You did not tell? No, no. You didn't know. But my family doesn't know. They couldn't know it either. It rests with me. With me."

"Looks like they knew everything, judge," observed Sargent.

"Sir, when I want your opinions, I'll ask for them. Do you hear?" He looked briefly and contemptuously at the county detective, clipping his words sharply. Then his smeary eyes searched our faces, trying to stare us down, trying to keep out fear, but not succeeding. . . .

"All right!" said the coroner. "Just the same, they do. Damn it, Matt Quayle, don't play Shakespeare in front of me! We're not lying. If you're afraid of somebody dressed up in a sheet, like a little kid; if you're afraid of this white marble hand——"

The judge had been trying to drink chicken-broth with dignity, but his hand was shaking so much that he had to put down the cup. He stared.

"Who said anything about a——?"

"White marble hand," repeated the coroner, emphasizing each word with gusto. "Can't you even say it? Why, just about the whole family, that's all."

The judge said hurriedly: "Then they're all in it. All of them. But I'll fight them. I'll show them . . ."

He was breathing hard, and I feared he might collapse again. But the coroner's bright little eyes did not waver.

"Listen to me," Judge Quayle went on, steadying himself. "There has been murder here; yes, and attempted murder. I will spare no energies towards running down the person who did it. If you have any questions to ask me, gentlemen, I am ready. But understand me now, once and for all: I will not have *that other subject* mentioned again."

There was no battering down that jaw. Reed was a fool. He was drilling like a clumsy dentist, boring nerves with a grind and whir you could almost hear. The man was clearly trying to test some theory of his own, irrespective of the murder. It was time to interfere. I said:

"Yes, judge, that other subject is off the track entirely. But there are a few things in connection with the poisonings Mr. Sargent would like to know. Do you feel strong enough to talk about it?"

"I am glad you have the wit to see that, sir," said the other, regarding me with cold courtesy. "Yes. Go ahead."

"I suppose you know what poison was used in the attack on you?"

"Yes. It was hyoscin hydrobromide. An ususual poison." He spoke levelly, without emotion. "Crippen used hyoscin. I believe it is almost the only case on record."

This was unexpected. Reed scowled, and then glanced up sharply, at this mention of the little Anglo-American physician who had killed his wife.

"Are you familiar with such things, sir?"

"As it happens, I am very familiar with the—the literature of the subject. I began it long ago, as a hobby, when I was engaged in criminal practice."

He was sitting up straight now. His face was again the statesman's in the engraving, dour and incurious, but with a speculative eye. He went on:

"But my practical knowledge is small, and I frequently had talks with Dr. Twills on that subject. Why do you ask?"

"Dr. Twills told me last night that some member of this household had gone into his surgery and stolen six grains of hyoscin. It is not a poison the layman would ordinarily use, he told me. Did you ever discuss such matters before other people? Hyoscin, for instance?"

"To my knowledge, never. Never, that is, in general conversation. There were people in the house, of course, and passing through the room occasionally. Our talk was never a secret."

"So that anybody could have overheard you?"

"I dare say. It seems obvious that some one did." He pulled down the corners of his mouth. "In point of fact, he was explaining the properties of hyoscin to me not more than two weeks ago."

"Do you recall the circumstances?"

Sargent's chair creaked, and Sargent's large box-toed shoes were twisted round each other with squirming absorption as the county detective bent forward, frowning. Judge Quayle seemed annoyed at this turn of the questioning, but he replied equably:

As I remember it, we were discussing the Marquise de Brinvilliers . . ."

"Excuse me, judge," broke in Sargent, clearing his throat, "but who was he?"

Judge Quayle, fingers at temple, flashed him a sideways look such as he might have given a dull-witted attorney from his height on the bench. The projecting teeth showed a sour impatience.

"The Marquise de Brinvilliers, Mr. Sargent," he said, "was a woman. She was probably the most celebrated poisoner of the seventeenth century, along with her paramour, St.-Croix. I remember, I suggested to Dr. Twills that Dumas had probably got the idea for his romance *The Count of Monte Cristo* from the life of St.-Croix, who learned all his arts from a fellow prisoner in the Bastille; Dumas devotes an entire volume of his *Celebrated Crimes* to the marquise.

"That naturally led to a discussion of the Borgia—I presume you have heard of the Borgia, Mr. Sargent?—and Dr. Twills was ridiculing the magical qualities ascribed to the poisons they are said to have brewed. Qualities, he told me, as foolish and unscientific as those now ascribed to the East

Indian herb *dhatura*. He informed me that the Borgia in all probability used nothing but white arsenic, the most painful but least dangerous of all toxics."

Judge Quayle cleared his throat. He was the jurist now, speaking coldly, impassively, and without haste.

"He also informed me that, if he were to employ an effective toxic agent, he would use conine or hyoscin. Conine is, I believe, the active principle of hemlock. Its crystals are odourless, almost tasteless, and soluble in water; but it is slower in taking effect than hyoscin. Hyoscin paralyzes almost instantly, though it does not instantly kill, and its effects on the brain are such that the victim does not realize what is happening to him. Dr. Twills showed me the hyoscin he possessed." Slowly the judge moved his eyes back to me, and inclined his head. "Does that answer your question, Mr. Marle?"

"Admirably, sir," I said. Having accomplished my purpose, which was soothing down the atmosphere, I now wanted to step out of it and let Sargent continue the interrogation. Yet (had I known it at the time) that statement of Judge Quayle contained the most important clue we had yet uncovered.

Sargent observed suddenly:

"You had a mighty lucky escape, judge."

Peculiar inflection in his voice!—what was it? He was leaning forward, big hands clasped, looking up from under frizzy grey eyebrows. A warning jabbed me. These two had already antagonized each other. Sargent not unnaturally resented the other's manifest contempt, and the more he showed his resentment, the more contemptuous the judge became.

"I dare say," he said curtly. "I drank very little of it. However, I was not commenting on that. I merely gave the facts Mr. Marle asked for."

With an absolutely steady hand he pushed back the long hair from his forehead. Richard's himself again. Slide into the breach now! I said:

"I believe you told us, sir, that there was nobody else in the room when this conversation took place."

"You are mistaken. That is not what I said. I said merely

that I was not in the habit of discussing these things in general conversation." He considered, tapping his fingers slowly on the table. "In point of fact, I believe there was somebody here at one time during our talk. At just what juncture, I do not remember—possibly before or after mention of the hyoscin had been made. We were sitting in this room, about eight o'clock in the evening, and my son Matthew came in. He administered a final combing to his hair at that mirror by the door, preparatory to going out for the evening."

A sort of bleat came from behind us. We had all forgotten Matt, who had followed us in, and now Matt was making protesting gestures. He cried:

"I was only in here a second, and you know it! That's the only looking-glass there is downstairs, and——"

"You will speak when you are spoken to, sir," said the judge, looking up at him without interest. "Not before."

Matt muttered sulkily: "All right. I'm sorry. But nobody said anything about hyoscin when *I* was here. I didn't even know you were talking about poisons. And I went right out of the house, and Bob Smothers was waiting in the car, and he'll tell you——"

"Of course," I put in, "anybody could have overheard that conversation, I suppose? The door to the hall was open?"

"Undoubtedly. The household were all here."

"Can you by any chance fix the date of that conversation, sir?"

"As it happens, I can. It was Friday, the twenty-eighth of November."

"Judge," said Sargent, "how do you happen to remember that so exactly, anyway?"

The other swung round and studied him, head to foot. "It was my birthday, Mr. Sargent. If you were acquainted with my habits, you would know that, except on special occasions, I always write in my library from six-thirty to ten. I ventured to consider this a special occasion. My birthday apparently, was an occasion of rejoicing to at least one of my family; it showed some one how best to poison me. . . . Are there any further questions, Mr. Marle?"

Evidently he was determined to address himself to me. The coroner had already alienated him by those questions about the white marble hand, and Sargent he brushed aside. There was such dry vindictiveness in the way he said those last words, such a sense of sour chuckling under his buttoned stiffness, that I felt that in him dwelt a small, mad mirth. I risked a shot.

"Isn't it true, sir, that you're rather *relieved* at this attempt on your life?"

A bunched-up smile, now, but fierce eyes. "Not bad!" he said. "Not bad, young man! Yes, I am. If that is the best they can do——"

He spoke softly, nodding his head as though we shared an understanding. Now Sargent was determined to take over leadership.

"Judge," he said, "I've got to ask some questions. You don't have to answer, if you don't want to, but you'd help a lot if you did. You keep talking about 'they,' and you won't answer straight out. Do you know, or do you suspect anybody?"

"I do not."

"Well, then, does this mean anything to you?" The county detective drew from his pocket the copy of Heine's poems in which Twills had jotted those inexplicable words. "Dr. Twills wrote this before he died. He had an idea. Will you please look at it?"

I thought the judge was a little hesitant as he stretched out his hand. His eyes had lost their smeary uncertainty; they had grown bright and wary in a haggard face. Some tremendous force burned in the creaky body. He looked like one of the old warriors of whom his long thin hair reminded you. A Biblical warrior. Out of the blanket stretched a gaunt arm in a blue-and-white striped shirt sleeve, the unfastened cuff fluttering loose at his wrist. He took the book, and ran his eyes slowly down the flyleaf.

Silence in that dim room, where the light of the green-shaded lamp was reflected in the glass doors of book and instrument and bottle cabinets. Behind the judge loomed the white screen. He had lain there on the operating-table last night; and now he sat impassively scanning the last writing of the man who had saved him. . . .

"I can make nothing of it," he said.

As he handed the book back I felt a shock like a blow over the heart. For the cuff and part of the sleeve of his shirt had fallen aside, and I saw that the fleshy part of his lower arm was scored all over by the brown punctures of a hypodermic needle. . . .

Chapter 11

A Detective Falls Downstairs

I TOOK LEAVE of them all shortly afterwards. Our interview of the judge broke up at an impasse. It was past eleven o'clock, and high time I was getting home for a bath, a shave, and a change of clothes, no less than to explain my absence of last night.

"But you'd better come out here this afternoon," Reed said. "We'll want you. You can get them to talk. God knows how. Anyhow, you be here."

He said that he would wait for the basket from the undertaker's, and ride in with it to perform the autopsy. Sargent was silent and dogged. Although he had not mentioned what he thought of the judge's testimony, it was plain that he was determined to carry through his investigation. His first step, he said, would be to gather the Quayles together and make them go over everything they had previously told the night before. He walked out under the porte-cochère with me while I made sure my car had not been frozen up.

"Maybe I'm not much good at this detective stuff," he remarked, kicking absently at the porch steps, "and I hope doc's not around when I'm talking. He throws me off, kind of. But what I mean to say is—I'm no dumber than the next one. And I always sort of had the idea that if ever a big case broke, like this one; something real *big*, d'y'see —well, *you* know! I'd show 'em a thing or two. And, by God, maybe I will!"

The old hope. I did not like the look of his jaw, the rather furtive squint of determination his eyes were taking on. He was standing on the lowest step of the porch, staring out across a white-powdered lawn, as I drove away.

There were too many things to be considered. For instance, those needle-punctures on Judge Quayle's arm. Had Sargent noticed them? If so, he had made no comment.

There was nothing definite to connect them with the word Morphine, I told myself; and then said, "Liar," when I remembered that inexplicable question Clarissa had cried out the night before. "It wasn't the morphine, was it?" That was her first thought when they told her the judge had been poisoned. Was this the explanation of his whole behaviour: a morbid persecution-mania, drug-induced? He shivered and fought at mention of a child's bogey, the white marble hand; yet when the hand dropped hyoscin into his brandy, and persecution assumed tangible form in a stroke at murder, he regarded it with almost a sneer.

I was still puzzling at it when I returned at one-thirty in the afternoon. The snow had ceased. The sky was a murky grey, but luminous along the purple shoulders of the mountains where snow lay in dim, rutted trails. Fields were wasteland; the sharp highway which cleft them, as with smooth dark water, emphasized their humps and the spiky straggling lines of their trees. Through a white powdering the humps broke out; a thin wind whipped the waste and sent powder scurrying. That wind cut with the sharpest of edges, like a razor whose bite you do not feel until the blood comes. When I ran the car through the iron gates once more, I swung round the house towards the garage, which was a part of the old carriage-house. But there was no place to shelter the car against freezing. I threw a rug over the hood, staring at the big shingled place with the cupola, the boarded windows, and the crooked weather-vane. A decrepit door—by which, if I remembered correctly, you entered the paddocks where Judge Quayle had kept good trotters in the old days swung and creaked open. Then the interruption came.

I heard, from the interior, a muffled splintering noise, a series of thuds, and a crash. They were followed by an outburst of the most picturesque profanity (punctuated by the sounds of thrashing about) it has ever been my good fortune to hear. It dealt chiefly with the shockingly lascivious habits of staircases, and surged from the heart like a prayer. I hurried over, pulled the door open, and peered inside.

The sight was as extraordinary as the language. Grimy

light filtered through a high window; the place smelt of dampness, decay, and old hay. Past a line of ghostly stalls, a man sat on the floor talking to a stairway. In one hand he held an ancient board bucket, and in the other what appeared to be a decomposed stocking. A carriage-rug, crusted with stiff dirt, hung across his shoulder.

"—and furthermore . . ." said the man querulously, "furthermore——"

"Excellent!" I said. "Why don't you get up?"

"Eh?" said the man, twisting his head round. "Oh, righto."

He sighed and began to haul himself to his rather surprising height, slapping dust from his coat with the stocking. A disreputable hat, brim turned down, was stuck on the back of his head, and from his lower lip dangled the small stump of a burnt-out cigarette. Then he seemed to forget his disaster. He looked round with an air of refreshed and naïve interest, and the most good-humoured expression I have ever seen on a human face.

"Well," he said, contemplating bucket and stocking, "I got these, anyhow."

"What the devil," I demanded, "were you doing up there?"

"Investigating a crime," he answered, with the utmost seriousness. "You know, I don't think I should be much of a success as a detective if I popped in on the Master Criminal like this. It would be rather a problem to say, 'Throw up your hands, Michael Slade!'—with any degree of coolness and nonchalance—while you were falling downstairs." He added helpfully: "These are clues."

I contemplated the bucket, the stocking, and the lunatic.

"Clues?" I said. "What crime are you investigating?"

The stranger looked doubtful. "Well," he admitted, "I really don't know, you see. That's the difficulty."

"Oh!" I said, with commendable restraint. "But don't you think it would assist your investigation somewhat if you knew what it was you were investigating? I mean, you might find clues that were even more significant than those."

"This had paint in it," he confided, holding up the bucket; "though, of course, it may not mean anything. The point is, what sort of paint was it? What I really need is some data about the snow."

I had an impulse to grasp large handfuls of my hair and yank vehemently.

"Look here," I said; "who are you, anyhow?"

"It's all in the mind's eye," he assured me. "Chap in India showed me; Yogi fella. You close your eyes, concentrate on the truth, and . . . Oh, I say! I'm sorry." He appeared to remember my question and looked contrite. "My name's Rossiter. I'm a detective."

And then I remembered. That telegram last night, and Matt's talk of a loony Englishman. The stranger was about my own age, with a sleepy, genial, homely face, rather fine eyes, and that perpetual air of refreshed and naïve interest. He had the powerful, loose shoulders of a crew man; his slouching posture made his long arms seem even longer. His lean height was wrapped in a nondescript coat of faded and dusty green. His shoes, also nondescript, were among the largest I have ever seen; and he wore a dingy tie—with Harrow colours. The colours of that famous public school hardly seemed to fit into the picture Matt had drawn; besides, I was still staring over that proud statement of his, "I'm a detective."

". . . It's a theory of mine," he was continuing earnestly. "All in the mind's eye. You concentrate on the truth, you close your eyes, and walk blindly forward. And what happens?"

"Why," I said, "you fall downstairs, apparently."

"Righto!" he cried triumphantly, and beamed on me. "You fall, boppo!—right into the centre of truth. I don't mind hitting things, you see; I'm always doing that anyway. Posts, hoardings, walls—smack! I run into 'em all, without discrimination. It's the thought that counts. The thought becomes rarefied. People don't understand the pure ether of your conversation, of course, and so it's difficult to hold jobs." He frowned, meditating this unfortunate circumstance. "But, anyway, I'd always wanted to be a detective. So after I'd got the sack from every other job in New York, I had to give in. And I became a detective. I admit it wasn't very sporting of me, but I did."

"How?" I said, groping after sanity.

"I went to the Police Commissioner," Rossiter said gloomily.

This was going a little too far in the line of jokes. I was about to make various remarks, when I looked at Rossiter's face and saw that he was perfectly serious. He might be a lunatic, but he was not joking.

"He made me one," the young man continued. "As I say, it wasn't sporting. But he did. I'd show you my badge, but I lost it somewhere. Got my papers, though."

He sat down on the steps, entirely at home, with the dirty rug thrown over his shoulder like a cloak. Flipping the cigarette-stub from his lower lip, he produced papers and tobacco, and regarded them proudly.

"Good American," he announced. "I roll my own. Chap in Mexico taught me. Watch." He then proceeded to construct the most ungodly cigarette ever beheld. It resembled an undersized cornucopia, sprouting tobacco, and flared out like a torch when he lighted it. Puffing at it with the utmost good humour, he went on: "I say I'm a bit uneasy. I should have called at the house, you know. But I wanted to investigate here first, and I didn't want to get chucked out. It's no good trying to be diplomatic; I can't do it. Somehow, it never seems to turn out right when I try to be diplomatic. I say the wrong thing, or upset the soup, or something—can't imagine why. The old boy in there"—he gestured with his cigarette, which had taken on the general aspect of a Fourth-of-July sparkler—"the old boy in there regards me as pure Poison. Damn it." Suddenly he looked up in consternation. "Look here, you're not a Quayle, are you? I mean to say—"

"No. Just a friend of the family. You mean you haven't *heard*?"

"Heard what? . . . So long as you're not a Quayle," he grinned in his homely and likeable way, "why, that's all right."

"Listen," I said, "I'm a friend of the family, and a good

friend of Jinny Quayle, so don't think this is just inquisitive-
ness. But it may not be all right. She sent you a telegram,
didn't she, asking you to come on here, and saying something about 'our troubles will soon be over'? Didn't she?"

"Yes. Rather! Why?"

"Dr. Twills was poisoned last night, and an attempt was
made on the lives of both Mrs. Quayle and the judge."

There was a silence. Rossiter's motionless cigarette dropped
large glowing flakes on the floor. "Oh, my God," he said. . . .
"Tell me."

I sketched a brief outline. His face was impassive and
guarded, with a small wrinkle between the brows. When I
had finished, he only trod on his cigarette.

"That's bad. Very bad."

"She didn't get your wire. Twills burned it. I think that
possibly Jinny had some quarrel with her father, which
Twills knew about, and Twills was trying to protect her.
I haven't mentioned it to anybody, not even to Jinny. She
doesn't know you intended to come. . . . I don't suppose
you know the circumstances?"

"Decent of you. Look here—I mean to say, thanks. No,
I don't."

He got up and began to pace back and forth between the
wall and the dusty stalls with enormous strides. Momentarily his fogginess and Buddha-grin had disappeared; his
face was screwed up so that it looked squat and narrow,
and his shoulders swung like those of one who intended
breaking down a door.

"Lend an ear, old man," he said, turning suddenly. "I'll
tell you something. I know you think I'm potty. But I really
am in the Detective Bureau, though I don't belong there,
and the Police Commissioner really did give me the job. I
can't tell you why. Jinny doesn't know it; it would have
been a confession of failure, do you see? I don't think she
knows I'm working at all."

I didn't see, but I nodded, and he resumed his pacing.

"Her letters have been pretty hysterical, lately. When I
got that telegram, why, naturally I hopped off immediately.
Now I've got to decide what to do. Do you think you could

go in there and tell her to come out and see me here? Without any of the others knowing, I mean?"

I nodded. All his seriousness disappeared. Again he sprawled his great length on the staircase; one lank eye wandered over the ceiling, and he had the pleased expression of one who remembers a good joke. But as I was going out his thoughts seemed to be occupied with something else; he looked absent and witless.

"All in the mind's eye," he murmured to himself, frowning. "Was it a very *bad* snowstorm, I wonder?"

And the curious part about it, I thought as I left the carriage-house and went up the driveway again, was that he was not a shrewd man trying to act like a lunatic. His brain did wander in that dizzy fashion, in God knows what fanciful labyrinths. The erratic and amiable figure in the dusty green coat went sauntering along, tripping over everything, blundering in everywhere without noticing where he was going; and, if you asked him a question, he would with all seriousness and good faith reply with what he happened to be thinking about, rather than what you had asked him. He was interested in Ideas, not in people or places. What insane idea had been at the back of his mind when he went poking about in lofts, after buckets, stockings, and carriage-robes I did not know; but I felt sure he had been in earnest about it, and very delighted at having found clues.

It was Sargent who answered the doorbell. He looked depressed.

"Come in," he invited in guarded tones. "Come in, and help me out. I've been making notes on everything I've been told, but damned if I know what to think about them. Still, I think I've got an idea."

"What's up?"

"I've got doc's report. It was hyoscin, all right—though we knew that all along. He'd swallowed about a quarter of a grain; there was at least a grain in the bromide-bottle, and traces in the glass he drank from. . . . The syphon, the one Judge Quayle used, was loaded with it. Nearly two grains, doc says. Doesn't help us much, but we've got our feet planted now. Come on into the library. I'm going to have a talk with that maid."

"Then there'll be an inquest?"

"Yes. But not for a couple of days at least. Doc's still hoping something will break to save the family trouble. . . . Where are you going?"

"Wait a minute," I said. "Where is everybody? I've got to see Jinny."

The speculative, doubtful look was pinching down at Sargent's eyelids again. "Oh, the little one?" he said. "She's been acting kind of funny. She shut herself up in the parlour down there, where it's colder than hell, and she won't talk to anybody. She had a spat with the old one—Mary—and Mary called her a cold little vixen, and said she didn't deserve to have a father. H'm. What do you want to see her for?"

I made an evasive reply, hung up my coat and hat, and went down to the parlour, which was just behind the library. They rarely used it; in fact, I did not remember ever having seen it open except when there were guests to play cards. I opened the door on a room that was as cold as a grave-yard, smelling of wall-paper and unaired curtains. It was dim and ghostly, white, with gilt panels, a number of small marble statues, on mahogany pedestals, a mantel frozen round in white tile, pink drapes, and a large unmusical-looking piano. In the embrasure of a high window, curled up on the seat, Jinny stared out at the mountains.

It would have made a painting: the dusk of the white room, the tall window with a Japanese tracery of trees, the mountains blue as Vesuvius, and the snow. She sat against it in profile, hand on the curtain and head slightly back. She was spectral in a grey dress, with a design of steel beads; and she stared out unfathomably at the watery silver in the sky beyond Chestnut Ridge.

My footstep creaked on the door-sill. The silk colours were torn; she whirled, a shadow, and looked across the room tensely. . . .

"Who—? Oh, it's you, Jeff! What on earth are you doing, standing there?"

"Admiring you," I said. "You're like something out of Lafcadio Hearn." I went over and sat down on the window-seat beside her. "Listen, Jinny, I have news for you. Rossiter's here."

She did not move or speak, but her eyes suddenly grew as bright as though she were going to cry. Keeping my voice down, I explained everything. At the conclusion she was half laughing, and looking round rather wildly, and clasping her hands; such a weight had been lifted from her that she could hardly speak.

"That's it!" she said, "that's exactly what he *would* do! What—what do you think of him?"

"Good sort."

"Of course, he is. But he talks such nonsense, and you can imagine how he'd get along with father and Matt; and he says he's a great musician, and once he was trying to show me how to make musical-glasses, and he broke eleven of mother's best goblets, and said, 'Oh, I say, I'm sorry!' and broke the rest of them trying to put them away in the china closet. He can't stay away from anything that's childish. . . . He's exasperating, and a trial, and a nuisance, and I love him. They can't understand how I can love him and think he's ridiculous at the same time; but I do."

"Where did you happen to meet him?"

She looked out at the trees, wrinkling her forehead, with a little smile.

"He answered an advertisement for house detective at the Summit. Came clear across the continent from San Francisco to do it. I think he believed 'house detective' meant something like Scotland Yard. That's his firmest hallucination: that he's a great detective. And he's even more exasperating, because he never says anything about things he can actually do, but he gets as proud as Lucifer about the things he can't do any more than a mule."

I pictured the dusty green coat, the enormous strides, the earnest stranger falling downstairs and seriously talking non-sense; and I knew how impossible he was to fit into the Quayle household.

"I saw him," she was hurrying on breathlessly, "up there

on the links early one morning. He was shooting the course in par with only a mid-iron he'd borrowed from a caddy; and when I came up to him he looked guilty, as though he'd been caught at something, and mumbled something about 'chap-from-somewhere' teaching him, and hooked the ball out of bounds. Then, the same evening, he told father he was a great musician, and one of the finest pianists in the world; and he got us all in here to hear him, and made the most unholy racket I ever heard out of a piano, and beamed on everybody, as pleased as Punch. And . . . oh, well, you'll see."

She rose hurriedly, the same deprecating smile on her lips.

"I'll go on out now. I—oh, I do want to see the old fool so much!" she burst out, winking both eyes. She smiled again, apologetically. . . .

Then I heard her footsteps hurrying down the hall, and I was left in the dusky room remembering all the questions I should have asked: about how she came to send that telegram, and why she sent it only a few hours before Judge Quayle was poisoned, and other matters which were not now important to her. But (I reflected) detective work is a grubby business, and her eyes were very bright, and who the devil cares anyway? This afternoon (reflected grandfather) there will be for those two a small bright poignant moment in a dim stable smelling of dampness and old hay; the snow will fall softly, and doubtless the ghosts of vanished horses will whinny benevolently from their equine paradise. Blessed are the lunatics. Blessed are the lunatics, for it is they whom women love; and all doors fly open to them, and they shall inherit the earth.

I went slowly back to the library and a murder case.

Chapter 12

Stolen Rat-Poison

A VERY MUCH frightened Slavish girl stood before us in the library. The judge, Sargent had told me, was taking a nap in his room; Matt was in town to oversee the arrangements for Twills' funeral; and Mary was up with Clarissa in Jinny's room; so we had the library to ourselves. Sargent sat behind the centre table, his notebook ready. He glowered upon Joanna. She was a strong, heavy girl, with an oily face, a flat nose, and braids of hair strung across the top of her head. Shifting from one foot to the other, she ran her hands nervously up and down the sides of a gingham dress, smeared with flour, and fastened small suspicious eyes on the corner of the table. She had not minded a death in the house, but the presence of the police disturbed her. Sargent knew his tactics with this type of witness.

"Now then, Joanna," he said sternly, "you know who I am, don't you?"

"Ya, I know you," she answered rapidly, with a jerky rise and fall in her voice. "I got bru'ter Mike, he know you too. You put him in lock-up for he make whisky; he no make whisky. I no make whisky either."

"Never mind that, Joanna. I want to ask you about something else."

But Joanna had a grievance. Her sullen voice rose higher:

"You put him in patrol-wagon, you take him to lock-up. He no make whisky. Priest tell you he no make whisky, we good people, but you put him in patrol-wagon—"

"All right!" Sargent interrupted warningly, shaking his finger. He imitated her style of speech, as people always do when they want to be particularly impressive. "All right! You answer everything I ask you, you hear? Or else I put you in patrol-wagon, take *you* to lock-up. You hear?"

Her face hardly changed, but she was terrified.

"You ask me!" she challenged. "I tell you what you want know. Ask me! I not scared. I no make whisky."

Sargent nodded, and resumed his ordinary style of speech. "Last night was your night out, wasn't it?"

"Ya."

"Where did you go?"

"I go home, like I go every night out. I good girl. I no make whisky. I take eight-clock car, stay wit' my mud'er; I not come back till morning."

"Where do you live?"

She hesitated, with a characteristic reluctance to give definite information in the way of places or names; but she decided he must know already.

"I live Republic."

"Now, listen! Were—you—here—in—the—kitchen—here—all—day—yesterday?"

"Me? In kitchen?" Apparently it had not yet penetrated her mind what he was questioning her about, and she still suspected whisky. She was merely bewildered. True, somebody had swallowed something and died, but what of it? People were always drinking bad moonshine and dying. Why (she must reason) this talk? *She* hadn't given him bad moonshine. "Me? In kitchen?" she repeated, dully. "Me? No. I make beds, dust, sweep—"

"Were you in the kitchen all afternoon?"

She thought hard. "Ya. After lunch. All time."

"Joanna, you know the tin of rat-poison, rat-poison, in the pantry?"

"For kill rats? Ya, I know. Ya! I look for it yes' af'noon. I hear more rats when I go down cellar after apples, so I go look for stuff for kill rats, in pantry. It not there."

Feeling that she had successfully diverted the discussion from whisky, Joanna was growing voluble. Sargent was excited.

"Are you sure about that, now, Joanna? The rat-poison wasn't there early in the afternoon?"

"Ya! I no lie! I say to Miss Quayle, I say, 'Miss Quayle, what you do with white stuff for kill rats?' She say, 'You no bother for rats. You tend your cooking.'"

"Which Miss Quayle was that?"

"Eh? Oh, thin one."

"Miss Mary Quayle?"

"Ya, sure." Joanna was scornful. "She only one ever come in kitchen. I say, 'Somebody take stuff for kill rats.' She say I no tell truth. But I tell truth! It not there. . . . What you want it for?"

Sargent looked at me. "It was gone early in the afternoon," he said, "and it's still gone. Nobody in the house will admit they saw it at any time. . . . Joanna, who was in the kitchen besides you that afternoon?"

"Nobody, no time, I tell you!"

"And you're sure, now, you're *sure* you didn't see anybody take the rat-poison? You tell me the truth, or I'll take you to the lock-up."

She flapped her arms. "If I see take it, why I ask her who take it? I not see anybody take it, eh, or why I *ask*? Please, I got go now. I got pie. . . ."

"Just a minute, Joanna." Sargent ran a hand through his grey hair and brooded, his eyes on the notebook. Then he assumed a confidential air. "Listen. You know this family pretty well, don't you?"

"Oh, ya." She was noncommittal. "I guess."

"Tell me, Joanna: how do they get along? They fight, eh?"

This was getting into the realm of gossip, and, by the greedy expression on Joanna's oily face, it was obvious that she loved it. Whisky had been put aside forever. She grew expansive, and eager to help. But first she glanced over her shoulder, and then lowered her voice before she went on:

"Oh, ya. All time they fight. Judge, he fight pretty one. They all have big fight, two, three, four days 'go. No! Was two, three, four week 'go they have big fight. Ya."

"What was the big fight about? Do you know?"

But for the moment Joanna concentrated on "judge" and "pretty one," because it contained details of amatory interest. "Pretty one," I assumed, must mean Jinny.

"She like sit in parlour, where nobody go. Cold in there,

too. She like play piano. Bloof!—what good you play piano if you no got people round sing?" demanded Joanna. "Sometime' judge he go in—I see when I dust—he look funny, he not speak loud. Not like my pop. My pop he come home drunk he lick me he think I not good, eh? Ya." She nodded, with pride. "Well, judge he say, 'Why you no play t'ings I like?' And maybe she play t'ings he like, and he sit and look funny. . . . I know. I like t'em tunes. I sit on stairs and listen."

(An old man, hesitant, groping after his family, his austerity fiercely repressed; stooping and pitiful, sitting on a chair in the cold parlour. He would ask her to play his favourites: hymns, and old homely songs which, in our smug damnable superiority, we have almost forgotten. I remembered, from the past, how he had loved "Lead, Kindly Light," and "Drink To Me Only With Thine Eyes," and Jinny, as a large-eyed child, played and sang.)

". . . while I listen, she ask him somet'ing, and they go argue. And first she try play gain, and hit piano hard, and then she get mad, and he get mad too, and she say, 'I will marry him! I will marry him, when he has job.' And first he try be nice, and he say, 'But who he *is*—you know?— and then he get made and say, 'Don' you talk to me!' . . . and she start bawl . . ."

Sargent glanced over at me, his eyebrows raised.

"That's all right," I said. "Fellow she's in love with. Arrived here today." I added, hoping for the best: "He's a detective."

"A detective, eh? Where's he from?"

"He's an Englishman. And," I continued—God help us if it wasn't true!—"he's a special friend of the Police Commissioner in New York."

"Hmf!" Sargent grunted. He shifted in his chair, frowning. Clearly he didn't like this. He wanted nobody horning in on his case, especially somebody who sounded impressive. I resolved to lie up-hill and down-dale.

"He's a little eccentric," I explained, tapping my forehead. "But sheer genius. That's why they've got him as special investigator. . . . And he never wants any credit, Mr. Sargent. He likes to work entirely unseen. He could give you a lot of help, without appearing in the case at all."

Sargent considered this, and was not displeased. "My colleague, a friend of—" Well! He nodded.

"Never heard of him before," he grumbled nevertheless. "I didn't know Miss Quayle knew such people. . . . Now, then, Joanna. Tell us about this 'big fight' you mentioned."

Joanna had been very bored and restive during this talk. She opened her mouth eagerly to reply, and then discovered she had very little to say.

"Why . . . fight," she explained. "You know. Fight. Was at din'r-table. They start, but they not say much when I come in with plates."

"What was the fight about?"

"I not know, for sure. Was 'bout money, I t'ink. They talk 'bout money, so I listen. You know? They talk 'bout somebody call Tom. And judge say soup too hot; make me take it back to kitchen, and—"

She paused, frightened. The stolid expression hardened on her face like putty; she folded her big hands. Mary Quayle had come stalking in, her flat-heeled brogues making hardly any sound. Mary's high nose was carried even higher, like her shoulders.

"Joanna," she said coldly, "go back to the kitchen."

The girl began backing away, her eye on Sargent.

"It's all right, Joanna," the county detective told her. He spoke with repressed anger, and kept nodding his head. "It's all right. Go ahead. Miss Quayle will answer the questions I was going to ask you. Go ahead."

"Well, I never—!" cried Mary.

"Now, Miss Quayle, you listen to me," Sargent said, "You people don't have to answer questions yet. But if you do, I'll tell you this: I can save you a whole lot of trouble at the inquest. It won't do you any good to act the way you're acting."

Mary pulled herself up. "Goodness knows, Mr. Sargent, *I'm* not trying to interfere with you," she snapped. "Go right ahead and ask me what you want to. But I won't have servants discussing . . . Close the door, Joanna! . . . I won't have servants discussing our business in public, that's all."

"All right, Miss Quayle. Then suppose you tell me: What was this quarrel at the dinner-table, about money and somebody called Tom."

Growing nervous, Mary looked over appealingly at me. I said:

"Better tell him, Mary."

"Well—good heavens! If you've got to know *everything*, it was about my brother Tom."

"Yes?"

"He's a waster, and a no-good, and a failure, and he's driven papa nearly insane, that's what he's done! And papa had been so kind to him, and gave him everything—*you* know that, Jeff! Then he had the nerve to write to us, all of us, and try to beg money. Mind you, the first line we'd heard from him in three years; wanting money! And saying he was broke, and sick, and everything. Lot of lies, that's what it was. But Jinny always sided with him, and so did Clarissa, sometimes; and of course mother, only she didn't dare stand up to papa."

"And they were urging him to send Tom money?"

"Jinny was, yes. It wasn't a fight, really. That Joanna is a spiteful little—"

"Wait a minute, Miss Quayle! Did the judge refuse?"

"Matt certainly told Tom off!" Mary announced with satisfaction. "Matt said just exactly what he should have said; he sided with me, and said let Tom go straight to the devil, where he'd always been headed. Mind you, I'm not the one to hold grudges, but after the way he'd treated papa . . ." She was so full of injury that she forgot her reticence. "Well! I said it would be shameful. Absolutely shameful."

Thus Mary, who found it very easy to be severe at a distance; but who, when she saw somebody in difficulties before her eyes—particularly sickness—would kill herself with ministrations, reserving the tirades for afterwards. She pitied a person only when the person was helpless: in which case her pity became more suffocating than her previous condemnation.

"But that wasn't what I was asking you, Miss Quayle," Sargent said patiently. "I wanted to know whether the judge refused."

"Refused—?"

"To send Tom money."

"Oh! He didn't say anything at all. He just got up and left the table, and when I saw the expression on his face I could have killed Tom. We knew he wouldn't; we knew he just wouldn't discuss it."

He wouldn't . . . And suddenly I saw why. "The expression on his face." He must have been pale, and his stiff lip drawn in, when he walked from the table, tightening his pride like a belt across an empty stomach. He wouldn't send money because he couldn't; he had none to send.

"We were all upset, and mother was crying, but we knew better than to cross papa," Mary went on. "All the same— I'm not sure about this, but I think it's so, because I saw a letter on the hall table—I think maybe Walter did send the money anyway, and signed papa's name to a letter. Walter would never talk about things like that. He always was soft like that. If he did send it, he didn't tell us." She sniffed. "I'd have more spunk!"

The county detective fell to making aimless marks with his pencil, apparently feeling that he was off on the wrong track, but not quite knowing how to approach the right one. At his elbow lay the yellow-bound Heine in which Twills had written those inexplicable statements; he picked it up dubiously.

"Mr. Marle," he said, "I've asked everybody here about the things the doctor wrote. And nobody has any idea what they mean." He looked sharply at Mary, as though he felt he had been talking too much in public. "Are you *sure*, now, Miss Quayle, you don't know? 'Burned in the fireplace' . . . h'm."

"I've already told you I don't! Walter was probably just dreaming, as usual."

Sargent opened the book and studied the flyleaf again. " 'Was it hope of money, or growing canker?' " he read slowly. "Whose money? Twills'? Do you know whether he made a will, Miss Quayle?"

"How on earth should I know?" demanded Mary, stiffening. "I'm sure I haven't the faintest idea. I dare say he'll leave Clarissa very comfortable, if that's what you mean. I . . ." She stopped. Alarm showed in her eyes at some thought which had just occurred to her. She glanced at Sargent, rather nervously, but he was absorbed in scowling at the book. "And if you're thinking about asking papa, I'm sure he wouldn't know either. He's much too busy to be troubled with things like that; and, anyway, Walter would never have mentioned it."

"All right, Miss Quayle. Thank you."

Mary said something about pies in the oven, and hurried out. For a long time I had been wanting to ask her something, but I had hesitated. A certain inconspicuous remark of Joanna's had made me remember something Matt had told me the night before. At the dinner during which this disturbance had taken place, Joanna said, the soup had been too hot, and the judge had ordered it sent to the kitchen for cooling. And, according to Matt, it had been at dinner that "one of the girls" had told that Roman story of the poisoned water-cooler which had been, in all likelihood, the murderer's inspiration. It seemed probable that the hot soup had suggested the story to somebody. Which one? I had hesitated, because I did not want to involve Jinny. Matt thought it might have been she. But sooner or later the question had to be asked. Meantime . . .

"I've got a statement from everybody," Sargent broke out suddenly. "But it doesn't help much. The same old stuff. I'm not very good at cross-examination, I guess. And, somehow, I can't get tough with these people." He brooded, his head in his hands. "Trouble is, my hands are tied until we get a murder verdict on this business. I'd like to search the house. Somebody's got a tidy lot of poison hidden here. If this were a city, I suppose I could go ahead, and damn the consequences. But the judge knows his rights, and if Doc

Reed won't string along with me . . . I'd—I'd kind of like to talk to this detective friend of yours."

"Did you learn anything new in your examination?"

"Only about the judge's movements," Sargent replied, leafing over his notebook. "I suppose you remember what they all said? They said that at half-past five last evening—that is, just after Clarissa brought home the syphon and gave it to Mary, who took it to her father in here—the judge went down into the cellar. Nobody saw him until shortly after six, when Matt met him on the front stairs.

"Well, it seems the judge is great for pottering around the house and repairing things. He's got a carpenter's workshop fixed up in the front part of the cellar. For the last few days he's been making a set of shelves for some preserves Mary's been busy with; so late yesterday afternoon he went down and worked for a little less than half an hour. Then he got a bottle of brandy, came up the back stairs, put the bottle in the library, went up to his room to wash his hands, and met Matt when he was coming down afterwards. That was when Matt was carrying up Mrs. Quayle's tray. . . . You see, you don't have to go through the kitchen in order to go down the cellar stairs; they're at the back of the front hall, giving on the pantry, and they continue as rear stairs to the second floor. That's why nobody saw him during the time."

Sargent rose and began to pace about the room, flourishing his notebook.

"I've got it all down here, tabulated," he said. "Shall I read it to you?"

I nodded, and he traced out the words with his forefinger as he read:

5:15. Clarissa arrives home in the car with groceries and the syphon. Mary takes syphon to Judge Quayle, remains until 5:30. Syphon has not been tampered with yet, since judge drinks with soda from it. Clarissa goes upstairs to her room and lies down. Maid is in kitchen. Dr. Twills in his surgery. Virginia does not remember precisely where she was, but thinks she was in her own room reading. . . .

"She wouldn't be definite about that," the county detective announced, looking up. "All she remembers is that she wanted the car to go into town after a book from the lending library. When she heard Clarissa's voice downstairs, she came down, took the car, and left. She thinks it was about five-twenty-five. All right." He resumed:

5:30. Judge Quayle leaves library and goes to cellar. Matt arrives home on bus and sees him going in direction of kitchen. Mary is in kitchen, helping maid with preparation of evening meal. Twills still in surgery, wife in her room upstairs. Mrs. Quayle in sick-room.

5:30 to (about) 5:55. Judge in workshop, others in rooms as indicated above. Matt comes downstairs about 5:50, goes to kitchen, loiters there while Mary prepares Mrs. Quayle's tray.

5:55. Judge comes up cellar stairs with brandy-bottle, leaves bottle in library, goes up to his own room to wash.

6:00. Dinner-gong sounds. Matt carries tray upstairs, meeting judge coming down. Judge stops to look at tray. Matt places it on table, not waking Mrs. Quayle, who is dozing in chair; then goes downstairs.

6:00 to 6:10. Tray untouched on table while Mrs. Quayle dozes. Judge and Matt alone in dining-room. Clarissa still upstairs, Mary and maid in kitchen. Virginia out with car.

6:10. Virginia arrives home. Mary goes upstairs, rouses her mother, watches her start to eat, and then comes downstairs. Clarissa down from her room, Twills out of surgery.

6:45. Dinner over. Judge goes to library, Twills to surgery, Mary to kitchen to assist with dishes, Virginia and Clarissa upstairs to dress, Matt to sit with his mother.

Sargent flicked the page gloomily. "There you are. Mary let the maid out as soon as the dishes were finished. Mrs. Quayle was taken ill about seven-thirty, but the doctor said it wasn't serious; so Mrs. Twills went to her ladies' club meeting in the car, and Virginia kept her date with a young fellow named"—he glanced at his notes—"Kane. You got here at eight o'clock, and you know the rest."

We were both silent. The room had grown more shadowy as the afternoon deepened. From the snow outside was reflected a spectral light, which mottled the glass doors of bookcases in weird patches, and brushed the walls with the outline of branches. Portraits were now only dark blurs palely rimmed in gold, the curtains lifeless and dingy. But, by some trick of light, the dull red flowers in the carpet had kept their colour. When Sargent paced against the line of the windows, he seemed to be tramping an ugly garden. I sat listening to the faint wind, which sounded horribly like somebody fighting for breath in a sick-bed. Yesterday afternoon, about twilight, somebody had crept in here, where the syphon stood on the centre table, and unscrewed the metal top, and dropped in two grains of hyoscin. Now the table stood up dark against the windows, with the topheavy piles of books from which Judge Quayle had been making notes. I could see the little iron press for clipping fasteners, just as it was the night before; the brass fasteners, the pens, pipes, and tobacco-jar; but where the syphon had stood now lay a yellow-bound book in which Dr. Twills had scribbled inexplicable accusations. . . .

"Who's guilty?" I said.

"I don't know," Sargent muttered, coming to a stop and staring at the yellow book. Then he glanced at Caligula's statue, in the corner by one window where the light fell bluish across its side. He gestured. "With one exception, I could make out a case against anybody. The only one I'm sure isn't guilty is the little girl—Virginia. She was out of the house between five-thirty and six-ten. And it was during that time that somebody undoubtedly poisoned the syphon, the milk-toast, and the bromide-bottle in Twills' room. *Everybody* had an opportunity. I . . ."

He paused, his back to me; paused with a little jerk in his throat.

What Sargent felt at that moment I do not know. But something fell in my stomach; fell, and then rose with a constricting rush of sheer terror.

I was looking at Caligula's statue, its dim and goggle-eyed smirk visible in the blue-grey light from the window. A moment before, the rectangle of the window, framed in its draperies, had been empty. Now a hand was pressed against the pane.

Its fingers were flat, palm towards us, an unhealthy white. Then the fingers began to scratch and drum on the pane.

Only for a moment I looked, the hot fear in my throat preventing an outcry. Then terror was lost in a gust of relief and anger. Muffled but distinct, a familiar voice outside cried querulously:

"I say, open the window, won't you? I can't hang to the side of the house all afternoon. Open the window!"

Chapter 13

Wherein We Draw Some Pictures

I STRODE OVER, unlocked the window, and pushed it up angrily. There was a scraping, and two hands appeared. Up over the sill appeared Rossiter's face.

"It's quite all right," he assured me, clinging there in some mysterious fashion and speaking as from a pulpit. "Sorry if I gave you a turn, old man. I was only trying to find out how much of the room I could see. I walked around a ledge here, and I rather think I've broken some wires or something."

His battered hat had now accumulated some ancient cobwebs, which draped down over his face like a veil. Another stump of a cigarette dangled from his lower lip. He was very contrite.

I explained, briefly but violently, what I thought of him, and requested without gentleness that he come in and close the window. He was craning his neck to peer about.

"Do you mind," he said, "if I swing up to the roof and crawl about a bit? I'm in rather good training; I think I could make it, and—"

"Come *in* here, damn it!" I said.

"Oh, righto," he agreed sadly. There was a sort of silent explosion among the curtains, a series of bangs and thumps, and then he unfolded his great height on the floor as I slammed down the window. That ominous statement, "I rather think I've broken some wires or something" came back to me, and I went over to test the electric lights while he was slapping dust from his coat. He was quite right. The lights refused to work. He had probably blown out every fuse in the house.

Sargent, who was sweating a little, had regained his composure. He glared at Rossiter. It was scarcely an auspicious time to introduce my Great Detective, but it had to be done. Sargent looked from Rossiter back to me, startled and obviously not knowing what to do. His suspicious gaze intimated that somebody was joking, and he coughed and jerked his head formally, and I grew a trifle uneasy.

"Where is Jinny?" I asked.

Rossiter was removing his hat and green topcoat, to display a grey worsted suit of good cut, but in an appalling state of disrepair. His tie was now skewered under one ear.

"She went up to pacify the old man," he said, frowning. "I don't want to get chucked out, you know." Then he beamed on Sargent. "Oh, I say! Stupid of me! You'll want to see my credentials, won't you?"

He began taking things out of his pockets, and he had accumulated on the desk a sizable pile of letters—chiefly unopened ones, of which he explained, "Bills, you see," very apologetically—before he found an ancient leather wallet, which he handed to Sargent. Then he sat down like a collapsing clothes-horse, and blinked about with sleepy good humour.

"Why," said Sargent hesitating, "this . . ." He rubbed his chin vigorously, looking even more startled; "this seems to be a certificate signed by . . . well, it says 'High Commissioner, Metropolitan Police, New Scotland Yar—' "

"Oh, God!" said Rossiter, jumping up out of his chair. "Wrong place. That's not it. Other flap. Oh, dash it. Got the thing?"

Turning over the wallet, after another bewildered glance, Sargent nodded. Rossiter relaxed with a sigh when the wallet was returned to him.

"Well," said Sargent, still bewildered, but eager to make amends, "of course, we're mighty glad, mighty pleased . . ."

"Not at all," said Rossiter absently. He was concentrating on the table, and looking like a slightly intoxicated crystal-gazer. In a moment he roused himself. "Look here, Mr. Sargent, if *you're* satisfied . . . I mean to say, do you mind not mentioning it to the others? Thanks awfully. . . . Curious things, those what-dye-callems. Very suggestive. Ve-ry suggestive, eh?"

Sargent blinked, seeming uneasy. "What what-dye-callems?"

"Little brass thingummies. *Pop!*"

"What in the holy hell—!"

"Pop!" explained Rossiter, bringing his fist down out of the air as though he were hammering something. The expression of rapt interest came back to his face, like that of a child with a new mechanical train. He bent over the table. "Little brass thingummies. You use them to clip papers together. First you put the papers under that press, and then you put the thingummy in, and then you press the handle . . ."

"You mean the fasteners?" I said.

"Rather. Let me illustrate. I know how. Chap in a law-office showed me."

"Well, of course. But . . ." Sargent moved his hands in a dubious way. The fiery enthusiasm of this extraordinary young man was impressive, but puzzling. Sargent watched with growing uneasiness while the stranger entangled his fingers in the mechanism of the press, shot three or four fasteners high in the air, upset some books, said "Hell!" with recurring frequency, and finally looked up apologetically.

"Anyhow, you observe the principle of the thing," he said, taking comfort. "It's all in the mind's eye."

"I suppose it is," said Sargent. "Well—"

Guiltily Rossiter tried to hide the press behind some books. "I should be very much obliged to you," he continued, as though eager to change the subject, "if you'd give me the facts in this affair. Just tell me slowly and carefully, you know, so that I can concentrate. Eh?"

This was more to Sargent's liking. He lost a little of his dubiousness, sat down with his notebook, and began a painstaking recital. During the recital, Rossiter stalked up and down the room, still imbued with his fiery energy. His loose figure clumped down big shoes, his jaw was poked forward, and on his face was that rapt expression of the intoxicated crystal-gazer. I studied him in better light than there had been at the carriage-house. He had long hair, of a dark grimy yellow in colour, which kept flopping into his eyes at every third of the gigantic strides, and which he pushed back nervously with a hand that might almost have palmed a football. When all the evidence had been reviewed, he turned uncertainly.

"You didn't need to tell me very much," he said. "You see, I know quite a lot already, probably more than you do yourselves. Jinny's letters . . . When a woman has something on her mind, she always writes a long letter about something else; and that's how you get to know." He drummed on the edge of the table. "But you made that suggestion about a will, for instance . . ."

"I've got to find out about that," said the county detective. "Do you think Twills made one?"

Rossiter looked at him vaguely. "Twills? Oh! I don't know, I'm sure. I wasn't thinking about Twills."

The county detective did not seem to hear him, for Sargent was holding to the arms of his chair; he was staring across at the empty fireplace, and moving his head in a curious way.

"You act kind of crazy," he said flatly, "but I see something. I've been thinking about it all day, and it scares me. Just the same . . . Dr. Twills *did* make a will, I'll bet you my last dollar. There are those fasteners for legal documents on the table. And the judge would have drawn it for him. 'What was burned in the fireplace, and why?' And then: 'Was it love of money . . .?' "

"Wait a minute, though!" I said. "You don't know to whom Twills might have left his money."

"That's just it." Sargent nodded slowly, and then lifted cold eyes. "That's just the point. He mightn't have left it to the Quayles."

I shivered. From such a starting-point, a person's fancy might put any face on the shadowy figure who crept about in this house, and who the night before (if we were to believe the nurse) had giggled over Twills' writhing body. I steadfastly refused, as yet, to put a face on that figure . . .

For a long time Rossiter had been looking dreamily at the sky. He woke up.

"I say!" Rossiter called out. He came round from behind the table and looked at us anxiously. "There's something very important we've been neglecting, and we've got to do it now."

"What's that?" demanded Sargent.

"It's all in the mind's eye," the other explained carefully. "Here—pencils and paper. Do you mind? Now, sit down and concentrate."

"Say!" protested Sargent, backing away as the young man excitedly thrust a sheet of paper at him. "Say, *listen!*—"

I found a pencil in my hand, and myself pushed down into a chair. Loose-jointed, one arm waving, Rossiter stood before us. "Ready?" he asked. "Good man! Now . . ."

"Well, go ahead," growled the county detective. "I'm as bug-house as the next one. What do you want us to do?"

"Draw a picture," said Rossiter triumphantly.

"*What?*"

"Draw a picture," the other repeated, in a tone of firmness. He grew earnest. "Man, man, don't you see the importance of drawing a picture? Don't you see the momentous and appalling issues which hang on your drawing a picture? Don't you perceive the profound psychological bearing it will have on the solution of this case when you draw a picture?"

"No, I'll be damned if I do," said the county detective. "What picture?"

"Any picture," said Rossiter.

"Oh, Jesus!" said the county detective and flung down his pencil.

"But look here," I suggested, with as much calmness as was possible, "what's the sense of this? I can't draw, and I don't think Sargent can either."

"Ah! But that's the whole point, don't you see?" Rossiter turned to me earnestly, and spoke with an appearance of easy good sense. "If you could draw, I shouldn't be asking you—should I?"

Sargent's sense of humour was entirely gone. There was a malevolent look in his eye. But at bottom, I think, he had an uneasy suspicion—based on what he had seen in Rossiter's wallet—that this might be some insane English method of police procedure with sound reason behind it. Such are our beliefs, nowdays. We are so enlightened and progressive that we cannot even have any superstitions unless they are scientific ones, so we have created a voodoo called Modern Psychology, and tremble before its divining-rods. This is, in short, the Self-Conscious Age, wherein mumbo-jumbo has acquired a dignity never possible to the earlier witchcraft. And I could see superstitious doubt in Sargent's face despite his anger. So I said:

"All right. Let's try it. I suppose this is a psychological test?"

"Lord, no!" said Rossiter. "All I know about those things is that they always come out the way the examiner wants them to, no matter how you answer the questions. Rather a one-sided business, don't you think? They cure you of diseases you never had, and then send you away thinking you still have 'em. . . . No, no! This isn't a test. It's a clue."

Sargent blurted: "O.K. Shoot. I'll draw you some pictures. Was there anything in particular?"

"I knew you'd see the importance of it," said Rossiter, beaming on him. "Excellent. The only specification is that you do it rapidly—just rough sketches, very hasty. Draw me a house, and a man, and a woman, and a dog, or anything else that occurs to you."

Picking up his pencil, Sargent went to work with a sour expression, and I applied myself solemnly to the task. I drew a very drunken-looking house, with smoke coming out of the chimney, then a man whose face got all out of proportion, a woman with luxuriant hair like the excelsior out of a packing-case, and a saw-horse dog. Tinges of lunacy, I felt, were creeping into my own brain. Rossiter stood over us like a benevolent schoolmaster. When I was just adding large rabbit's ears to the dog, I became aware of sounds in the hall. Dr. Reed came bustling in at the door, followed by Jinny.

"I just dropped in," sniffed the coroner, "to tell you— what the devil are you people doing?"

"Sh-h-h!" Rossiter admonished. "They're drawing pictures."

Sargent's face had turned noticeably pink, and he was making strange noises. Reed stuck out his neck.

"They're—what?"

"Drawing pictures," said Rossiter cheerfully. "They mustn't be disturbed."

"Well, well," said the coroner. "Have a good time, Joe. Shall I get you some nice blocks? Or a nice popgun, maybe? —What the hell is this: a playroom?"

"It's a clue," explained Rossiter. "Good of you to come in and help, sir. Here's another sheet of paper. *You* draw a dog."

"I will not draw a dog!" howled Reed, striking the pencil away. "I don't want to draw a dog! Young man, who in—"

"Oh, all right," said Rossiter, "if you must get shirty about it, *don't* draw a dog, then. You're only obstructing justice, you know." He took the papers from our hands and examined them. "Good. This is exactly what I want. Talent, you know. Sheer genius."

"Obstructing . . ." Reed began with a kind of violent and terrifying calm. Then he whirled on Jinny. "Virginia Quayle, will you be good enough to tell me who that young fool is?"

Jinny was half angry and half tearful. Her green eyes darted at Rossiter, who had begun to look uncomfortable, as though he had been caught stealing jam. "Pat Rossiter," she said jerkily, "I should have enough consideration for all of us, at a time like this! . . . Please don't mind him, doctor. Please! He's a friend of mine, and I've just been to all the trouble of calming papa down—!"

"He's a detective," Sargent contrived to say. "For heaven's sake, doc, don't fly off the handle. We're mixed up enough as it is. He's a detective; he'll show you. He's got cards from Scotland Yard and—"

"Oh, my hat," said Rossiter dejectedly. "That tears it."

The next few minutes were chaotic, with Reed exclaiming "Stuff and nonsense!" and Jinny still looking angry, naturally convinced that Rossiter was off on another piece of nonsense. Out of the babel piped the doctor's wheezy voice calling for silence.

"I don't care *who* he is," snapped Reed, "or why he's here, or anything about it. If you people want to sit around drawing dogs, go to it. I've got more important things to do. Now, then . . ."

He leered about him. Rossiter had drawn Jinny into a corner, and was whispering earnestly.

". . . now, then," the doctor went on, "this thing is all over town, and it's a murder case straight out. I don't know whether you feel as certain of yourself as you did before, Joe," he looked malevolent, "but you got what you asked for. There will be an inquest tomorrow afternoon at two o'clock. Have you got all the testimony for me?"

"Yes. I've seen everybody but Mrs. Quayle. Is she in shape to talk?"

"H'm. Well, we'll go in for a few minutes now. And hurry up; I've got to get back to town."

The county detective, despite his recent humiliation, seemed secretly much impressed with Rossiter. He glanced over at the latter in a dubious way.

"I don't suppose," he said, "I—er—do you want to come along, young fellow?"

"Do you mind if I join you later?" asked Rossiter, pushing a handful of hair out of his eyes and blinking at us in a rather blind fashion. "I—er—I've got a lot of explaining to do." He looked at Jinny. "It takes me such a confoundedly long time to explain things, somehow," he added apologetically. "She keeps asking me what I mean. And, after all, it's comparatively simple, don't you think?"

"Oh, yes," I said. "It's all in the mind's eye. All right; we'll see you later."

Reed, Sargent and I went out into the hall. The long afternoon shadows were gathering more heavily; the hall was an ice-house, filled with a mustiness as of old coats. Reed looked at the county detective and growled in his throat.

"I don't know what this is all coming to," he snapped, "when you let crazy people like that young fellow smack into the middle of everything you're doing, and sit around drawing dogs, and . . . hmf. Stuff and nonsense. Drawing dogs, indeed; I'm telling you, Joe Sargent, that—"

A voice, just behind the coroner's ear, suddenly hissed:

"I say!"—

"Gurk!" said Dr. Reed, jumping involuntarily. He whirled a fiery and whiskered face. Rossiter was standing in the door of the library, looking very mysterious. "Oh, it's you, is it? Look here, young man," said the coroner heatedly, "I've had about enough of this! Don't stand there looking like an Italian conspirator!—what's the idea?"

"I say, I'm sorry," said Rossiter, "but I had to know." He addressed himself to me, lowering his voice after a cautious look over his shoulder. "I forgot something. It's very important. There's a question I wanted to ask you, Mr. Marle; after all, you knew him pretty well—"

"Knew who pretty well?" I demanded.

"Tom Quayle. Jinny's brother, you know."

"Yes, I used to know him. What did you want to ask?"

Again Rossiter glanced carefully over his shoulder. Then he bent forward in the gloom, and questioned in a tense whisper:

"Was he very fond of walking?"

Reed slapped his hands together and made weird gestures. But, under the eagerness of Rossiter's gaze, I answered solemnly:

"Why, no. As a matter of fact, he hated it. He would never walk any distance if he could avoid it."

"Ah," said Rossiter, in a tone of profound satisfaction, "that's what I thought."

He slid mysteriously back into the library and closed the door. . . .

Chapter 14

Dreams and Coffins

IN MRS. QUAYLE'S room the shades were half drawn, and the whole room seemed as tired as the dull winter afternoon. There was a stuffy smell of medicine. The wall-paper, with staggering flowers like blue cabbages, was cracked in several places, and there were damp brown stains on the ceiling. It had that air of secrecy belonging always to the rooms of those who live alone; of small trinkets jealously massed, and pins stuck everywhere, and china ornaments strung along the mantelpiece, and tall creaky rocking-chairs where a woman could swing by the hour at useless sewing.

Mrs. Quayle looked very small in the large walnut bed. Her grey wool nightgown was buttoned up around the throat; little corkscrews of greyish hair tumbled stringily about her face, which peered out from the depths of enormous pillows. Faded, the face was, with an uneasy mouth; but it still retained traces of a bright, sparrow-like quality, and the watery eyes followed your every movement. So shrunken were her arms, outspread on the patchwork quilt, that the hands looked big and bony in contrast. Over in one corner of the room, the nurse was making up a camp-bed.

"Come in," she croaked, fumbling for eyeglasses among the covers. It was one of those thin but insistent voices which, in health, would go prattling on, clickety-click, clickety-click, while she smiled rapidly and continuously, in time to the creak of a rocking-chair.

"She's much better now, doctor," Miss Herries told us.

"Here's the chart, if you'd like to look at it. As soon as I've given her the opiate, I'm going to get some sleep."

Reed nodded briskly, and Sargent and I made a show of profound understanding. Mrs. Quayle had unreeled a length of wire from an apparatus like a black campaign button, and fumbled with the rimless glasses until she got them on her nose. Her eyes were vague and frightened. She made an effort to cry out, but her voice rose not much above that same croak.

"Miss Herries! Miss Herries! I don't know these men! What are they doing in my bedroom?"

"Have you told her?" Reed asked the nurse.

"About Dr. Twills only," said Miss Herries, slapping a pillow composedly. "I didn't think it was my business, doctor. But she kept asking for Dr. Twills, and . . ."

"Oh, I know you!" squeaked the woman in the bed. "Dr. Reed! Oh, I'm glad you're here. I'm glad you're here! Did you hear about Walter?" She began to whimper, and her watery eyes were fixed on him piteously. "Walter was my friend. He read the newspaper to me. The serial story in the newspaper. Do you read it, Dr. Reed? Who are these other men? What are they doing in my bedroom?"

She fumbled; the glasses tumbled off her nose, and now she seemed blind and scared. Even though the eyes followed you in that birdlike way, they were very dim.

"Now, now, ma'am, be quiet!" Reed urged querulously. He studied her for a moment. "You knew he was killed, didn't you?"

"Killed? Killed?"

"Murdered. Somebody gave him poison."

Mrs. Quayle gave several quick nods, so that the corkscrew hair whirled. "And I can't see anything" she mumbled. "If they give me something, I just have to drink it. Unless it's right under my nose. And every time I eat or drink something . . ."

"Excuse me, ma'am," put in Sargent. "Now, don't get upset! I'm Dr. Reed's friend. Do you mean you're nearsighted? Do you mean you can't see across the room?"

"I can see *you*," she said defensively, as though he had implied some slight. (We were all standing near the head of the bed.) She blinked up at him and clenched her hands.

"Well, I mean," insisted the county detective, "can you see the door from here? Could you recognize somebody who came in?"

"I'm old! I'm not young like you! You couldn't expect me to——"

"Stung," said Sargent in a low voice. He turned to us, and indicated a marble-topped table over by the door. "That's where Matt Quayle said he left the supper-tray last night. And she was sitting in a chair by the window. I was in hopes she might have been half awake and seen something. . . . Ma'am, do you remember eating your supper last night?"

Again she gave that series of nods, which were now mere slight jogglings. Her mouth looked terrified. Sargent was growing very sympathetic; that remark "You're young" had pleased him immensely.

"Did you see your son Matt bring up the tray?"

"Eh? . . . Why, I—I don't know who brought it up. I didn't know it was here until Mary touched me on the shoulder and told me to eat it."

"Were you asleep, then?"

She was clearly bewildered by all this, and still afraid of Sargent.

"I don't know. I was sitting down. Why do you want to know? Doctor, please tell me—who are these men?"

"Now, ma'am, won't you wait a minute?" urged the county detective. "Did you see anybody before Mary woke you up?"

Mrs. Quayle fumbled at her lip. "No. But one of the girls was here before that. I heard her walking. I called out, but she didn't answer. And then I got scared . . ."

Involuntarily Sargent snapped his fingers. He bent his big grey head forward tensely, and tried to keep his voice steady.

"Now, ma'am! That's what we want to know. How do you know it was one of the girls?"

"Why . . . wasn't it?" she asked, bobbing her head at him as though she were trying to strengthen her watery eyes, bright and blind. "I—I don't know. I thought it was. My ears are good. It wasn't heavy, like Matt or Mr. Quayle. It was light and quick steps." Her forehead wrinkled up, with an intense effort at concentration. "I was sleepy; maybe I was wrong. It was dark in here—sort of grey—I couldn't have seen much anyway. But I heard somebody come in. And I said, 'Who is it?' and there wasn't any answer. And I got frightened. I don't know why. Except that for a long time now, since I can't see very well, I've been awful scared somebody will grab me in the dark, or put poison in something I eat. But I only get that way when I'm alone, or it's dark, and I forget about it afterwards."

She wheezed slightly after her long, rattling speech, and sucked at her lips. Then she smiled apologetically.

"Bosh!" snorted Dr. Reed. "Why should you feel like that?"

"I—I don't know. But that's the way you feel. Really it is!"

"Excuse me, doctor," the nurse put in, in a low voice. "I believe it is her physical condition. Dr. Twills mentioned it. Peripheral neuritis. Morbidity, melancholy . . . I've been trying to argue her out of it, but she won't listen."

"Mrs. Quayle," the county detective insisted, "what did you do when you heard this person walking around in here?"

"Eh?" She had been staring at the bed-post, her mind far away, but now she tried to concentrate again. "Why, nothing. I—I felt so awful bad that I—I just didn't care. Sick. I pulled up the quilt around me, and then it got nice and quiet and drowsy again. . . . I—I used to have nice flower-boxes outside that window. Geraniums.— If they wanted to hurt me, I didn't care. I felt so tired."

She shivered. Her face had grown grey, and her eyes weird with that creepy expression which comes to those on a sick-bed; as though they could see through walls and follow the movements of phantoms.

"I'm going to die," she added, without any emotion, but merely nodding her head as though to confirm it. "I know it. I dreamed the other night that—"

"Rubbish!" said the doctor. "You won't die. You must know by now that somebody tried to poison you, but you didn't die; and somebody tried to poison the judge, and *he* didn't die . . ."

There was a pause, an emptiness of all movements, while Mrs. Quayle's face wrinkled up into slow and grotesque folds. Her eyes became the eyes of an idiot, and she groped along the patchwork quilt as though to understand. Her voice crept out eerily:

"Tried to—poison *him*? You say they tried to . . ." She was growing breathless, beseeching Reed. "Oh. Yes. I—I knew it. I dreamed that, too. I dreamed he was dead, and Tom—my little Tom—was standing by the coffin. But he didn't, did he? He's all *right*?" The voice rose fretfully. "You knew that, nurse. You knew it all the time, didn't you? But you didn't tell me. Nobody ever tells me anything; they just let me sit in here, and rock, and worry my heart out! . . .

"I could see him just as plain," she muttered, in those queer, intent, far-away tones. "And then I dreamed Tom was standing at the foot of my bed and smiling at me. He's all I've got to live for. My little baby . . ."

It had become a yearning, drowsy murmur. She turned her face over in the pillows, and seemed to be watching, through half-closed eyes, the window and the mountains beyond. I became aware that it was very hot in the room; that I was standing almost beside an oil stove, and that the palms of my hands were clammy. The nurse said gently:

"Don't you think, doctor——?"

"Humpf. Oh, all right," growled Reed. "Better pamper her. We'll go out. Give her her medicine, and let her get some sleep."

"There's just one other thing—" said the county detective. "Mrs. Quayle! Mrs. Quayle, listen, please: will you?"

A tremulous glance: blankness and wrinkles as she peered up.

"Mrs. Quayle, this person you heard in here—could it have been a man walking on tip-toe, instead of a woman?"

"Eh? What person? I—I thought you'd gone. Why don't you go? Nurse, make them go, won't you? . . . I wish they'd tell me things. They just come to the door and say, 'Mother, you're looking fine!'—no matter how I feel, and then they hurry away. . . . You've got too many covers on me, nurse; I don't want so many covers." She tossed weakly. "Read me a story, out of one of his books. I wish *I* could. I feel so tired."

We went out softly. There had been little comprehension

in that round, wide-open, unsteady stare, shrinking back among the pillows, and the tremulousness of the jaw. Though it was not yet four in the afternoon, a wing of twilight had begun to brush the panes. The blue cabbages had grown blurred, the ceiling drooping with shadows. At the core of this thick, alcohol-smelling heat, the little oil stove flickered yellow. . . .

We were never again to see Mrs. Quayle alive.

Out in the hall again, we shivered in the cold. Reed opened the face of a big gold watch and then shut it up with a snap.

"Waste of time," he said petulantly, but he kept his voice low. "Now let me see those notes of yours, Joe. I've got to get back to town."

"Better come downstairs. Why don't they put on lights in this place, anyway? You can't . . . *who's that?*"

The whole atmosphere had gotten on Sargent's nerves more than he would admit. His voice rasped as he looked over his shoulder in the gloom, and his face looked damp. But it was only Mary, trying to walk carefully on a creaky floor.

"Jeff!" she called. There was urgency in that whisper, and I stopped. "Jeff, may I see you alone a moment? Please . . ."

I dropped behind as the others tramped downstairs. She waited until they had reached the lower floor, and then put her hand on my arm.

"Jeff, you've got to do something. It's awful. Clarissa's drunk."

"Drunk?"

"Yes. And I'm scared of her. She's still up in Jinny's room, and I'm afraid she'll go out, and papa will see her. Oh, it's awful. There was about half a pint of whisky left in a bottle she had in her bureau, and she got it, and——"

I hesitated. "Well," I said, "maybe it'll do her good if she locks herself in and gets thoroughly under. It may help her forget this thing."

"Oh, no! She's worse! She's talking wildly, and she's hid the key so I can't lock her in, and she's drunk enough so she wants some more. I'm afraid she'll go down in the cellar after some of papa's liquor, and he'll meet her. That would be worse. Why do they leave *everything* in this house to me? Won't you go up and see what you can do?"

There was nothing I could do, of course. But I remembered a certain well-known Latin proverb, and thought that some truth might be stimulated out of the stately Clarissa. So I followed Mary upstairs.

For some reason it is impossible to define, I shall always regard that walk—up the attic staircase, along the matting and creaky boards, in the weird dusk of coloured glass—as the real prelude to the horrors in this house. Nothing was to happen up there, nothing was to happen at all, until the hands of the clock pointed to half-past four. But, instead of a clock ticking, I became at this moment conscious of some beat like the clicking of train-wheels, at a distance, becoming slowly louder and faster, louder and faster, as the clock-hands crawled, before it overtook us. Had I been given then a glimpse beyond the clock, I know that I would have cried out with terror in the shadowy bleakness of the attic. For this glimpse would have shown a carpenter's work-bench, a candle burning upon it, and a *hatchet*.

Now my knocking rattled on the door of Jinny's room. Mary remained outside, her hands clasped together, as I went in.

"Oh, hello! It's you, is it?" Clarissa greeted me, twisting round. "Come in, great detective. Come right in! Ha-ha."

Her négligé somewhat disordered, she was sitting in a wicker chair before the gas grate. Her eyes were smearily bright, and her mouth somewhat loose; but she was even more the Great Lady, and blinked upon me with slightly amused patronage. Sitting very straight, with her arms out stiffly and fingers grasping the ends of the chair-arms, she had the posture of one on a throne.

"It's all a lot of apish nonsense, isn't it?—Have a chair," she invited, indicating one with a queenly gesture. "A lot of apish nonsense. Ho-ho. Sit down, do. I'd offer you to have a drink, only there's just a drop left."

"Feeling better?"

"And I shall stay the way I am, because I do not give a damn," she said, quoting vaguely but with the utmost satisfaction. "Walter's dead, but what of it? I don't feel it at all now. I liked Walter.—Did you know that?"

"Yes, of course."

"I liked him," said Clarissa, nodding and staring very hard at the fire, "but, tck!—he wasn't any dashing Don Juan. I like Don Juans. It's all a lot of apish nonsense. Ha-ha. Isn't it?" She began to laugh; then checked herself and turned loftily. "But they'll do what *I* say around here, from now on. Walter was a wealthy man. He left everything to me. I know he did. Well, there'll be no more complaining and fighting when I want to take a little drink, like a civilized person. I'm civilized. They're not. *I'm* the head of this house now! Ho-ho. It's funny . . ."

From laughter, while she hit the chair-arm decisively, she stiffened, and her eyes were suddenly full of tears.

"But they won't talk that way about Walter. If mother and father had been dead, we could've gone away. But while they're alive—I couldn't. If they were dead I could, but now I can't. I don't know why; sometimes I hate 'em, but I can't. That's what I've thought. Only I wouldn't like to travel with Walter. He makes me ashamed of him. Oh, damn it. I want to go alone."

"Steady!" I said, as the whining voice rose higher and higher, and she began to blubber in my direction.

"That's why I was afraid they'd think *I* did it," she went on. "Because I had the chance. And I've often thought if father and mother and Walter were all dead, I could go away, and say 'Ha-ha' to the rest of them. I'd thought that. And I thought everybody was reading my thoughts . . ."

"Pull yourself together! Do you hear?"

She blinked at me. I had made a mistake in coming up there. Alone, she had let the whisky pad her brain warmly against ugly fears; but now she had begun talking herself into hysteria. At my snappish command, she drew herself up, looked fearful, and tried to recover her poise. I felt a little sick.

A silence, while the gas hissed. She groped beside her

chair, brought up a tumbler half full of whisky and water, and drained it.

"Well," she said finally, with a kind of grim bravado, "I won't be as easy as Walter was, I'll tell you that. *I* know Matt's been faking Walter's accounts; you can't fool me; *I'll* find out. I won't be cheated. And there won't be any more fancy dresses for Jinny—little numbers that cost one and two hundred dollars . . ."

I soothed her down presently. Trying to extract information from her wild and stubborn talk was useless; nevertheless, I thought, she had inadvertently made a few remarks which might prove very valuable.

"What's more," she whirled to say, raising her voice as I was going towards the door, "what's more, I've been thinking a lot since this morning. And I have a pretty good idea who *is* doing all this . . ."

I stopped.

"No, I'm not telling," she snapped. "I wouldn't tell. Not now. All in my good time, maybe. But you just remember I was in the room next to the bathroom when somebody poisoned that bromide-bottle. It was in the afternoon, and I was there, all right!"

"If you know anything, Clarissa——"

Her lower lip folded over, and her face grew ugly with sullenness. Tact and browbeating were both unavailing to make her talk. She would just glance slyly out of her blurred eyes, contemplate her glass, and mutter. I left her laughing a little, huddled before the yellow-blue fire.

Mary was waiting anxiously in the hall outside. In the dull light she looked even more upset; but she agreed that there was nothing to be done, and that the only possible course was to leave Clarissa to her tipsy meditations.

While Mary went to the kitchen once more, I descended to the library. Somebody was lightly touching the keys of the piano in the parlour—Jinny or Rossiter, probably. At least, I hoped that Rossiter was not plaguing Reed and Sargent. He might be a fool or he might be supremely clever, but his effect on the hard-headed people with whom he came in contact was always explosive. Also, his habit of appearing suddenly in impossible places, to greet you with some extraordinary question, was hard on the nerves. It was like being followed by a clumsy-footed ghost.

Voices were upraised as I opened the door to the library. Reed and Sargent were arguing, the former pacing the room with his sharp terrier-friskings, the latter seated glumly in a big chair by the table.

"Shut that door," Reed ordered, thrusting out his neck. There was a momentary silence while he glowered at me through his gold-rimmed glasses. "Now, then. Where have you been?"

"Seeing Mrs. Twills."

"Well?" demanded Reed, knocking his knuckles on the table. "What?"

"She knows something," I said. "Or else she's just drunk, and thinks she does. There are possibilities. She got half a pint of whisky somewhere, and it looked like a good lead; but just when she got to the edge of being talkative, she shut up again."

"H'm," said Reed. He made an effort to chew at his whiskers. "Joe and I have been talking. So far, we've done nothing. We haven't even said anything. But we're all thinking. And it strikes me that it's time to put the cards on the table. . . . Can anybody overhear us now?"

"I don't think so."

Reed put his head on one side and spoke with great intensity.

"All right. You say you've been talking to Clarissa. . . . What do you want to bet *she* isn't the poisoner. Eh?"

Chapter 15

Blood and Whisky

THAT WON'T WORK!" protested Sargent, his voice growing high. "It won't work, I tell you, doc. You haven't got a thing."

"Trouble with you is," Reed snapped at him, "you don't understand her case. I do. I've known her all her life. All they've got to do is show you a pretty face, and simper, and show you what a great big man they think you are, and you . . . Bosh!" He snorted.

"Prejudice aside, doctor, what have you got against her?" I asked, sliding before Sargent's impatient reply.

"'Mf. That's better. Now, Joe, get this romantic stuff out of your head, and listen to me. That woman's a dangerous case. She's got Queen Elizabeth ideas. She goes and sees these damned movies about people on the Riviera, and titles, and suitors who wear dress suits and talk with mush in their mouths; and she thinks she's queen of all of 'em. Well, she had a husband who wasn't like a movie hero, and parents who didn't treat her like a movie heroine; and she got sick of it. . . .

"Wait!" he ordered, waving his hand irritably at Sargent. "You're going to ask me why she didn't just go away? Eh? Well, that's the hellish part of it. I've known these cases before; don't think I haven't. Little fifteen-year-old girls at the coke-works, who want to go to the big city. As long as their parents were alive, they'd rage and storm, but they'd feel duty-bound to stick by 'em—work in a store till they dropped, for five dollars a week, so they could help support their families. And here's the funny part: they'd rather kill their parents than refuse to help support 'em! If they were dead, they'd be off the girl's conscience! They'd be past help. And the girl would kid herself it was the judgment of God, or something like that; and decide she was free now, so she could go ahead. It's the *ties* that count. They don't want to be merely free of their own accord, like running away, for they'd still worry; and they'd still feel the presence of ties. And conscience wouldn't bother them half as much if the parents were dead. . . . Humf. I'm not much good at talking or explaining. Leave that to the lawyers. But I can see it, just as plain as daylight."

"You mean," said Sargent, "you honestly think Mrs. Twills would be capable of doing a thing like that, loving her husband and her parents——"

"Bosh! She doesn't love anybody. It's the best-developed case of its kind I ever saw. I could give you physiological reasons for it, if you could get 'em through your head. But I'm telling you, it's a fact. They've been brought up with family-ties drilled into 'em; they wouldn't think of doubting their duties to their relatives, like more sophisticated people; but all of a sudden they'd go crazy and just wipe them out. And *this* woman stood to get a fortune all her own. . . . What do you think, Mr. Marle?"

I hesitated. It followed so uncannily in the line of what Clarissa herself had been telling me, the small alcoholic slips wherein she admitted her secret wish to have her parents and her husband dead, that I grew uneasy. Its possibility was manifest even in the coroner's disjointed explanation. Amazingly, Clarissa had never in the least doubted the ancient dictum that the family is sacred. To commit the crime of murder might trouble her conscience less than to rebel against her emotional beliefs; and a dead face might trouble her less than a reproachful one in poverty. While she preened herself on the Riviera, there might always rise in her mind some sentimental cinema conception of the Poor-house—ludicrous to others, but powerful to her. Whereas the grave would be final, solid, impossible to remedy.

I looked at the coroner, who had thrust out his neck and was glowering through half-closed eyes.

"It's possible," I said. "But that's only a theory. You'd have to prove it."

"Right. Right. But let me ask you," he returned doggedly, "who had the best opportunity? She had; right next door to her husband, where she could have poisoned the bromide-bottle without anybody knowing. Nobody saw her all yesterday afternoon from half-past five to six o'clock. She was supposed to be lying down in her room, but who saw her? She could have put the arsenic in her mother's tray before she came down to dinner. And her mother heard 'one of the girls' in that room.

"Who was closest to Dr. Twills, and could have pumped him about poisons without his knowing? She was.

"Who knew that Twills was in the habit of taking a bromide every night of his life? She did.

"Who knew that there was a fresh syphon of soda-water in the library, right handy and convenient? She did; she brought it home herself."

"Hold on a minute!" Sargent protested. He had been sitting with his hand shading his eyes; he jerked it away and made a frantic gesture. "Mary knew about that syphon too, don't forget. She took it in to the judge, and was there while he took a drink."

Reed snorted. "Bosh! Utter tommyrot!—Next to Virginia, Mary has the most complete alibi of anybody here. She was in the kitchen with the maid from half-past five to six o'clock. . . . Now, then. Who stood to gain from Twills' death? Clarissa did. Eh?"

The county detective had drawn himself up squarely in the chair, his elbows stuck out and his hands on the chair-arms, in the fashion of one who has put himself on guard. The wrinkles were deep round his pale eyes.

"Don't forget, doc," he retorted, "that she almost drank from that bromide-bottle herself."

"Joe Sargent, sometimes I think you're a child. A moron. Utter, wild, screaming drivel!" squeaked Reed. "The woman's not an utter fool. That's the kind of childish cunning she *would* use. Exactly. She lets somebody see her about to drink a bromide . . . but you'll notice she doesn't drink it. That's movie stuff too. She knew she couldn't kill herself with a bromide; she knew there wasn't any danger from an ordinary dose. But she poured it out, all the same. Eh?"

"Because . . ." I said slowly.

"Because she knew it was poisoned."

Sargent got up slowly, lumbered round behind the table, and picked up the copy of Heine.

"All very good, doc," he said bitterly. "Now suppose you explain what's written in here. What Twills wrote himself. Can you? I'll bet you can't."

"Don't be too sure, Joe Sargent. Hmf. Well, look here. 'Am I sure I know poisoner?' Mind you, he's sitting by his wife's bed while he writes that; he's looking at her, and wondering, and not positive . . . I'll come to that in a minute . . ."

"Not so good, doc."

The coroner's voice rose shrilly. "God damn it, will you shut up a minute and give me a chance? I know what I'm doing. 'What was burned in the fireplace and why?' I'll tell you. It was the doctor's will. If he died intestate, she got everything. *Eh?*"

"That will has something to do with it, I'll admit. But——"

"Look here," I said, "why are you people assuming there *was* a will? We haven't heard of any. But just as soon as we heard of something being burned in the fireplace, everybody jumped to the conclusion that it was a will. That's what always happens in the stories; but what other reason have we got for thinking so?"

Sargent had the appearance of a man growing dizzy. He raised his hands pleadingly, steadied down, and then replied in a quieter tone:

"Well, for one thing, that fireplace over there—in this room—is the only one in the house where anything *can* be burned. I've looked at the others, and they're gas. Whatever was burned, it wasn't anything solid, which would have left traces; I've been all through the ashes from last night. It must have been paper. . . . For another thing, that young fellow Rossiter, crazy as he sounds, had a good suggestion. I mean the brass fasteners there on the table. They're only used for clipping sheets of legal paper together. And he made the suggestion that they might have been used for making the doctor's will, right here in this room . . ."

"Oh, I say!" a voice protested suddenly, in very distressed tones. "It won't do, you know. I never said anything of the kind."

We all jumped. Reed whirled with a somewhat homicidal expression on his face, and glared in the direction of the voice. None of us had heard Rossiter come in. He was perched on the back of a chair like a large-boned goblin, holding his chin in his hands and blinking at us.

"Much as I regret the necessity of breaking in on your conversation," he continued, "I can't let myself be misquoted. Bad for my reputation." He smiled vaguely, and squinted at the table. "I'm almost certain something was burned. And I did mention a will. But I never said anything about Dr. Twills. Really I didn't."

"Well, who else would make a will?" demanded Sargent. "Judge Quayle? He hasn't anything to leave; anything much, that is . . . And there wouldn't be any point in burning *that*."

Rossiter looked thoughtful. "Quite. That's the interesting part of it. But, as a matter of fact, you can use those little brass thingummies to clip other things besides legal documents, you know."

"Well?"

"Chapters," said Rossiter.

There was a pause, while Sargent turned to stare at the desk. Then Rossiter continued, blinking at the chandelier:

"I know I shouldn't intrude, of course, but I really think there are too many of those little brass thingummies spilled all over the table. I mean, if you were merely going to clip one document together, you wouldn't need so many, would you?" He rumpled his hair. "I say, Mr. Marle, you came out here to have a look at the judge's manuscript, didn't you? I wonder where it is?"

Sargent's mouth was slightly open. His eyes grew fixed. He walked swiftly around and pulled open the table drawer.

"It's in a devilish mess, isn't it?" asked Rossiter. "I looked there. Somebody seems to have been through it before us. . . . But there isn't any manuscript. I rather think it's been burned."

Another pause. Reed was breathing hard through his nostrils; the sound was sharp in this shadowy and quiet room.

"Well?" Reed cried. "What's that got to do with the case? Why should anybody burn his manuscript? You mean it hasn't got anything to do with the will?"

"It has quite a lot to do with the will, I'm afraid," said Rossiter. "But I may be wrong. You might ask Judge Quayle."

Sargent pushed the drawer shut. "I'll get him," he said. "Wait here."

When he had gone, Rossiter slid down into the chair. He produced his tobacco and cigarette-papers, and his speculativeness was lost in naïve pride as he constructed another of those weird cigarettes. Behind that fiery beacon he smoked with evident enjoyment, one long leg flung over the arm of the chair. Reed seemed irresolute, plucking at his whiskers.

"Young man," he said with asperity, "I don't get you. I don't understand you at all. And if you're acting the fool . . . Come on, now! Out with it! What have you been up to?"

"Getting information about Judge Quayle's parents," said Rossiter. "And his nurse. Especially his nurse: the one he had when he was a child. Of course, I didn't know he had one until Mrs. Quayle told me; I thought it was probably just his parents, and I fancied she would know . . ."

"You've been disturbing Mrs. Quayle?"

"Oh, I say! I mean, hang it all!—I'm the only one she *will* see. We get on famously. I showed her some new card tricks . . ."

"Card tricks?"

"Card tricks," affirmed Rossiter. "I'm tremendously good at it. Chap in a medicine-show taught me. I used to do them for Mrs. Quayle hours on end." An experimental gleam crept into his eye, and the coroner backed away. "I wish you'd let me try some on you. You mustn't mind if they don't come out right the first three or four times. Mrs. Quayle never did. I have the cards here, if you———?"

"I don't want to see any card tricks! What I was asking you——"

Rossiter looked doubtful. "You're sure, now," he persisted, "you wouldn't like to see the Jack Who Lost His Latch-Key Coming Home From the Pub, and how did he get to the top of the pack? . . . Ah, well. Mrs. Quayle did." He brightened, and added reflectively: "She's the only one who would ever let me perform my Scenes from Shakespeare, too. I rather fancy myself as an actor. You should see my Shylock. And my Hamlet, particularly in the more epileptic scenes with the Ghost. My Lear also has been favourably commented on, though the force of the interpretation is weakened by the frequent necessity for removing my false whiskers in order to get the hair out of my mouth. This sometimes leaves the audience in doubt as to whether I am playing King Lear or Sherlock Holmes. My Othello, with the assistance of a little burnt-cork——"

"I don't want to hear about your Othello, either," said the coroner desperately. "I want to know what you've been up to. Stop it, will you?" he cried, as Rossiter seemed about to launch into another speech. "I won't have you snooping around, do you hear? I suppose you heard everything I said about Mrs. Twills."

"Oh, well," said Rossiter, "if you insist in talking about the dashed case . . . I overheard you." He shook his head sadly. "It's all eyewash, sir. All eyewash. I'm terribly sorry to have to tell you, but that's what it is. Eyewash."

The coroner had jumped forward in belligerent reply when he saw the door opening, and stopped like a terrier caught on the leash. Rossiter got up, spilling fire all over the rug from his lopsided cigarette; he looked very uncomfortable when he saw Judge Quayle.

"Good afternoon, gentlemen," said the judge. "Ah. Good afternoon, Mr. Rossiter. My daughter told me you were here."

He spoke with a sort of grim affability. He spoke, in fact, almost too affably; there was about him a sort of dry and brittle brightness, a jerky movement, and a sense of that small, mad, repressed mirth. I remembered the needle-punctures in his arm, and wondered. But the nap had done him good. He was freshly shaven, his long hair was brushed stiffly, and he wore his best black clothes; with a black bow tie, and an enormously high collar. He was almost as tall as Rossiter. When they shook hands, you could not help noticing the difference between his rigidity, his puckered sharp eyes, and the slouching uneasiness of the big Englishman. Bowing to the rest of us, he went over and sat down behind the table.

"Now then, gentlemen," he continued, clearing his throat dryly. It was the voice of old times, which I had not heard last night: sure, rasping, resonant. He looked from one to the other of us. "Mr. Sargent tells me you have some further questions to ask. I am happy to say that I feel much better. I am entirely at your service."

"That's good, judge," said Sargent. He came in, closed the door, and hesitated. There was a silence . . .

"Well?" said the judge, a trifle impatiently.

"Got any other ideas on this thing, Matt?" asked the coroner. "We thought when your brain was clearer . . ."

"My brain was sufficiently clear this morning, I think."

"What we really wanted to ask you, judge," said Sargent, coming forward, "is this: Did Dr. Twills make a will?"

"He did. I drew it myself."

"Where is the will now?"

"In the possession of my son Matthew, at his office in the safe."

"Do you mind telling us what the provisions of the will were?"

Judge Quayle's eyelids drooped slightly. He turned his head a little sideways, in that familiar movement, to regard us obliquely.

"It is not ethical for me to answer that question, Mr. Sargent. However, since Dr. Twills never made a secret of its contents, and the present circumstances are unusual . . ." He lifted his shoulder a trifle. "Aside from a few small bequests the bulk of the estate was left unreservedly to my daughter Clarissa. He had no surviving relatives, with the exception of two aunts in Florida who were already wealthy in their own right."

"None of the other bequests were large, you say?"

"Certainly not large enough to have inspired murder, Mr. Sargent. In any case, there were no bequests to members of this family."

"Dr. Twills was a wealthy man?"

"I believe so." There was a slight hesitation. "But I am not in a position to state accurately at the present moment. My son Matthew will undoubtedly be able to tell you. He handled the doctor's financial affairs. My son-in-law had inherited his money; it did not interest him in particular."

"Then your son had his power of attorney?"

"Yes." The judge showed no annoyance, but his fingers began to tap on the edge of the table. "As I say, you must apply to Matthew. I have been occupying myself with literary work for so long that I have lost touch . . ."

Sargent drew a deep breath. He came closer.

"Speaking of literary work, judge," he said casually, "I understand you had a book—a manuscript, or something like that—you wanted to show Mr. Marle. Is that right?"

The old contemptuous expression, which had been so manifest that morning when he spoke to Sargent, returned briefly.

"That is true. But I fail to see how it could possibly interest *you*, Mr. Sargent."

The reply was beribboned, but it was none the less a whip. For the first time (and heaven knows why) he had really infuriated the county detective. Sargent waited a moment until he could speak smoothly.

"Well, it does interest me, judge. I read books occasionally. When did you finish it?"

"Is this necessary?"

"Yes," said Sargent. His pale eyes were squeezed up.

"My daughter Mary typed out the final draft of the last chapter two or three days ago," Judge Quayle answered, with ironical amusement. "If you are interested, Mr. Sargent, please let me show it to you."

He leaned over and pulled open the drawer of the table. . . .

A silence. We were all bending forward, and the judge must have felt the tensity. But he did not look up, and we could hear his hands moving among papers with a dry noise like snakes in leaves. It was growing darker in the library. Past the windows, the mountains were dull purple. Lights had winked out at a filling-station. It was so quiet that we heard the whir of a car grow loud on the highway, swish past, and die away in faint droning. . . .

The judge's hands still moved mechanically, shifting papers, long after he had ceased to search. He did not look up. He merely sat there, dark against one window. His head was still bent, so that we could not see his face.

The quiet grew unbearable. Now at last even those hands had stopped rustling among papers. They were limp. Sargent's voice sounded crude in the hush when he said, too loudly:

"It might have got misplaced, judge."

And Reed's bark was even worse. "Stuff and nonsense!" he snapped. "You can write it again!"

Suddenly Judge Quayle got to his feet. His hand made a short but fierce gesture, and then sagged down limply. He remained standing straight against the dying light, a silhouette without a face . . .

Somebody's chair scraped. That gaunt figure moved out from behind the table, slowly, and slowly walked over to the door. It turned there, as though against its will. The eyes moved, and looked out at the mountains, but saw no light. When he spoke, it was a steady, husky voice.

"I am afraid you do not understand, gentlemen," he said. "I am not concerned about the loss of the manuscript."

He turned his back to us, and laid his hand on the knob of the door.

"But they must—*hate me—very much.*"

The door closed. We heard the footfalls of an old man going slowly, steadily, blindly down the hall.

There was a long silence. The echo of those strange, damned words hung in the twilight, shaking the nerves of all of us. They had struck deeply, and they still drew blood. Sargent remained standing by the table, motionless, his grey head slightly bowed.

"Well—" the coroner said at last "Well . . ." He tried to snort, but he did not quite succeed.

The county detective raised his head. "I haven't eaten since morning," he muttered. "I'm hungry as hell. I think I'd better ride in town and get a bite." After a pause he added irrelevantly: "I've got two boys. One of them's at Annapolis. I—Will you drive me in town, doc?"

Rossiter was still sprawled in the chair. He did not move when I accompanied Reed and Sargent out to the door. Reed twisted on his muffler like a man set on hanging himself; he jammed his slouch hat down on his eyes and went hurrying out to race the motor of his car viciously. Following at a slower pace, Sargent assured me that he would return before long; he shook hands vacantly several times, and he looked almost comical in a derby much too small for him. . . .

The coroner's old sedan went grinding and bumping down the drive. I stood on the porch, breathing gratefully the bitter cold air. The grounds were beginning to swim in a dusk like dirty water so that bushes were distorted; but over towards the west, in a dinginess of spiky trees, the light still lingered, and the trees looked gigantic. There was a small filtering of red in the sky, which touched the cavern of the dry swimming-pool, silhouetting the jagged rocks round the edge and the white paint of the basin. Car-lamps moved on the highway. A horn called mournfully; there was a rasp of somebody shifting into second gear.

I paced up and down the porch, my footsteps knocking sharply on the brown boards. A thin sweeping of snow was cut into writhing patterns by a gust of wind, and blown off the porch. Darkness, pressing closer—a sense of terror —why?

I stopped pacing, and whirled round. For a moment I

could have sworn I saw somebody moving on the shadowy lawn, over there where the forlorn cast-iron dog kept watch along the driveway. I peered again, but I could see nothing. It was rather terrifying to imagine eyes watching you from round the corner of the cast-iron dog. Then, too, over at the side of the porch just in front of the porte-cochère, a tiny flickering light seemed to be playing along the ground. It did not come from the sky. . . .

Then I remembered. The cellar, of course, where Judge Quayle had his workship. When he left us, he had probably gone down to be alone, and that light was from the cellar window. Which reminded me—the lights had not worked in the library when I tried them some time ago; Rossiter had probably blown out the fuse. We must have them repaired, or the women would get hysterical. In that senseless way with which the mind will hammer at a small point, I wondered what kind of light Judge Quayle had in the cellar. It fluttered along the ground, against the ugliness of the pale red sky. Preoccupation was bad; I had grown nervous myself. My hands were numb with the cold, and I found myself shivering. I could imagine a thousand monstrous shapes for a figure which *might* be crouching behind that cast-iron dog. The wind seethed faintly.

I went back into the house. The wind had caught the door; it was almost jerked from my grasp, and it banged with a hollow slam which went quivering along the hall, suggesting broken glass. . . .

Fumbling for the light-switch on the off-chance, I pressed it. There was no response. For some reason, I abruptly felt that we needed light; we had to thrust away these shadows. On the wall just by the library door there was an ancient gas-bracket, with a lopsided mantel inside its globe. I felt it carefully. It even seemed to take a great while to find matches in my pocket. The match rasped and spurted up; a fluttering yellow-blue glow trembled out in the hallway, showing the brown staircase, the dull grey carpet, the gilt frames of the paintings . . .

And then I heard the scream.

It did not seem to come from anywhere. It seemed to rise, shrill but muffled, from somewhere behind me; it jabbed into my nerves as suddenly as a gust of wind, and all the hall was full of it. My hand jerked on the gas-fixture, rattling the globe; I whirled, with a horrible falling sensation. . . .

The hall was still empty, dingy and feebly lighted. Nothing stirred. It was as though all the members of the house had been struck dead, and I was alone. I started to run toward the stairs, and then realized I did not know from which direction the scream had come. Its echo remained, drilling the ear-drums. Turning back, I saw with another sensation of shock Rossiter standing in the doorway of the library. His face was white.

"What—" he said, "what was——?"

Somewhere in the house, there were footsteps. Heavy, echoing, and hollow footsteps. They seemed to move, disembodied, in the hall itself; then they grew louder, and I knew that they had come from the cellar. They began to ascend the cellar stairs . . .

Rossiter jumped forward, and then halted with his hand half lifted. Down at the end of the hall, the door to the cellar stairs was being slowly opened. It was so shadowy that we could see only the outline of a figure grow huge there, though we could see the pale glimmer of a face. The footsteps began to creak on the floor of the hall, coming nearer.

His face bloodless and his eyes red, Judge Quayle loomed up gaunt out of the depths of the hall. He seemed to be walking in his sleep. His upper lip was lifted in a ghastly fashion, so that he almost seemed to smile. . . .

"Judge!" I shouted. "Judge Qu——"

Rossiter jerked my arm. The big figure, a shadow following it along the ceiling, came nearer at its stumbling walk—into the uncertain glare of the gas, staring at the light with blind eyes, passing us, speaking no word. I felt Rossiter's fingers grow crushing on my arm, and I looked where he pointed. . . .

Thump, thump, thump—the beating of those slow, hypnotized steps; *thump-thump.* Then I saw his feet had left a trail of small dark smears on the grey rug. Still with that ghastly half-smile, he lifted his hand to wipe it down the front of his coat; and I saw in the eerie light that it was stained with blood.

Chapter 16

The Hatchet

ROSSITER made the first move. I felt the thud of his big shoulder as he bumped past me; then I was stabbed into motion, racing after him down the hall towards the cellar door. Breath hurt my lungs. His big shoes banged on the floor. We were through the door almost together, into a landing smelling of whitewash, and crashing down a wooden staircase, into darkness.

"Which way?" he demanded breathlessly. "Which——?"

"Over there!"

The place was stuffy from the furnace, full of a smell of apples, and dampness, and coal; but far ahead, along ghostly whitewashed lanes, I could see a gleam of light. It flickered, and in that momentary rising I thought I could see blood on the floor. . . .

We were blundering forward on stone; Rossiter stumbled on a basket, kicked it out of the way, and plunged on. The front of the cellar was set down in a depression, and reached by three steps. We came to the edge of the steps and stopped. In the angle of the left-hand wall, at the front, was set a heavy workbench, with shelves along the left-hand wall. Beside these shelves, the wall of the coal-bin stretched out four or five feet, and threw dense shadow. A candle in a tin holder was burning on top of the work bench; it threw gleams on the vise beside it, and illuminated the whitewashed angle of the walls, and the dusty pane of a high cellar window over the shelves. For an instant we stared at the yellow undulation of the candle-flame. Then our eyes were attracted by motion; by the motion of a shining dark fluid which was crawling along the stone floor from the shadow of the coal-bin, with the smudges of footprints leading away towards us.

A damp and crawling moisture was on my skin. I felt

physically incapable of motion; I felt that the whole scene was shredding down in tiny flakes like scales of whitewash, and that some horror was breathing in the very flame of the candle. Nothing looked real. It was not true. A little rivulet of blood shot out at angles from the stream, and seemed to dart towards us. My stomach was a wet rag, being slowly squeezed. Rossiter pushed my arm, but I could not go forward. The heat of the furnace rolled in damp waves . . .

Rossiter's big figure went blundering down three steps; it moved into the shadow of the coal-bin. My legs were unsteady, but I could do nothing but follow him.

"There—there's the handle of something here," he said. His voice boomed in the confined space. "It feels like a hatchet."

He thrust out his face, looking ashy-green, and began to rub his hands together fiercely. "It *is* a hatchet . . . It's been driven—in the back—of her head. It's Twills' wife. It's Clarissa. You'd better come down here."

It was horribly like what you see when you are not used to glasses, and you put on somebody's spectacles and try to look through them. The floor seems to have risen up in a blurred and spectral way; you are wading in the floor, and everything is out of its place. That was the way the scene looked now, in the eyes of horror. I heard Rossiter's words, but I didn't believe them. It was a bit too monstrous. Rossiter's feet crunched on some coal; a small landslide came rattling down, and a lump or two bounced out on the floor. This seemed to disturb the flame of the candle. There were, I noticed, cobwebs in the angle of the wall. Desperately I kept staring at these details, trying to wrench away fear.

Then Rossiter struck a match. After the first shock of the sight, it was easier . . .

Clarissa dead. It thumped at my head like the noise of the judge's footsteps in the empty hall. She lay with her feet towards the coal-pile, spread-eagled in the black négligé, and limp as a sack. Her legs, in black silk stockings, were sprawled; the arms were twisted backwards, palms exposed;

and just beside her lay a smashed bottle. The fluid was not all blood, for there was a heavy odor of whisky. Fortunately, the long black hair covered most of her face as she lay with her cheek against the stone floor. But the blood had not stopped seeping. The hatchet had gone into the brain just above the right ear, and it was still wedged there; its weight had dragged the head over on the right until the tip of its handle rested against the floor. Worst of all was the horribly flaccid and broken appearance of the body; she had simply collapsed like a burst tire, *spilling* to the floor, when the hatchet-edge had cleft her skull. In this shambles of blood and whisky, I discovered that my own shoes were soaked, though I had come no nearer than a few feet.

I heard my own voice speaking—eerie and unnatural.

"She wanted more whisky," I said. "She was drunk, and she wanted more whisky. So she came down here, and——"

"Lock that door," said Rossiter. "Lock the cellar door! Don't let them come down here. Hurry!"

I stumbled back up the three stone steps, blundered along the length of the cellar, and up the wooden stairs. Now somebody up in the house was screaming hysterically, and there was a movement in the hall. In the dim gaslight I saw somebody running towards me; but I did not wait. I snatched the key from the outside of the door, locked it on this side, and then leaned against the wall to wipe cold sweat from my forehead. On elongating and shrinking legs I went back. Rossiter, with the burnt match still in his hand, was standing a little distance from the coal-bin; his gaunt, humped shadow lay across the floor. You could hear a whining of wind, and through cracks in the furnace door the fire winked demoniacally.

I could not think of Clarissa, the tipsy, scared woman I had last seen sitting in front of the gas-fire, fallen with a cloven skull—suddenly pitched out into darkness—dead—knowing the answer to all the riddles now. But there she lay, with her trumpery garters showing, the whisky-bottle broken beside her, and her black hair stiff-matted in blood. It was too sudden. It was . . .

My eyes had strayed to the grimy window above the shelves. Again the spasm gripped my chest. I cried, "Rossiter!—" but it ended in a croak.

There was a face looking in at the window. I could see the white tip of a nose flattened against the pane, and eyes.

"Above you!" I yelled. "The window—look!"

He whirled, straightening up. Still I could hear the screaming upstairs. Rossiter glanced up stupidly; then I had run past him, jumped on top of the workbench, and begun to wrench frantically at the fastenings of the window. The face was gone. I was hampered by the tins of old paint on top of the shelves; my fingers were clumsy, and it was a long reach; so that it seemed minutes before the window jerked out with a hideous long-drawn screech. I swung up to the top of the shelves, knocking paint-cans off with a crash, and wriggled blindly through the cellar window. Cold air gushed in. The candle fluttered and went out.

My hands were raked by gravel as I pulled myself up. Faint vestiges of that weird pink-and-white light streaked the west, the trees stood up dim and spiky, and just ahead of me—streaking off towards the swimming pool—I saw a running figure. From the cellar came muffled bangs and crashes; I had just started to run when Rossiter was beside me.

"Head him off!" I yelled over my shoulder. "To the left! I'll take the right . . ."

My words were choked by the wind-knife. I hurdled a line of bushes and cut towards the front of the lawn. The figure ahead, black against the dying light, was running erratically, zigzagging from one side to the other. I shouted at him, but he did not pause. Then I saw Rossiter sweep round ahead of me. I am counted fast on my feet, but never have I seen a man travel as he did then. He drew in on our quarry; I lost them in the shadow of some chestnut trees, but I could hear the flying thud and crackle of their feet. There was a sobbing gasp, a cry, "No!—" Then a thud, and silence.

"I've got him," called Rossiter from the shadow. "Over here."

Roots were hard and brittle under my feet. I brushed away a dead branch, and saw, very dimly, a figure lying on the ground. Rossiter was standing over it, his hands on his hips. The figure drew gasping, shuddering breaths. It was a terrifying silhouette, with the branches and a faint pinkish light beyond. We were close to the iron fence and the highway; I heard the whir of an automobile growing louder close at hand. The figure on the ground tried to rise. It seemed to be sobbing and mumbling incoherent words. Painfully it pushed itself up on one knee. Then through the iron fence glared the lights of the passing car. The shadow of bars whisked momentarily in the face of the stranger, and I saw that it was Tom Quayle.

Tom Quayle. There could be no doubt about it, though the face was dark in the next instant. I stared, stupefied. Tom Quayle, with sickened fright in his eyes; very pale, and thin, and ill, and with a cut lip where he had fallen . . .

I said his name aloud.

"Who—who's there?" he cried. "Who is it?" Then his voice broke. "Oh, God. Oh, my God . . ." he kept repeating, in a kind of chant, and rocked himself backwards and forwards. "I can't stand it! I can't——"

Rossiter's voice, suppressed but fierce, snapped out of the gloom.

"Is this the chap who ran away?"

"Yes," I said. I could not understand the note in his voice. "Tom! Brace up! It's Jeff Marle, Tom. You remember me, don't you? Steady, now!"

"Help me up," said the other. "Oh, my God. I'm sick. I shouldn't have run. I just got out of the hospital. Who did you say you were?"

He was gasping at a half moan and half shudder, and he staggered as I extended my hand.

"I was afraid to go in," he continued in a whisper. "I didn't know whether they'd want me. I—I'm cold. I haven't any overcoat. It's cold . . ."

"Oh, dash it," Rossiter said uncomfortably. "Here, take it easy. Let's go inside."

Together we supported the small, thin figure across the

lawn. We could hear his teeth chattering. Rossiter took off his own jacket, with a growled curse, and put it over Tom's shoulders.

"I was afraid to go in——" Tom kept repeating, over and over.

When we rang at the front door, footsteps came running. Jinny, very pale and wild-eyed, flung the door open; she began to talk, but stopped when she saw the man between us, and her lips shook.

"There's no time to talk," I said. "Here he is. He's come back. Never mind how. Where are the rest?"

"I'll get back through that cellar window," said Rossiter. "You stay here and try to explain things."

He had gone when I closed the door. Jinny was pulling fiercely at her fingers, as though she were really trying to yank them from the sockets. For a moment she could not talk.

"Father——" she whispered. "Father!——"

"Where is he?"

"Who is it, Jeff? Is it Clarissa?" She paused, squeezing up her eyes and stiffening as another shrill cry came from upstairs, and we heard hurrying footsteps. Mary appeared at the head of the stairs.

"Quiet!" I said. "Quiet, for God's sake! We'll attend to this——"

Mary screamed from the top of the stairs: "He's all over blood! He's hurt! He's all over blood. Oh, Christ . . .!"

"Jinny," I said desperately, "if you ever did anything in your life, if you ever showed any guts, do it now. Do it now, or we'll all go crazy. Go up and quiet her. Can you?"

With an unsteady hand she pushed the bronze hair back from over one eye. Her words were almost incoherent in a mumbling mouth, but she smiled.

"I'll try. I'll try . . ."

"All right. Go up there, then, and after that come in the library."

I turned to Tom, who had been leaning stupidly against the wall, and hustled him into the library. He stood where

I pushed him, just inside the door, and did not move. I stumbled across the room, struck a match, and lighted the three mantles in the chandelier. Tom blinked for a moment; then slowly he sat down in a chair.

His actor's jauntiness was gone. His sullenness and fire were both gone. Sitting there clasping his hands together, his narrow shoulders trembling, he could still not keep his teeth from rattling together. His lips had a bluish tinge. The dark curling hair spilled out from under a greasy cap; he had a wool muffler wound round his throat under the coat of a loud-striped shabby suit. His dark face was as handsome as ever, but pinched with illness, and prematurely old.

"I've got no guts," he said suddenly. Somehow, the word I had used to Jinny in the hall had stuck in his mind. He repeated it, staring blankly across the room. "No guts . . . Here I am again."

He looked round incuriously. Then the shivering took him again.

The keys of the bookcase desk, where the brandy was kept, were still in my pocket. The brandy was harmless, we had discovered that day. I unlocked the cabinet, took out the bottle, and handed it to him. First he regarded it as though he could not believe his eyes, and then drank greedily. He put it down, drew a deep breath, and drank again.

"Go easy," I said. "When did you eat last?"

"Yesterday afternoon." His voice was husky. He shook to a last spasm before the warmth of the brandy eased him; he relaxed. "That—was—good. I feel—much better. It's been pretty bad. I—I didn't say hello to you, Jeff. Didn't recognize you, at first. What—what's happened?"

"What were you doing looking in that window?"

His laboured breathing was loud. "Listen! Listen. Tell me something, now. Am I light-headed?—I mean, did I just think I saw something—down there? I couldn't tell. Oh, my God, I may be losing my mind! . . . I think I must be . . ." He reached out trembling fingers, begging; then suddenly he covered his eyes with his hands.

"What did you think you saw?"

He took away his hands. The eyes were wide-open and glassy.

"Yes. I just imagined it. Low vitality. You see things. Your head buzzes. I lied to the doctor in the hospital. I lied to everybody; I said I was rich . . . When I looked in there, I thought I saw somebody—Clarissa; my sister Clarissa—hit with—something. I saw *blood*."

"Did you see who hit her?"

"No. I didn't see anybody. That's why I know I must have imagined—" Again he jammed his hands over his eyes. "And yet I even heard them talking. I saw things as plainly as . . . Listen. I've got to tell it. I only got here this afternoon. I walked all the way from Cleveland. I was afraid to go to the front door, so I just walked around the house, and it was cold . . . it was so cold, and I was so cold, that I decided to risk it. But the house was all dark, except a light in the cellar window. I looked down in there as I went past . . ."

"Well?"

"Listen. There was a candle on that workbench. I saw Clarissa come over from the other side of the cellar. She had a look on her face as though she'd heard something in the corner where I was; yes, and she had a bottle under her arm. She said, 'Who's there?' I swear to God I heard her say, 'Who's there?' and look in the direction of the coal-bin. She seemed—kind of scared, and wobbly, as though she—well, as though she was drunk."

He swallowed hard, lifting his thin shoulders. "I just looked. It was all so queer. She went over and looked in the coal-bin . . . I mean, behind the board partition. I couldn't see what was on the other side of the partition. Then I lost sight of Clarissa for a second. But I heard Clarissa say something, as true as I'm telling you . . .

"She said, 'Oh, my God, *you*?' "

Tom threw out his arms. "Then there was a sort of scuffling, and something fell out and went *plunk* on the floor. It was something made out of tin: a can of some kind . . ."

(The can of rat-poison, knocked from the murderer's hand behind the screen of that partition, where Clarissa was looking upon the face of the poisoner at last.)

"I heard it hit and wabble and roll around on the floor," Tom rushed on. "And then there was some more scuffling. Clarissa was saying something I couldn't hear. Then I saw Clarissa for a second. She'd started to run out from behind the partition . . .

"I *heard* the hatchet hit," he said wildly. "I'll swear I heard it. A kind of a crushing noise. It was a hatchet. I saw it. And a couple of drops of blood spurted so far that they sizzled in the candle-flame. I know it. Maybe I'm seeing things. But I never saw anything so horrible, so awful and *real* as that was . . . I even saw somebody dragging her back when she was on the floor. I didn't see anybody, but I saw her body being pulled back. That finished me—seeing that thing with the hatchet in its head moving backwards along the floor. . . ."

"Did you scream?" I demanded.

"No. I—I was too scared. I stumbled, and started to run away. But I couldn't get any farther than a tree, and I just lay there shaking. Lay on the ground. Still nothing seemed to have happened. I saw people come out on the porch, and two men get in a car and drive away. Then I saw somebody walking up and down on the porch, and I hid behind the iron dog . . ."

He shuddered. "I got to thinking I was crazy. Lightheaded. I thought maybe I might die right out there on the lawn, and it would serve them all right when they found me next morning . . ."

A fit of coughing struck him. The brandy had gone to his head, and there were tears of self-pity in his eyes. He looked even younger, more childish and petulant than in the old days, and his quavery voice had taken on a self-righteous whine. "I thought I'd just imagined it. I knew I had. So at last I thought I'd go back and look in again, and if I didn't see anything then I must have been seeing things the first time . . . You chased me when I looked in . . ."

He shook his head despondently. "Everything's all wrong. Everything's crazy . . ."

The door opened. Tom jerked round nervously as Jinny entered. She looked him over from head to foot; she took in the frayed clothes, the hangdog air, the pleading and uneasy expression; and then she came over to put her arm around him.

"You look bad, old boy!" she said, murmuring into his ear. "No, don't get up! Dear old—I can't welcome you much, Tom. It's too awful here. But everything's all right for you, now." Her smile brimmed into tears as she looked at me across his shoulder. "We've got him back now, Jeff. We'll keep him. It's all right, Tom. . . . Now tell me." Her arm tightening around him, she looked at me steadily. *"What's happened?* I've got to know. How did you find Tom? What's down there? Don't be afraid. I can stand it."

"Clarissa is dead," I said slowly. "There is no doubt that it is murder again."

Tom half jumped up, disengaging her arm. "Clarissa—" he mumbled, "Clarissa . . . Then I'm *not*—I'm not crazy! I'm not! . . . Who—oh, I can't stand this! What are you talking about? What do you mean, 'again'?"

Slowly Jinny moved off the arm of his chair. While Tom ranted out gibberish, and appealed to her for sympathy, and groped after the bottle beside her chair, she remained standing motionless. Her green eyes were filmed and enormous.

"But why?" she demanded abruptly. "Why . . . kill Clarissa?"

I did not answer that question. I only said:

"It's difficult to face, Jinny. There may be any number of reasons."

"Well? For instance——?"

Still I hesitated. The obvious conclusion was there, from Tom's story; and yet there might have been a deeper cause. And, in either case, every indication seemed to point inexorably to one person. . . .

"It might have been," I said, "because the murderer was recognized by Clarissa. She said she had an idea who it was, anyhow. And also . . . the murder of both Clarissa and Walter Twills may have been part of a prearranged plan. Twills had the money, and died. Clarissa would have had the money, to do with as she wished . . ."

"You're still holding back something, Jeff."

"I'm not holding anything back. I hate to say it. But you saw who came upstairs from the cellar with blood on his hands, didn't you?"

There was a foolish, raucous noise of Tom sucking at the bottle, which made my words seem all the worse by contrast. Jinny fell back a step.

"You don't mean," she whispered, "that father——?"

"I tell you, I hate to think it. And I don't really believe it, either. But Sargent is suspicious already. With this . . ." I shrugged. "Where is your father now?"

"Upstairs. I had gone to see Clarissa, and she was gone. I saw the bottle she'd been drinking from, and I was afraid she'd started out after more liquor. I sat there and tried to read, but I couldn't. Then I heard somebody cry out. For a while I was too frightened to go out. But when I came downstairs from the third floor, I saw father . . . washing his hands. And the water in the bowl was . . ."

"Steady!" I commanded, as her voice grew more hysterical. "You'd better take Tom out in the kitchen and get him something to eat. He hasn't had any food since yesterday."

Tom was sunk into a half stupor. He had tried to understand what we were talking about; but cold and hunger and weakness, combined with the last terrible sight he had beheld, were too much. She roused him, and led him out unresisting. He was mumbling something under his breath. Once more somebody had almost seen the murderer, and still the murderer's face remained a blank. . . .

Bewilderedly, almost insanely, I hammered my knuckles against my head. It was narrowing down, but to what? There now showed a ghastly bestiality in the murderer's makeup, worse by far than the sly cowardice of the poisoner. Something much more savage, and grim, and relentless than anything we had imagined, to have wielded a hatchet in that fashion. In this house there was literally an evil spirit. It prowled and prowled; and then suddenly the poison-tin rolled on the floor, and the sharp hatchet swung. I remembered that giggling laughter which the nurse had heard in Twills' room last night, and my brain cried out in despair. Tear off these cardboard masks! Drag the devil out from behind its kindly face; but how to find the devil?

Where had the members of the household been when the killer struck? Judge Quayle . . . it was inconceivable. We had to start all over again. I walked back and forth under the dim gas-lights. It was entirely dark outside now, and I had a premonition that even worse things were coming this night. So entangled in my brain was the vision of the murderer with the thought of a beast, that I thought: He's tasted real blood now. He will want more butchery.

I jumped involuntarily when the door opened, and Rossiter entered.

Chapter 17

The Hand

I've locked the cellar again," Rossiter said, closing the library door after him. He looked unsteady, and his hair was rumpled wildly. "Where is the other chap—Tom?"

"Getting something to eat. He'll be back shortly. What did you find out?"

I offered him my cigarette-case, because his hands were not quite calm enough to roll a cigarette of his own. Lines were drawn slantwise under his eyes, and I saw that his hands were new-washed and shining.

"Not much more," he answered jerkily, and drew smoke into his lungs with relief. "There were some crates split up for kindling-wood just behind that partition. The hatchet must have been lying against them. The murderer must have been hiding there, and picked up the hatchet on the spur of the moment . . . What did Tom Quayle say?"

I narrated the conversation. His eyes had become blank again, and his long figure was sprawled in a chair.

"The wine-bins," he said, "are over on the opposite side of the cellar. I say," hesitantly, "about that candle: Was Clarissa carrying it?"

"No. Tom mentioned that it was burning on the work-bench when he first saw Clarissa."

"I found the tin of arsenic," he said. "Buried in the coal-pile. There wasn't much of an effort made to hide it . . ."

"You think it had been there all the time?"

"No. Anybody shovelling coal this morning couldn't have failed to see it if it had been there before. No. I—I rather suspect it had been somewhere else, and the murderer just shoved it into the coal after Clarissa had been killed. . . . But there wasn't any hyoscin bottle. I'm very much afraid the murderer isn't through."

Though I had been expecting this, the words struck me with a chill none the less.

"And why isn't he through?" demanded Rossiter, sitting up straight. "That's the hellish part of it. It's inescapable. It's so obvious—and so ghastly—I say, I'm tempted to wash my hands of the whole business. I'm tempted to take Jinny and get out of here . . ."

"Why?"

"Because if I stay," Rossiter said in a queer voice, "I shall have to tell them the truth."

I stared at him. The expression of the intoxicated crystal-gazer had come back; he seemed even more blundering and foolish, knocking fire from his cigarette all over the chair; but there was something in his hushed nervousness which made my throat dry and tight.

"You—you think you know?"

"I'm afraid so. Good Lord, why doesn't somebody else see it?" he cried and slapped the arm of the chair. "Why don't you see it? Why doesn't Sargent see it, or anybody except me? It's so dashed, infernally obvious! Why must *I* be the one? I can't do it. I'll be damned if I do it. And yet, sooner or later, I've got to."

"It looks bad," I said, "for Judge Quayle."

"Yes," he replied. "Yes. Very bad."

"And if Sargent can prove he did all this; Sargent suspects him anyway, I think . . ."

Rossiter jumped as though he had been stung. He glared at me with an idiotic expression, "Judge Quayle?—Who said anything about *him* being guilty?"

"Didn't you?"

"Oh, I say!" he cried, with a distressed gesture. "I never said anything of the kind. Hang it, why has everybody got to get me wrong? I never in the world thought the old boy did it. Whatever makes you think so?"

I mopped my forehead. "Why, look here . . . I thought you——"

"You mean," Rossiter interrupted, struck by a new angle, "you mean you think he deliberately poisoned himself, to avert suspicion?"

"I'm not telling you *I* think it," I said sharply. "It's what Sargent probably has in his mind . . . Well, then! Suppose the whole plot, from the beginning, was directed at Twills and Clarissa? The poisoning of Mrs. Quayle, and then poisoning of himself, constituted a blind entirely. He gave Mrs. Quayle arsenic, knowing that Twills would detect it and prevent her death. He took hyoscin himself, when he knew Twills would be at hand, instantly suspect hyoscin, and save him. Remember this: he only *sipped*, very sparingly, that drink he poured for himself—and carefully left almost all of it untouched on the mantelpiece. Had he swallowed a heavy dose, he would have died . . ."

"Wait a minute!" begged Rossiter, waving his hand. "How did he poison Mrs. Quayle's milk-toast? He didn't have access to it at any time!"

"Have you forgotten," I said, "that when Matt was carrying the tray upstairs, Judge Quayle was coming down? He stopped Matt; he lifted the cover of the tray and put his hand inside . . ."

"I see," Rossiter nodded. His forehead was wrinkled. "Go on."

Even as I was speaking, every small point began to dovetail in my brain with damning significance. So long as I had refused to admit the possibility that the judge might be guilty, I could resolutely close my mind to these details. But, now that the words were said, they gathered up everything . . .

"If," I went on, feeling that I was somehow carried along in an irresistible stream, "if we conceded that Twills *suspected this plot*, everything that Twills said and wrote grows clearer. To begin with, did you know that the judge has been using morphine?"

Rossiter put his hand over his eyes. "I don't know how you knew that," he said dully. "Jinny told me she suspected it."

"It brings dreams, and fancies, and a distorted outlook. It is a derivative of opium. Suppose the judge imagined that somebody was trying to scare him to death with a white marble hand? In the light of this morphine-knowledge, we can doubt whether there ever *was* such a thing as a white marble hand! Dreams! A hallucination so strong that, though he would discuss who might have poisoned him, he refused to discuss the white marble hand at all. He crumpled up at the mention of it, and I myself saw him reduced to a maudlin state of terror over a knock at the door. . . . Who else has ever seen it in this house? Nobody. Mary halfway fancied she did, but what she saw could just as easily have been a piece of wrapping paper blown by a wind in the pantry.

"He conceives that the whole house is leagued against him. He told us as much, straight out. In addition, he has lost his money, and he broods over that. If he can get back his money, he can regain his old power over his family—he can whip them into submission, as he wants to do. Finally, as the last straw, he thinks they have burned his manuscript. Maybe somebody did! Or maybe he burned it himself, for he seems not to have been overly interested. Or maybe the whole thing is another drug hallucination . . ."

Rossiter stirred uneasily.

"I say," he muttered, "you're piling up a lot of mixed motives. So you think he conceived a plot to kill Twills and Clarissa, and Twills knew this all the time?"

"Remember what Twills kept saying at the very beginning. The first thing I heard him say was, 'God forgive me, I think I'm responsible.' And then there was that conversation he had with the judge, outside the library door, which I didn't hear. Twills refused to talk in anybody's presence. Well, did he say, 'I know you gave her arsenic, judge'?—and was that why the judge came stamping back wild-eyed just before the poison got him?"

"Go on."

"Twills must have known about the morphine and its result. Remember, he of all people wasn't alarmed about the danger to other people. 'If they try to poison anybody, it will be me,' he told Clarissa. And he told me that he *expected somebody to call on* him that night. He sat up to wait for it—but the poison got him first, in a way he hadn't anticipated. He sat up to protect himself and Clarissa; but somebody did call on him, after all.

"As to the plot, Twills may have suspected this, or he may have suspected that the judge, in a kind of insane drug-induced revenge, wanted to kill everybody in the house. Either interpretation is possible . . . but, in either, Twills knew he would be the first victim. Because he had told the judge all about the properties and effects of hyoscin; he had even shown him the bottle and where it was kept—when there was nobody else in the room at the time."

"I think I see what conclusion you're leading up to," said Rossiter. "That last point is a bit difficult to answer. Anything else?"

"Only a mental one. You know the judge's personality . . . his stiffness, his conception of family duties, his whole outlook . . ."

"Well?"

"The breaking-down of that personality by his family may have been what soured and tortured him, and drove him to striking out with murder. It may have been the root of everything: a tradition handed down to him by his fathers. And that is the crucial point, after all."

"Why?"

I took up the copy of Heine's poems from the table. "Remember," I said, "everything we've gone over just now. It answers each of the questions Twills wrote down.

> Am I sure I know poisoner?
> What was burned in the fireplace, and why? (O.K.)
> Could personality have made such impression? Medically possible? Psychologically? (Yes. See Lambert, Grafstein)
> Was it hope of money, or growing canker?
> What about $C_{17} N_{19} NO_3 + H_2O$? Influence?

I put the book down slowly. "And question number three, the root of the motive," I said, "is the only one answered with a 'yes'—by the authority of two famous psychologists."

There was a long silence. Rossiter ruffled up his hair again. "You don't believe all that, do you?" he asked.

"I didn't say I believed it. I said Sargent probably did. Yes, and Reed. Reed's an old friend of the judge . . ." I hesitated, thinking back over the morning. "Reed probably noticed the hypodermic marks on the judge's arm when he went in to see him first. I think he jumped to the conclusion that the judge might have gone crazy with drugs and done all this. He was certainly trying to shield the judge, and he worked like the devil to make everybody think Twills' death was suicide. That was what made Sargent suspicious in the first place."

We heard somebody descending the stairs, and we both fell silent. There was the shrill, protesting murmur of a woman's voice; then Judge Quayle's gruff tones. Rossiter got up, flung his cigarette at the fireplace, and stamped over to the window. He was staring out blankly when the judge entered. . . .

Old and hollow Judge Quayle looked now, his weak eyes blinking at the gas. He shook off Mary's hand, and said:

"I'm all right. I'm fine. Let go, do you hear!—Gentlemen . . ." he peered at us, shading his eyes with his hand, "gentlemen. I fear I was indisposed a while ago. Allow me to sit down."

He groped over after a chair. His long face had a decayed look, and his head bobbed nervously.

"The nerves will stand just so much, gentlemen. It is not given to many people to see what I saw—"

"Don't talk about it, papa!" cried Mary. She looked at me venomously.

"I bent over," said the judge, in a far-away voice. Stretching out his hand, his eyes fixed, he touched the air in a hesitant way. "I bent over . . . I—I presume, gentlemen, you have been to the cellar?"

The red-rimmed eyes wandered up to mine. I nodded.

"We have, sir. There—there isn't much to say, is there?"

"The strange part is," he went on, "that I cannot for the life of me remember how I got there. I recall leaving this room; I wandered into the dining-room, where it was full of shadows, and sat down. The next thing I recall"—his hand was pressed hard to his forehead—"I had started down the cellar stairs. I felt that if I could work with my hands . . ." Staring at his hands now, opening and closing them spasmodically, ". . . I could feel better. A saw, or a plane, or a ha——"

Mary gripped his shoulder as he half rose.

"No matter," he muttered, sitting back. "I went forward. I pressed the light-switch—but the lights refused to work. I did not even think that was curious, gentlemen; I simply took it for granted. There was some sort of light ahead of me. A candle. Then I stumbled on something on the floor, and put my hands down to feel it . . ."

"Was it you who cried out?" I asked hurriedly.

Still bent forward, he was moving his hands about grotesquely only a few inches above the floor, as though he were bathing them in a pool. Blood had begun to fill the big veins in his forehead. He peered up at the question.

"Eh? I don't know. I may have."

My old theories were being swamped out like sand-castles. He never once thought that he ought to be suspected. He never once protested his innocence, as a man with blood on his hands might well have done. It never occurred to him. And I thought . . . might these horrors have come about during blank spots in his brain, so that he had no recollection of them? I saw him tramping down the hollow-sounding stairs, gaunt and shaken in the twilight of the cellar. . . .

"When did you go down there, judge?" I asked. "Just before Mr. Rossiter and I saw you in the hall?"

"It must have been. I—I believe I was there only a moment."

"And you saw nobody while you were in the cellar?"

"I am afraid I don't remember. I have an impression," he wrinkled up his forehead, "that somebody passed me, brushed my elbow, just as I was going down. But I cannot be sure."

I turned to Mary. "You know what's happened, don't you, Mary?" I asked.

She nodded, dumb and miserable. All her terror and spitefulness had collapsed; she was just frozen, with her hand on her father's shoulder.

"Did you hear the scream?"

"Yes. Oh, God, yes!"

"Where were you then?"

"In the pantry, peeling potatoes. That was when I heard it. I couldn't move."

"The pantry door," I said, "communicates with the landing of the cellar stairs, doesn't it? Then you must have heard it more plainly than anybody. Did you go and look?"

"No! I didn't dare. And—and I didn't know it came from the cellar, either. I couldn't tell *where* it came from." She was twisting the folds of a large rubber apron, for housework, and you could hear the small rustling noise of the rubber. "I just sat there. Then I got up, and put the potatoes in the sink, and I was so weak I spilled them . . ."

"Had you been in the pantry long?"

"Twenty minutes, anyhow. Oh, Jeff—"

"And did you hear anybody go down?"

"Y-yes. I heard father, because I know his step. And two other people before him." As I took a step forward, excitedly, she backed away. "But I didn't see them, Jeff. One went down a long time before father, and another just a few minutes before father. They must have been Clarissa and
. . ."

"But you didn't see anybody?"

"No."

"Where was Joanna?"

"She was cleaning the silver, on the storm-porch at the back. But she was in and out of the dining-room a lot. She may have seen somebody."

I looked around at Rossiter. With his blank and foolish expression he was examining the table; that mask was up again, and I knew I should get no help from him. He spoke, sanely, when he desired to. Now he merely seemed to apologize for being there.

"Mary," I said, "will you please ask Joanna to step in here?"

"But—father—!"

"He'll be all right. Please!"

There was a difficult task ahead of me now. Judge Quayle was sitting back in his chair; he was impassive, but you could hear the wheezing of the breath through his nostrils. I went over and stood before him.

"I have some news for you, sir," I said. "Will you listen for a minute?"

A faint questioning crept into his narrow eyes, but his expression remained incurious. "I am in full possession of my faculties, Mr. Marle," he replied, trying to rasp out the words. They seemed to hurt him.

"Your son Tom is here, sir. Steady, now!"

His hands had gripped the chair-arms. But for what seemed like minutes he did not move or speak. . . .

"You—you don't mind, then?" I said.

Slowly his eyes moved from the other wall to me; they held a ruin.

"No," he said. "No. I do not mind. I confess I am somewhat glad."

His eyes closed. It had been a mere whisper, hardly louder than the wheezing of his breath. But the iron stiffness seemed suddenly to have gone out of his joints, and the wrinkles smoothed down, and he had the appearance of one who, after a night of horrors and smarting eyes, drifts into cool rest. Still with his eyes closed, he spoke:

"I trust my son is well?"

"He has been in the hospital, sir. But he is better now."

"Ah!" His fingers tightened a little. "Yes. He wrote us. I was glad to send him what money he needed. I could easily spare it."

(A little, pathetic, defiant lie, Judge Quayle. Twills sent the money, because you had none; and you pretended to disapprove, because you would not admit you were penniless. And now your fingers tap softly on the arms of the chair. And I can suddenly see why you cried out in anguish, when, last night, *I* rapped on the library door as Tom used to rap. Ever since he had left—secretly—you were thinking that it was you who had driven him away; and since that letter you were thinking of him ill and broken, in a strange place, and he thought you hated him. And you could not bear that, Judge Quayle.)

"He will soon be back on his feet, sir," I said. "I think he intends to remain."

The old man nodded, as though in slumber. Nothing more was said until the door opened to admit Joanna and Jinny; then the judge started, opened his eyes, and glanced round. He was still impassive. Yet he had wanted to see Tom. Jinny's glance, flashing at me, asked, "Did you tell him?" and I nodded. Joanna, her face waxen and pale, huddled back against the door.

"I want to talk to you, Joanna," I said sternly, trying to imitate Sargent's manner. "Do you hear?"

"Ya. What I do? I not do nothing?"

"Miss Quayle says you were cleaning silver on the storm-porch late this afternoon. Is that right?"

She stuck out her lower lip. "Ya! That right. I there all aft'noon. I no leave."

"Did you go out in the front hall at any time?"

"Front?—Oh. Ya. I go once. I think I hear someone at front door, and I look out. But it only two men leaving; that county detective, I know him, and other man, and you in hall. So I go back."

"Did you see anybody near the door to the cellar stairs?"

"Ya! I see somebody stick head out—like this." She illustrated.

I took a step forward, almost stumbling over Judge Quayle's foot. There was a sense of stiffening and tensity in everybody here. My own voice sounded unnaturally loud, almost incoherent in the hush.

"You saw somebody? Who was it?"

"Eh?"

"Who was it! Tell me!"

"Eh . . . Oh! That one," said Joanna, and nodded at Jinny.

Chapter 18

The Murderer

THE FIRST SOUND I can remember after that startling announcement was a kind of Gargantuan snore. It was Rossiter making a scornful noise as gently as he could. He stepped over from the window, looking very distressed.

"I thought I could keep out of it," he said sadly. "But, my hat! This is going a bit too far. I see I've got to explain things, after all." He looked at Jinny, his brow wrinkled. "My dear young idiot, I was congratulating myself that you at least had kept away from suspicion. Did you actually make the silly-ass mistake of going near those stairs?"

Jinny regarded me steadily. Her green eyes were unwinking, and her pale lips pressed together.

"I did," she said in a clear voice. "Jeff, that's the first thing I've omitted telling yet. And it's the first thing I get tripped up on—right away."

"Nobody's accusing you," I said, conscious of a sick feeling. "What did you do, precisely?"

"I didn't go down in the cellar. Believe me or not. I didn't. I told you I'd gone up to Clarissa's room, and so I had. I told you I thought she'd gone down in the cellar after whisky. So I went down the back stairs to see. I got just to the top of the cellar stairs, and I couldn't go any farther. I don't know why—*I couldn't*! I just stood there, frightened. It was all dark down in the cellar, and . . ."

She made a vague gesture.

"That's all there is to it. I looked out in the front hall, and saw Mr. Sargent and Dr. Reed leaving; I just hurried up the rear stairs again, to my room. And I didn't leave it until I told you."

"But why didn't you tell us this in the first place?"

Her lip twisted. A wry, humorous, far-away expression came into her eyes, and she nodded at Rossiter.

"There's the cause. I thought—so far, I haven't got tangled up in any of the dirty circumstances. And things are coming out all right for *us*—Does it sound awful of me to say that now?" she burst out. "Well, I don't care. I'm telling you what I thought, and not trying to varnish it up any. That's what I thought. And I didn't want to get myself implicated, when I'd come through the other part of it all right. And it would be hellish, to have them think I did it, now. Do you understand?"

"I've generally discovered," Rossiter said gloomily, "that it's the innocent people who feel most guilty; they think everybody is watching them. That was a bit idiotic, my dear. . . . You didn't hear anything or see anything, did you? In the cellar, I mean."

"I—I think I heard something," Jinny answered.

"What?"

"A sound like somebody giggling. I sort of halfway heard it, if you understand what I mean; I wasn't sure, but I think that's what terrified me most. Laughing."

She could not control herself now; her body was trembling, and she seemed perilously close to a breaking-point. "That's it," she said hurriedly; "the whole thing's like a joke—a joke—without any sense."

Judge Quayle stiffened in his chair. His eyes were still closed, but he lifted his hand. He looked like an old actor then, an old actor dazzled by footlights; and he spoke as though against his will, in two voices:

" 'Have you heard the argument: Is there no offence in't?' —'No, no, they do but jest, poison in jest; no offence i' the world.' "

Clumping forward in his mildly angry way, Rossiter hit the table a blow with his fist.

"Look here," he said, "this has got to stop. I'm going to stop it, before we're all potty. You're talking of jokes. Well, I'll show you what the real joke was. The real joke was that it started as a joke."

Jinny turned on him fiercely. "If you start any of your foolery now," she cried, "I'll kill you. I swear I'll kill you."

"Go out in the kitchen," Rossiter said to Joanna, "and tell that chap to come in here."

He seemed to tower in the big room. He was as close to wrath as his easy-going nature would permit; he looked suddenly dangerous, and his gesture was such that Joanna scuttled out of the room.

"Maybe you'll say," he told Jinny slowly, "that it takes a fool to expose a fool. Righto! But the person who's responsible for all this is your brother Tom."

Judge Quayle's eyes flashed open. . . .

"I don't say he committed the murders," Rossiter went on, "but I do say he's responsible for the white marble hand."

Mary let out a squeal. Rossiter's brows compressed; he clumped over and seized her by the shoulders, towering huge over her brown upturned face. He tried to shake her very gently, but the result was a clattering of teeth.

"I want *you* to be quiet," he said. "Not a peep. Not a breath. I want all of you quiet. Sit down in that chair, now." His mild glare whirled round the circle. He gave Mary a slight shove, and she toppled backwards.

Then Tom appeared. . . .

Pale, dark-haired, sharp-featured, in loud and shabby clothes. Something of the petted gangster there, something of John Wilkes Booth; arrogant and cringing, François Villon in loud and shabby clothes. His eyes blinked rapidly.

"There's your father," said Rossiter, pointing. "Go and apologize to him for what you did on the night he chucked you out."

"I'm sick," said Tom shrilly. He pushed his hand in front of him as though he were pushing somebody away. "I feel bad! Go away from me. I can talk to my own father without you butting in and . . ."

Rossiter took him by the collar. "There was a snowstorm that night," he said. "A bad snowstorm. Jinny told me so. You wouldn't walk two miles to town in the middle of that, and you didn't; you weren't fond enough of walking to go that far in good weather. But you had to make a good exit, didn't you? I rather think you slept in the carriage-house."

Tom let out a cry as Rossiter picked him up like a ventriloquist's doll. He was lifted across the room and deposited before Judge Quayle's chair.

"Look here, sir," the big Englishman went on, "I don't know why you were so afraid of the hand you broke off that statue, but this son of yours knew you *were* afraid of it. I'm afraid he's got rather an unpleasant disposition, and a vindictive one. And he's fond of ghost stories—or he was. He's a good deal like a child; I know, because I am too. And while he was out there in the carriage-house, weeping over the way you'd handled him, I fancy he got the notion of scaring you once before he left town . . ."

Judge Quayle was sitting bolt upright, a witless look in his eyes. Still squeaking like a ventriloquist's dummy, Tom was being held in the air. Then Rossiter released him. He plopped to the carpet in a sitting position; weird, ludicrous, and foolish.

"You know sir," Rossiter told the judge, smiling confidentially at him, "I'm a wizard, really. I'm an exorcist. Watch me cast out a devil: I just dropped him on the floor. And he looks a bit comical, doesn't he?—There's what's been frightening you for years."

His broad, homely grin expanded.

"He's like most devils, sir. He looks foolish when you pick him up by the collar or the seat of the pants and drop him out in the light. But as long as you kept him inside, and never talked about him, he was bad."

Judge Quayle started to rise, but he seemed to be incapable of motion. He looked at Tom. There was grease on Tom's mouth and his cut lip still bled a little. His eyes had a defiant whine.

"You mean—" said Judge Quayle.

"It's mostly supposition, of course," interposed Rossiter. "But I think he went round the house and tried to get in a window. He climbed up to that one over there"—Rossiter jerked his thumb towards the window through which he himself had made his entrance. "Jinny told me there was moonlight later on, and that you were sleeping on a couch in here. He probably saw you. I tried the effect of my own hand at that window, and it gave Mr. Marle and the county detective rather a turn. In the middle of the night, by moonlight, I expect the effect would be rather better. Particularly if he'd painted a glove white and used it, with maybe an old black stocking to conceal the rest of his arm in the shadow. If there had been a table or anything there, and you were lying down, you would probably have thought it was crawling across the table inside the room . . ."

Rossiter was rambling on in a casual manner, still with a sympathetic smile, as he might have explained to a child what had frightened it in the dark. Nobody else spoke. Rossiter had the stage, and he was enjoying it. He turned to me apologetically, struck with another idea.

"I say, Mr. Marle . . . it just occurred to me. You must have thought I was off my chump when you saw me prowling about in the carriage-house. I rather suspected what had happened, you see, but I wasn't sure just what was behind it. I said I was investigating. And you said, 'What?' I said I didn't know, which was true. But I'd found a bucket that had white paint in it, and an old black stocking, and the carriage-robe he must have used to keep himself warm that night; and I said it all depended on the snowstorm, which was true too; and, of course, Jinny had told me you people used to have a playroom in the carriage-house; and so . . ."

Tom started to get up, but Rossiter jerked him by the collar again and forced him down on the floor. Jinny began to laugh hysterically.

"Then," I said heavily, "there never has been any appearance of the—of the hand except that?"

"What puzzles me," muttered Rossiter, rumpling up his hair again, "is why you, sir," he looked sympathetically at the judge, "ever were afraid of *a* white marble hand to begin with. I knew you were, of course, because this cheerful little actor here on the floor made some remark about it on the night you threw him out. Nobody else seemed to know . . . I'm not certain why you feared it, but I think it would do you good if you told us."

Still the judge could not collect himself. He looked as dazed as though bright lights were in his eyes.

"My son—" he said, with an effort, "my son did that?"

"Let me up!" Tom complained, beginning to writhe on the floor. Rossiter stepped back. "I don't see why you make all this fuss over it!" Tom burst out. "I did it. Sure I did. But what of it? I'd forgotten all about the thing. I thought you were talking about something important . . ."

He looked round, appealing to all of us, and as he saw our impassive faces his pallor became more pronounced. "It *wasn't* anything, was it?" he cried. "For God's sake, don't look at me like that! I haven't done anything. That was years ago, and it was just a joke . . ."

"It's all right," said the judge. "It's all right."

Tom rose at the same time the judge did, though Tom stood humped. The judge remained looking down at him, in a queer and puzzled way.

He stretched out his hand. He patted Tom on the back.
. . .

"Then the other times——" he said.

"I know what obsessions are, for my sins," Rossiter said absently. "I know how they work. I know how they change everything you look at into the image of what you're afraid to see. And you, sir, if you'll pardon my saying so . . ."

Judge Quayle drew himself up.

"I cannot explain," he said dully. "I cannot tell you anything." He clenched his fists, and began to glare about him. "All of you are staring. All of you would be glad if I were dead. But you won't have the satisfaction. Get out! Get out, all of you—!"

As he swung round, his foot kicked the squat brandy-bottle from which Tom had been drinking earlier, and which still lay on the floor at the foot of the chair. It rolled across the rug, spilling its contents; and the judge stood staring at it in a puzzled way, as though he wondered how it came there. . . .

Rossiter seemed suddenly weary. He glanced at Tom, who had cowered back towards Jinny.

"All right," he said. "All right, sir. We'll go. But I warn you—"

"Thank you, young man. I don't think I need your advice," rasped the judge, clenching his hands. "My nerves are quite good, thank you. But if the pack of you won't get out of here! . . ."

His hands were quivering in bunched fists. Mary stepped forward to plead with him, but he shook her off. I could see another of those ugly scenes brewing, as usual in this topsy-turvy house, and I joined Rossiter in urging the two women to make an end of it. Tom had already bolted out of the room.

In the hallway outside I saw him making blind motions, hitting the walls like a bat, as though he were trying to find a way out. His stamina was nearly gone now. He ought to have been in bed, the bluish lines in his face smoothed out by comfort and warmth. But I could see the knifelike looks in the eyes of Jinny and Mary. Tom turned, to regard them in a way which was pitiful and a little contemptible.

"We'll talk to *you*," Jinny said, taking his arm.

Tom said: "You haven't got any right to kick me out of here. I won't go. He said it was all right. He said I could stay. Let go of me."

Mary was blubbering now, in a sheer hysteria of rage, or relief, or weakness, or all three. She leaned up against the wall and hammered her hands there until Rossiter quieted her. But Jinny just smiled tightly at Tom.

"Come into the parlour, little darling," she said. "We won't be disturbed there . . ."

Rossiter had, I think, the only cool head among us all. He shepherded us into the parlour lest the women should make more noise, and lighted the pale frosted gas-globes there. More than ever the place looked like a mortuary. Tom seemed to be staring round for a place to hide; then he burst out sobbing.

We were silent during a grotesque moment, while a shrewd rising wind came swooping against the windows. Then Jinny said:

"You're responsible. You made this place a crazy-house."
She folded her arms. "Now you're going to tell us all about
it."

"Tell you—what?"

"Why you did that. Why father was frightened."

From sobbing, Tom began to laugh hysterically. He turned
out his hands, palms uppermost. He looked ill, and blue, and
silly, under the pale gas-globes. You felt that his hands would
be as cold to touch as the white statues on their pedestals.
He was shivering.

"But," he whispered, "that's the crazy part of it. I could
laugh. There isn't any cause. Father was just born to brood
over something. And he wrecked himself by brooding over
something he did when he was a kid."

"If you don't tell the truth—!"

"I am telling the truth! That's what he was like. Fear inside him; nothing but fear. He could keep it from most
people. But I knew."

"Fear of what?" Jinny demanded.

"Of anything. Oh, my God, I see you don't know what
I'm talking about! He had to have something to worry about,
always. But he never would talk. Everything worried him,
a speech, or a decision, or even a casual word on the street.
He's as neurotic as an old woman, only you never saw it.
That's what's so funny." Tom began to laugh again.

Jinny started after him, her fingers suspiciously like claws;
and then Rossiter caught her, and we were all breathing
hard. But Tom's expression had became vacant.

"He was brought up that way. He could have helped himself if he'd only have talked. But—do you get the crazy
humour of this?—he regarded merely *nervous worries* as
weak, and womanish, and unworthy. So he wouldn't even
mention them. He thought any mental goblin was fit only
for women. And so the goblins ate him."

Mary cried out shrilly: "Tom Quayle, if you don't stop
that simple talk and—"

"It isn't simple talk. It's the truth. It's what his father
taught him . . ."

"Easy," said Rossiter. He spoke gently, but Tom looked

at him in fear. "I rather think it is the truth, you know," the Englishman added. "He's the type. And I know the type pretty well. *I* have an old man, too."

Rossiter looked suddenly despondent. Tom was licking the dry blood on his lip, and breathing hard.

"He broke the hand off that Caligula statue when he was a kid," Tom went on huskily. "And that's all there is to it. It's funny, isn't it? I told you it was. And he had a nurse, a Scotch nurse . . ."

"Yes," Rossiter said, nodding. "Mrs. Quayle told me something about that nurse. . . . Look here." He turned to us, somewhat fiercely. "There's a lot of tosh written and said about people being haunted by crimes, and stricken by conscience, and things like that. I dare say you expected this to turn into something melodramatic, like a man he'd killed, or a murderer he'd condemned who had sworn to get him. Well, it's much more personal, and terrible, than that. I've generally found that a man with meanness or courage enough to commit something choice in the way of crimes isn't bothered much with conscience after it. The things that really drive a man mad are fears of nothing at all . . . little fears that grow, and grow until they transform everything he looks at, and he sees his fear in the smallest shadow. It may be money, or it may be jealousy, or it may be just a phantom."

"And in this case?" asked Jinny. Her wrath seemed to have dried up; she was studying Rossiter in a curious way. "In this case?"

Rossiter stared at the floor.

"He'd just lost all his money. His family was getting out of hand. He had been neurotic all his life, and it was beginning to crush him. I'm not sure of it, but I think something popped into his mind that had been worrying him all his life. He'd laughed at it, but it never does any good to laugh at devils; the contrast makes them seem all the worse. . . . And," Rossiter muttered, "you say he had broken the hand off that statue?"

"You're no fool," Tom said. "You're no fool."

"That nurse," Jinny said, "died before I was born. But

I've heard of her. You mean—a bogey. She was the hell-fire type. 'Thrawn Janet.' I've always thought of Thrawn Janet when somebody mentioned her."

They were speaking slowly, with a kind of ghastly impersonality. Even Mary, despite her bewilderment, was silent. Tom seemed to take courage from the fact that nobody was abusing him. He grew eager, almost vociferous.

"She had him under her thumb until he was ready to go away to school," he said. "I know. I've talked with old Marlowe, who was a kid with dad. Marlowe knew. She'd nursed him. But she scared him with every horror threat she knew. And I knew, because I've seen him when I used to tell ghost stories . . .

"I know where I get my love for that stuff!" Tom said, almost as a screech. "He's not a lawyer. He's an actor. Like me. And that's why I'm his favourite, and he'll take me back any time I want to come back, do you hear?" He glared at us with a kind of weak triumph. "You've been talking about Thrawn Janet. Well, it was a ghost story that first put me on to what was scaring him. It was a story called 'The Beast With Five Fingers.' And one night when I told it he was there. He talked to me afterwards, when I asked him what was wrong. For he'd turned all white and sweaty . . ."

Tom shuddered. Beyond this white room with the pink curtains, I was looking at that portrait of the nurse, hung in the library.

"He was only a kid when he did it," Tom said vacantly. "He had a fit of temper, and smashed that statue's hand with a hatchet. . . ."

"With a hatchet?—"

I found myself blurting out the words. Tom nodded. He drew one frayed sleeve across his nose, and his snuffle was very loud.

"And she told him it would come back some night, and get him."

"But, listen!" Jinny cried desperately. "A thing that occurred when he was a kid—!"

"He didn't think of it much, really, until the devils began piling up," Rossiter said. "But it had always been there, because the nurse saw to that. And then he lost his money. And his family began to disintegrate. And then he began to take morphine . . ."

"As long ago as *that*?" I demanded.

Uncomfortably Rossiter shifted from one foot to the other. "Hang it," he protested, "I don't like to talk about it, but surely you know one thing! When a person begins taking morphine, he doesn't use it hypodermically. He takes it through the mouth, as a sedative. He doesn't begin using the hypodermic until . . ."

"Well?" I asked.

"Well, until it's no longer powerful enough in the other form. Until he's got so habituated to the drug that it has to be used that way to get its effect. . . . Oh, I say!" Rossiter burst out. "This is all guesswork, of course. I'm not trying to insult anybody. All I say is that I think he'd started using the morphine after his money was gone, and the old-time hobgoblins started coming back. Then he had this quarrel with Tom, and that finished him. Look back over his whole behaviour, and see whether this isn't the only explanation that will square with everything."

Wind was growing louder at the panes. Rossiter moved across the chill bright room, his head down.

"I wish I'd never pried into this," he muttered.

After a long silence Jinny said in a queer voice: "Then—that night Tom played the fool was the only night a hand ever . . ."

"Yes. The rest was all his damned imagination and the morphine, seeing a hand everywhere."

"But Mary saw—"

"No, I didn't," Mary said huskily. We whirled on her. . . .

"I just said that," she went on. "I was so sick and half-crazy, and I'd heard about Jeff doing all that police-work, and I was afraid he'd been brought out here to play detective; and I wanted to pump him, and see what he thought of it, without telling him anything more than I had to." She began to beat her hands together. "The minute I saw you that night, Jeff, the very *minute*, I thought papa had sent for you, and I was afraid of scandal . . ."

I remembered her frightened face in the hall, when she had let me in. She made a gesture, appealingly. Jinny was staring from one to the other of us.

"Then," Jinny cried, "these murders have nothing to do with the hand at all?"

"I'm afraid not."

"But what motive . . . ?"

Rossiter turned. His face was rather pale. "I've got to tell you," he answered. "The motive was money."

A suspicion, a ghastly idea, stirred at the back of my brain; first it was only formless, and then it began to take shape like a face peering through curtains. Jinny had retreated, her hand jerking at her forehead. Then, from an immense silence, she spoke.

"Where—is—Matt?"

Mary let out a cry. Rossiter had taken a heavy step forward, causing the light-globes to tinkle. They seemed to cast a devilish, unholy brightness, to bring out wrinkles, and guilt. The piano was a huge, shining, ominous hulk, like a coffin for this white mortuary room.

Then I realized that a voice was crying out in the house.

. . .

It was calling, low but insistent, with a horrible illusion of seeming to come nearer and nearer, like a figure along twilight paths.

Springing past me, Rossiter flung open the door of the parlour. We could hear the voice plainly now. In the dim glow of the wall-bracket in the hall, we saw the white-uniformed nurse at the head of the stairs.

"Will some one please come up here?" She tried to keep her voice low, but there was too much horror in it. I saw her white hand on the banister-rail, horribly like the white marble spectre. . . .

"Will some one please come up here? Mrs. Quayle's gone into the bathroom, and I can't rouse her out. We may have to break open the door."

The white fingers twitched. The nurse had had her fill of murder also. For a moment Rossiter stood motionless, staring up, his grotesque shadow reared up across the wall. With his wild hair and great shoulders, he looked like a Norseman. His voice fell, vacant and hollow, into the brown gaslit coffin of the hall:

"The murderer's loose . . ."

A crash, and a cry. I whirled, stark mad by this time; for the crash had come from the library. Rossiter swung about and plunged towards the library as though he meant to carry the door off its hinges. I was just behind him when he threw it open.

Only one low burner was aflame with pale yellow-white. Judge Quayle, with blood on his face, stood behind the table. He looked at us once, uncomprehendingly; then his eyes were obscured in a gush of blood. He half twitched, and pointed into the shadows just before he fell.

He was pointing at Caligula's statue. There was something rustling and crouching behind Caligula's statue now; something hiding there. . . .

With a steady step Rossiter walked over towards it. My feet crunched in pieces of a broken bottle, the brandy-bottle, which had been used as a weapon, and which now lay thick with dark splatterings on the floor. The murderer was there now. The murderer was behind Caligula's statue.

Then Rossiter leaned over and shot his hand into the dark pocket of shadow behind. . . .

"You had better come out, Mrs. Quayle," he said. "Your work is finished."

Epilogue

The Clock Ends Its Striking

EIGHT, sounded the clock. The echoes fell away, settling softly into the quiet Vienna streets. Through my mind, almost in an instant, had twisted the evil images which were contained in the pages I had already written, and which now lay under Rossiter's hand. Still the air quivered, as of something lost and damned, when the clock ceased striking.

". . . for instance," said Rossiter, drawing deeply on his cigarette, "when you spoke of Judge Quayle, and the possibility that he might have poisoned himself to divert suspicion, you should have realized that the probability was just the other way round. Hyoscin's effects are almost instantaneous. Nobody would swallow hyoscin and trust to luck that somebody would discover it and pull him through; it would be insane. Moreover, nobody would poison that syphon and then run the risk of killing an innocent outsider—yourself—which is what would have happened if you had accepted soda-water. If a murderer weren't deterred by conscientious scruples about killing the outsider, he would at least have refrained because he would need somebody to give the alarm and save him from his self-inflicted dose.

"*But*, you see," he continued, "it is very probable that a woman might give herself arsenic to divert suspicion. It is fairly slow, its symptoms are unmistakable, and, since Twills was constantly in attendance on her anyway, she would run no real risk. But she took no chances, you'll observe. That was what first made me think of the possibility. She definitely told Twills she was being poisoned. Now, after all—that isn't very natural, is it?"

He took a sip of his kümmel. "I know she was suffering from peripheral neuritis," he said. "We'll come to that in a moment. Let's look at the question of arsenic and hyoscin for a moment, right from the beginning. I—well, I may not be a wizard, but, hang it, look at the thing from the poisoner's viewpoint! When you've got six grains of a swift, almost certain poison, hard to spot and as deadly as anything in the drug line, why do you want to mess about with a clumsy and uncertain thing like arsenic? Hyoscin would be much better. We know the murderer must have got all this knowledge from overhearing the conversation between Judge Quayle and Twills. Well, Twills definitely said that arsenic was 'the most painful but least dangerous' of all toxics; so what was the murderer's idea in using it, *if the murderer really intended to kill the one to whom the arsenic was given*? Furthermore, after you've pinched enough hyoscin to kill everybody in the house, why run the terrific risk of being seen pinching a tin of arsenic—hard to hide, and not half so effective as what you've got—from an open place like the pantry, where there was somebody present nearly all day?"

Rossiter spread out his hands into the light which fell across our marble-topped table. I could not see his face, but I could sense the wrinkle between his brows.

"And not only that, but why act so inconsistently as to give two people hyoscin and one person arsenic? The hyoscin had already been planted the afternoon before anybody was poisoned, so it wasn't merely a case of discovering that the arsenic didn't work. (For that matter, neither did the hyoscin—on Judge Quayle.) You see," he fidgeted, "I happen to know rather a lot about poisoners' ways myself. If they have one distinguishing characteristic, it's this: they always use the same poison, no matter how many people they try to kill, or how many other drugs they have at hand. Look at the list: Buchanan, Armstrong, Hoch, Louise Vermilya, Bowers, Waite, Bertha Gifford, Mrs. Archer are a few modern examples of people who took more than one life, or tried to. They all used the same toxic agent, and—"

"Where the devil," I interrupted, "did you get all this information?"

"Eh? Oh. Chap at Scotland Yard showed me," he explained. "I'm not such a fool, really. . . . So, you see, the business looked fishy from the very start. But wait. Before we get to a consideration of the motive, let's look at another angle of the thing. Mrs. Quayle was dangerous—devilish dangerous. I'm not sure, but I rather suspect she was a necrophile. You might consult Krafft-Ebing. I'd sooner drink castor oil than read the chap's stuff, myself, but sometimes he's extraordinarily revealing. By necrophile I mean a being who's fascinated by death and the dead; enthralled by them, in fact. Necrophiles love to be in sick-rooms, and to prepare the dead for burial, and they delight in the tasks normal people shudder at. A number of famous women poisoners have been in this category, like Mrs. Vermilya, and Bertha Gifford, and the cheerful lady they called The Angel of Allegheny. It's a gland or nervous disease. In Mrs. Quayle's case, it may have been accentuated by her neuritis —melancholia, depression, and hatred of her husband and by the effect of having been exposed to Jane McGregor. You notice (you've got it down here) how her thoughts always kept running on death. Even her dreams dealt with it, though there we're on more debatable territory. Her first thought, when her husband kicked Tom out of the house, was to poison herself. She disguised this tendency, when she spoke to you, by pretending she was in fear for her own life—but she wasn't, and I rather think I can prove it to you, presently.

"Look here! The motive was the clearest thing of all," Rossiter said earnestly. "You knew it. Who definitely did have a poisonous hatred for Judge Quayle? Everybody knew she had never forgiven him for what he did to Tom; it was the beginning of her illness. And you saw how that degenerated. She could think of nothing but Tom. Without this tinge of morbidity and madness, she mightn't have gone so far as murder. But it grew, and grew, and became inflamed until she conceived the idea of poisoning her husband. Good Lord, man!—I mean to say, it's so dashed plain!"

He picked up the yellow-bound book, the copy of Heine's poems, with those strange words on the flyleaf. He had been speaking querulously, and now he flourished the book in my face. He went on:

"How else can you explain these words: *'Could personality*

have made such impression?' Well, it couldn't have been anybody else than Tom, could it? It's perfectly simple. But you tried to make something abstruse out of it, and its simplicity got lost. Twills knew, of course. I fancy he'd seen her pinch the hyoscin out of his surgery; or, if not that, he had a pretty fair suspicion it was she. That was why he knew instantly, when he saw the judge fall, what the poison was. Where Twills messed everything up was in failing to suspect that she might already have planted hyoscin where he, Twills, could take it. She'd already poisoned the bromide-bottle, of course. But he thought that, due to the arsenic, she couldn't act for a day or so at least, and that everything was safe enough for him until he decided what course to take. You see, he still wasn't sure—witness the first question he wrote in the book. He couldn't quite believe it even then. But she had put hyoscin into the bromide-bottle at the same time she poisoned the syphon. . . ."

"When was that?"

"While the rest of them were having dinner. Man, she had a clear field, without anybody in sight, for over half an hour; and no chance at all of anybody catching her! Twills had to die. She had no particular animus against him, but he had to die, because he knew. I suspect Twills must have dropped a pretty strong hint to her while he was attending at her bedside. I think he gave her a chance to come in and return the poison voluntarily—after the others were in bed —and that must have been why he was waiting up. You mention that in your record. She had no intention of doing it, of course . . ."

"But the motive!" I interposed. "It couldn't have been mere revenge. You said it was money."

Rossiter slumped back in his chair. He lit a cigarette, and the gleam of the match lit a queer, baffled, ironical expression on his face.

"Yes," he said. "That was the dead give-away. That was what pointed so clearly to Mrs. Quayle. It *was* money. Where all of you went astray was in jumping to the conclusion it was *Twills'* money; and Twills' will, and all that kind of thing. Hang it, I tried like the devil to tell you differently—

you've even written down what I said, and I leave it to any-body whether that at least wasn't plain—but still you tried to involve Twills. He didn't figure in Mrs. Quayle's plans at all, except that he had to be eliminated because he was suspicious . . . It wasn't *his* fortune. It was Judge Quayle's fortune, to be given to the disinherited son Tom."

"But Judge Quayle," I said, "didn't have any fortune. He had no money at all."

"Righto! *And Mrs. Quayle was the only one in the whole house who didn't know that.*"

One after another, lamps were coming out on the street. In the café behind us a waiter began kindling gas-globes, and we heard fiddles being tuned. Rossiter, his hat stuck on the side of his head, appeared as a slightly embarrassed goblin. He began to roll another of those unholy cigarettes.

"I'm sorry," he said, after a pause. "I tried to tell you, you know. Clarissa made special point of mentioning that fact. Of all the people there, only Mrs. Quayle hadn't been told that the judge was on his uppers. That was why Twills wrote, 'Was it hope of money, or growing canker?' She saw no sign of the judge relenting—and so, when they got this pleading letter from Tom asking for money, she must have gone a bit mad. She pictured him as ill and broke, and she couldn't stand it. It led directly to the attempt at murder. She destroyed the judge's will, because she was afraid it might contain a clause against Tom; otherwise *she* would inherit, and she could bring Tom back with what she thought was the judge's wealth. . . .

"Don't comment on this irony. That was the futile thing about the whole business."

"And she did destroy the will?"

"I don't know; probably we shall never know. But she searched for it, and naïvely looked in the drawer of his writing-table. That was where she found his manuscript. And she hated him so much that she burned it. Perhaps it was merely a means of venting spite when she didn't find the will. Perhaps she thought she was destroying what he loved most in the world, and had taken his affection for Tom. Perhaps both. But it was a lead. Of all the people in the house, she was the only one who disliked him enough to burn his manuscript. Maybe she burned both of them; Twills, you see, wasn't sure himself, and he was wondering about it.

"You tried to work out some fantastic theory of the judge directing a plot against Twills, and against Twills' money. I say, excuse me!—but it was ridiculous, you know. Twills wasn't thinking about any future attempt on his own life when he wrote 'Was it hope of money, or growing canker?' Was, *was*, WAS—that's the word he used, referring to the poisoning of Judge Quayle, referring to what had happened in the past. And it was another glaring, immense sign-post. Who on earth would poison Judge Quayle for money, except the one person in the whole house who didn't know he was bankrupt?

"You've only got to interpret those questions written in the copy of Heine in the most obvious way, and you have the whole truth. It shrieks out at you. That was why I kept saying it looked bad for the judge; *he* was her objective, and she was determined to kill him." He hesitated. "Clarissa's murder . . ."

"Clarissa's murder," I said, "was committed while she—apparently—was up in bed with the nurse in the room."

He grinned wryly, and tapped the sheets again. "Yes. You've got the explanation here, only you didn't know it at the time. *I* didn't know it myself until I read this. Damn the luck. If I had been with you and Sargent and Reed when you interviewed the old lady, I believe I could have prevented Clarissa's death. But, of course, like an ass, I was mooning about downstairs. . . .

"Mrs. Quayle's behaviour, from your record, is as clear as daylight. She didn't know she hadn't killed the judge, until you told her! She thought her work was finished. Of course, nobody had mentioned it to her before, and she didn't dare ask. Then Reed said—it's right here—" he fumbled at the sheets, "yes. Reed said, 'Somebody tried to poison the judge and *he* didn't die.' And she nearly broke down. You say so yourself. She answered, 'Tried to—poison him? You say they *tried*—' Tried, tried! It's practically a confession. She attempted to cover it up in an instant, and immediately shifted to her favourite topic of death. . . .

"Follow what went on in her mind! After saying that, the first thing which jumps into her head is—Tom. She has failed Tom. She hasn't done her work. So she begins mumbling about Tom, and growing so incoherent after the shock that you had to leave her. Previously, you'll notice, she had made an effort to throw suspicion on one of the girls by that incredible story about somebody sneaking into her room and not replying to her question—"

"Why 'incredible'?"

"I'll show you in a moment. It ties up with why she really wasn't afraid of an attempt on her life all along, despite what she said. The old lady was a dreadfully bad liar, you know. I can tell she was, because I'm such a poor liar myself." He shook his head sadly. "That's why I get myself into such hot water. I never can tell a convincing lie, so I just have to keep quiet, and it makes people think I'm a bit cracked, sometimes. But about Mrs. Quayle. I think she was vaguely trying to throw suspicion on Mary. She disliked Mary, you see, because Mary had always been so bitter against Tom; besides, Mary had the most opportunity, and so was the first person who jumped into Mrs. Quayle's mind."

"There were times," I said, "when I felt more than a little suspicious of Mary myself. If she hadn't been so clearly fond of her father . . ."

He nodded. "Well, Mrs. Quayle told that story. Now mark this. She says she is terribly afraid she may be poisoned. They bring her dinner up. She says she heard a suspicious movement in the room; a person there for no good purpose, who doesn't answer her when she calls out, and who is probably trying to do her harm. Almost immediately afterwards, Mary calls her attention to the milk-toast, and urges her to eat it. . . . Good Lord! Do you think that, if she had really been afraid of poison, she would have touched that meal? Do you think that, if she really thought she had heard somebody in the room bent on mischief, she wouldn't have cried out and alarmed the whole household? It isn't consistent. It's a palpable piece of bunkum.

"No, no. She poisoned her own milk-toast. She thought everything went well. But then you came in the next day, and brought her universe down by telling her she hadn't poisoned the judge after all. You'll notice she immediately lost interest in this story of the mysterious intruder, and wouldn't even talk about it any more. She was figuring out ways and means of getting the judge.

"She'd hidden the poison in the cellar, because she thought she had no further use for it. Now she had to go and get it again. How? Why, the nurse told you, didn't she, that she was going to give Mrs. Quayle a sleeping-pill, and then lie down to sleep herself on that camp-bed? The nurse was exhausted; she'd been up all night, and her nap would be pretty sound. It isn't difficult to palm a sleeping-pill and only pretend to take it; I'm a good amateur magician myself," Rossiter said complacently, "and I know.

"You'll notice the difference in her technique now. She was desperate, and almost mad. Her self-control broke. She had nerved herself to do this poisoning, and now she had to do it all over again. She *would not* be balked. It's the hideous crazy determination of the woman which is so appalling. When the nurse was napping, she slid out quietly, and went down the back stairs. Clarissa caught her probably with the arsenic and the hyoscin both in her hand. Clarissa was drunk, and ready to scream an alarm; and the old lady *would not* be balked. . . ."

Rossiter's cigarette was flaring now. All the pale lights at the café were on; the tables mopped, the floor inside swept and watered. The orchestra was still plunking experimentally. A low hum of movement had commenced along the street. There was laughter, the swishing of feet, and flickers of white from women's dresses among the trees. My companion stared vacantly at his glass.

"And," he said in a low voice, "I dare say you, as a novelist, would appreciate what happened. The son for whom she was doing these things was looking on at the cellar window . . . if he had known it.

"She was stark mad now, of course. She didn't care what happened. Her attempt at secrecy was all gone; she was opening the throttle wide and tearing straight for destruction. Before that, she had tried to shield herself with what she thought was great cunning, but why bother now? She got back to her room somehow, though she almost ran into the judge coming up the cellar stairs. The commotion roused the household, including the nurse. I rather fancy there was blood on her, too, and she hid it under the bedclothes. When she made her attempt on the judge, she just went into the bath between the two communicating rooms; locked one door, and went out the other. The nurse didn't see her slip downstairs. She must have drawn a wrapper over the blood on her nightgown. . . ."

I shuddered. Rossiter looked at me with a pinched and sombre expression.

"I'm sorry, old boy. You asked for the gory details. There was blood on her when I found her dead body behind that statue. The exertion, probably, was too much for her heart at last, in her weakened condition. It was a blessing, anyhow. And since the judge didn't die from being cracked over the skull with that bottle . . . well, if she had lived, she would probably have made a third attempt."

He hesitated.

"Look here. I haven't thought about these things for a long time, and I get a bit on edge. I've been trying to keep it away from Jinny's thoughts as much as I can. We shall be going to the hotel to see her soon, and I know you won't mention—eh? After all, this is our wedding-trip, you know; she wouldn't like to be reminded of what happened."

"Of course not," I said. "And I haven't yet offered my congratulations." I looked at his reasonably neat tie, and clothes which were almost pressed. He no longer had quite so apparent a look of being blown through the world by a tipsy wind. "You're looking domesticated already. And rather more prosperous. Are you still in the detective business?"

He shifted uncomfortably.

"Oh, dash it. I mean—well, I gave in. After seeing all that unpleasant business at the Quayles'—I mean to say, my own old man . . . well!" He threw out his hands. "I knew I should probably give in when I took that job in the police department. My old man learned where I was, naturally, through the American commissioner, and he got in touch with me. . . . I mean to say, he's a good sort, and I only got him humped when I tried to mess things up at Scotland Yard. You see, the governor is High Commissioner of the dashed place. That was why they did me a favour in New York. We had a row, you see. My well-meant efforts to help him practically paralyzed English justice, *he* said. I'll tell you about it sometime. But, well—after all, he wants somebody to keep his damned old baronetcy going, and I'm it. And so . . ."

He gestured plaintively, and then finished his drink.

"Let's go along to the hotel," he said, "and pick up Jinny, and then we'll make a night of it. She's fine and blooming; she'd enjoy a bit of a tear. This thing," he pointed at the yellow book, "we'll burn. I didn't know you'd held it as a keepsake."

"Willingly," I said. "But if a person could look at it in the abstract, it would be a good case. You have a certain Mr. Joseph Sargent believing you're the greatest detective in the history of the world. He didn't believe it when you had us drawing pictures, for instance. . . . By God! Wait a minute! In retrospect, it's fairly easy to see everything except that. Why the pictures?"

Rossiter grinned. "I'm a student of scribblography," he replied.

"Of what?"

"Scribblography," he repeated, with relish. "I couldn't tell you why I wanted to do that, or it would have spoiled things. You'd have got self-conscious and botched it. . . . You remember, I asked you to draw various things: a house, a man, a woman, a dog? Well, you all did. And your rough drawings were all practically the same; but I had to have it demonstrated. When you drew a woman, you made a rather funny-looking face with spirally blobs for hair, like excelsior shavings . . ."

"Well?"

"So did Twills," said Rossiter.

During a silence he pushed across the yellow book. "Look at it! You haven't forgotten those absent-minded little sketches Twills drew before he wrote, have you? You've certainly explained them in great detail in the manuscript. There's a great deal of truth in the absent, apparently meaningless sketches a person will scribble on a sheet of paper. Twills was thinking of Mrs. Quayle. Look at that sour face. Look at the ringlets. But even if I could demonstrate that *a woman* was what he had drawn—not a man—it would be enough to confirm my explanation of what he wrote. I asked you to draw, very sketchily and roughly, a woman— and you all did just as he has done. Each of those scribbled things, the OOO's the bird, all of it, had a meaning; but the woman was all I wanted. Study it up sometime. For the present, we *must* all go out and get drunk, what? The place at home, where my old man has us living with him, is a cheerful little bird-cage with fifty-four rooms, and I'm not exactly suited for the gentle life, you know. I pine. I become elevated. Presently I bust. Yes, I think we'd better get tight."

I think he was staring out somewhat wistfully at the wide lands he had tramped over, in a dusty green topcoat and a battered hat.

He removed his own Burlington-Arcade headgear, properly creased, and eyed it with something of disfavour. The café tables were beginning to fill up.

"There are just two more things," I said, "that I'd like to ask . . ."

"Eh? Oh, carry on! I'll answer 'em, if I can."

"Well, then—that question in Twills' book about the morphine, for instance."

"I've been wondering about it too. And here's the explanation, I think. Twills, you know, really believed somebody was continuing to scare the judge, all those years, with an imitation of a white marble hand. We can be pretty sure the only time it was actually tried was when Tom did it;

but the judge, doped up as he was, probably saw it in every corner afterwards. Twills, when he wrote that, very likely suspected that it was Mrs. Quayle who was scaring him with the dummy hand; and what he wrote had reference to how frightened the judge might be, because of the influence of morphine. Of course, the old lady wasn't interested in any play-acting. All she wanted was the return of Tom. I fancy that a good many people in the house believed their mother was a bit off. Not to the extent of murder, of course . . . but off all the same. It may serve to explain their attitude. They accused each other, rather than have anything said about their own parents."

"The last thing in the case," I said, "the crux of it, and what seemed to me the horrible part . . ."

"Well?"

"It was the laughter. You remember? The nurse hearing laughter in Twills' room? It haunted me. And everybody kept talking about it; the way Judge Quayle suddenly came out with those lines about 'poison in jest' . . . Ugh! But the nurse swore Mrs. Quayle was safely in bed when the laughter was heard."

"She was," he replied sombrely.

There was a silence. Rossiter rose to his great height, towering over the hedge. He stuck his hat at an angle on his head, and took stick and gloves—foolishly incongruous things in his hands—from the chair beside him. Behind him, in the café, I could see waiters bringing beer. The orchestra was settling into its music racks, tucking fiddles under chins. . . .

"Twills loved this city," my companion went on suddenly. "He wanted to come back here and realize all his dreams. He was still thinking about it when . . . Did it never seem strange to you," he broke off, staring into the warm, lamplit dusk, "that Twills didn't save himself? He felt the poison getting him. He must have known what it was. There was still a little time for an attempt to combat its effects. But he didn't. He was just tired, old man. He was just tired, and he didn't care. . . . It was Twills they heard laughing. He was laughing at his own destiny, when he lay there in his peppermint-candy pyjamas, and waited for death."

Slowly, with a dimming vision of that cold house, we walked out into the shadowy street. The orchestra-leader lifted his baton; the surge of a waltz rolled out across the tables, above the clatter of glasses and the low hum: *"To thee, beautiful lady, I raise my eyes. . . ."*